HEART OF
THE DEMON

*The classic first novel in the
DS Hunter Kerr series.*

Michael Fowler

Fiction aimed at the heart
and the head...

Published by Caffeine Nights Publishing 2012

Published in Great Britain by Caffeine Nights Publishing

www.caffeine-nights.com

British Library Cataloguing in Publication Data.

A CIP catalogue record for this book is available from the British Library

ISBN: 978-1-907565-26-7

Cover design by

Mark (Wills) Williams

Everything else by

Default, Luck and Accident

PREFACE

Heart of the Demon, is the first novel featuring the central characters Detective Sergeant Hunter Kerr and his working partner DC Grace Marshall.

It was originally published in paperback in October 2010.

This latest edition is a revised version of the original novel.

MICHAEL FOWLER

Michael was born and grew up in the once industrial heartland of South Yorkshire and still lives there with his wife and two sons.

He served as a police officer for thirty-two years, both in uniform and in plain clothes, working in CID, Vice Squad and Drug Squad, and retired as an Inspector in charge of a busy CID Department in 2006.

Aside from writing, his other passion is painting and as a professional artist he has achieved numerous accolades. His work can be found in numerous galleries throughout the UK.

He is a member of the Crime Writers Association.

Michael can be contacted via his website at:
www.mjfowler.co.uk

This one is for Liz who has always been a part of my dreams

Acknowledgements

My gratitude goes out to all those who have given up their time to bring this work to fruition, in particular Alan Twiddle who read the original manuscript, and the first published edition and gave me invaluable advice which enabled me to make this revised version stronger.

To Stuart Sosnowski, Crime Scene Supervisor, South Yorkshire Police who helped me with my crime scene forensics.

To Margaret Ardron and Janet Williamson who gave me expert guidance and critique on the original manuscript.

To the Rawmarsh Writers Group who continually encouraged me to deliver.

And finally to Darren Laws, of Caffeine Nights Publishing, who made it all possible.

Heart of the Demon

PROLOGUE

25th July 1988.

Gripping one shoulder firmly, with a quick sawing movement he began to slice into the first layer of flesh with the curved edge of the blade.

Tough little bastard.

He had thought that it would be easy to separate the head from the body with the Bowie knife he had recently acquired. However, the neck tissues and sinews were far tougher than he expected and he had to drag the blade repeatedly against the leathery skin. As the knife finally tore into the vertebrae, drops of warm sticky blood splattered his hands and his clothing.

Not such a tough little bastard now, are you?

He had hoped to torture the creature a lot longer but it had brought about its own death much quicker than he had wanted.

A little earlier, he had chuckled whilst watching the rabbit's brown eyes almost bulge from its sockets as he had twisted the leather leash tighter around its neck. His own heart had pumped so fast he feared it would burst through his chest and it had felt as if his head was ready to explode.

The rush had been an almost unbelievable experience and had made him exert even more pressure on the leash. That's when the *tough little bastard* dug those buckteeth into his clenched fist, drawing blood - his own blood. He'd almost released his grip on the thrashing rabbit nearly allowing it to escape. In a flash of anger, which he later cursed himself for, he had grabbed its twitching back legs, swung it around and smashed its fluffy head against a tree stump.

That had put paid to the life of the New Zealand dwarf.

Sarah is going to be really pissed off when she finds her pet gone. High-faluting Sarah, with her lispy posh voice who thinks she's a cut above the others on the street. Yes she is really going to be pissed when she finds her little 'Bob-Tail' gone. Little Bob-Tail, with its posh imitation jewelled collar,

11

which she walked around her garden - on a leash, of all things.

He had listened to her repeatedly clucking her tongue against the roof of her mouth and shouting for 'Bob-Tail' to come for his 'din-dins'. It really irritated him. Many a time he had wanted to rip that clucking tongue right out of her snooty little mouth. Luckily for her she lived too near. She didn't realise just how fortunate she was.

She won't be acting so highfaluting when she finds her dear little 'Bob-Tail' in pieces. Spoilt little brat.

* * * * *

12th October 1993

He drew heavily on the cigarette he had pinched from his mother's packet; the packet which was always tucked between the cushion and arm of 'her' chair. He had been hiding in the bushes for over half an hour and had a good view of the front doors of the block of flats when he spotted the regular visitor lock up and leave his car in the unlit car park.

He took a final drag on his cigarette, flicked the remains to the floor and ground it underfoot. Glancing quickly at his watch, and knowing that this guest would be at least another hour and a half, he put on a pair of leather gloves and moved slowly from the bushes towards the Ford Fiesta. Taking half a tennis ball from his jacket pocket, he placed it over the lock on the driver's door and with a quick bang forced out the air. The suction made the plastic locking mechanism shoot up and the door opened without a sound. He forced a screwdriver into the ignition barrel, turning the handle as he would a key. The car's engine fired first time and taking a final look around he slid into the driver's seat. As he reversed a smile ripped across his face. No doubt about it the CID officer was going to be well and truly pissed off when he came out of that flat.

* * * * *

Head bowed from hunched shoulders, jaw resting between his hands, elbows on desk, Hunter Kerr chewed on the end of his pen whilst double-checking the contents of his most exciting arrest file to date. This was the most tedious part of the job but also the most important and being on the evening shift helped his concentration. It meant a virtually empty office; no incessant chatter or the ringing of phones to distract him.

Momentarily closing his eyes he massaged his eyelids and pushed himself back in his chair. Wiping away the tiredness overcoming him he forced them open and re-focussed on the document on his computer screen. Then clicking back into gear he commenced tip-tapping the keyboard, putting the finishing touches to the arrest summary.

Over the past week he and his partner had cleared up twenty three burglaries committed by a team of four teenage tearaways who were now on remand in a young offender's institution. And that was only what they were admitting. It had been amazing that since their arrest only two house break-ins had been reported. It was obvious that the team were responsible for a lot more, but he guessed he would only know that when they were sentenced and begged him for a prison visit to 'clear their slate,' so that they wouldn't be arrested again when they were released.

Hunter was in the final month of his six month CID aide period and things had gone very well. The contacts and informants he had built up from his previous three and a half years working the streets in uniform had ensured an impressive number of arrests. The Detective Inspector had already congratulated him on many occasions on the quality of his 'collars' and he had also been promised a good report and an early entrance into the Criminal Investigation Department at Barnwell.

The strident ringing of the phone on his desk made Hunter jump. He pulled the pen from his mouth and snatched up the handset from its cradle. "PC Kerr, CID" he announced.

"Hunter," an excited voice rasped down the line. He immediately recognised the high-pitched voice of his working buddy, Paul Goodright.

"Listen I'm up shit creek, the car's been nicked."

Hunter clamped the handset between head and shoulder and with pen poised over a pad of paper made ready to jot down information.

"What do you mean nicked?"

"Just get the other car and come and pick me up on Church Street."

For a few seconds there was silence, then Paul blurted down the line, "And don't say anything to uniform...yet."

The call ended.

Hunter rose quickly and began scanning the desks in the office for the spare set of CID car keys. He urgently moved crime reports and files around in other officer's trays knowing the keys would be somewhere amongst the paperwork. At the same time his thoughts rolled back to the conversation with Paul an hour earlier. His partner had smiled mischievously when he had mentioned he had an enquiry to do and would be back in an hour or two. Hunter immediately knew from the expression on his face that what Paul really meant was that '*he was off shagging*' and needed him to cover. And although deep down he had disapproved he had chosen not to voice his thoughts. After all, Paul was two years greater in service and an established detective. Besides that Hunter enjoyed having Paul as a partner. The pair had 'hit it off' very quickly and already established themselves as a formidable partnership within the department. And despite not having the experience of some of the more seasoned detectives' in the office both had more hunger and enthusiasm when it came to chasing villains.

Hunter found his colleague pacing excitedly on the footpath outside a block of flats on Church Street. As he pulled up beside him Paul flung open the car door and dropped into the passenger seat.

"This is my worst nightmare. I can't believe that some little bastard's nicked the car. I'll fucking kill him when I get hold of him. It was in the car park at the side there." He pointed back towards the flats. "Before I report it in we'll run round all the dumping spots and if we don't find it I need you to back me up with a cover story."

As Hunter pulled away from the kerbside he could see Paul anxiously wiping away beads of sweat, which had formed on his brow.

* * * * *

For half an hour he drove furiously around the twisting unlit country roads on the edge of town, roaring past slower cars and then cutting them up as he forced the Fiesta back into the correct lane. On several occasions he laughed loudly, even though there was no one else to hear. He wondered if that CID guy had discovered the car had gone yet. As he increased speed, so the sensation swelled inside. He felt wired. His alert eyes were as dark as the night around him, and he focused intensely on the surroundings as they flew by. Ahead lay a series of bends and he pushed the car's engine until he could feel it throbbing on its mountings. Then he eased off and decided to head back to Barnwell.

He was approaching the outskirts of town when he noticed her standing at the side of a bus stop. Carol Siddons. She was blowing into her hands and stamping her feet. He slung the car hard left and hit the brakes. The tyres squealed as he skidded to a halt beside her.

She looked up as he leaned across the passenger seat and wound down the window. Bending down she peered inside, squinting to see who the driver was. "Oh it's you," she said. "Where did you get this from?"

"Nicked it," he responded "And guess what, it's a cop car"

"Yeah all right, spin me another."

"Don't believe me eh? Well look at this then." He picked up the police radio handset from the dash and thrust it towards her. "Believe me now then?"

She started giggling "Bloody hell you're going be in some serious shit if they catch you."

"Naaw, no chance of that. Fancy a spin?"

"You are joking."

"No come on. I'm gonna dump it soon. I'll give you a run round and then drop you off home, before I get shut."

He sensed her hesitate. "Come on its freezing out there and the bus might not come for ages." He flipped up the door catch and pushed it open. The glow of the interior light shone on his grinning face. "Come on, live on the edge."

Carol Siddons looked around. Nothing stirred. She edged forward apprehensively, took another look around, and then slipped into the passenger seat, slamming the door behind her. "Come on let's get out of here fast you crazy bastard."

He forced his right foot onto the accelerator and the Fiesta screeched away.

As he tore around the country roads again he was conscious of Carol's excited jabberings, though he was unable to decipher exactly what she was saying as he concentrated on the narrow lane ahead, his focus shooting back and forth between road and rear view mirror. His arms ached as he gripped the steering wheel, and as he checked his speedometer he realized he was shaking and sweating profusely.

Throwing the car into a sharp bend, far too late he spotted the rear lights of another car. Instinctively, he smashed his foot down onto the brake. His effort was in vain and there was a spontaneous thump as the Fiesta smashed into the back of the other car. In a split-second reaction he swung the steering wheel to the right and the tyres protested with a concerted squeal. There was a loud scraping noise as metal gouged metal and the car in front bucked and slewed sideways towards a wall by the side of the road.

He felt the Fiesta's engine surge and almost stall as he fought to disentangle it from the other car. It crabbed sideways for several yards before he managed to bring it back under control and point it back in the direction he had been heading. Quickly glancing back, he saw that the other car had embedded itself in the stone wall. Without warning, there was a loud whoosh as the front of it exploded in a fireball. Within seconds searing incandescent gashes of red and yellow flame were licking from beneath the wheel arches and up onto the bonnet and windscreen.

"Fucking hell." Carol screamed.

He hammered his foot down onto the accelerator and with a squeal of rubber on tarmac, sped away from the carnage.

Every nerve in his body was straining and he became acutely conscious of every sound around him as he sped through the countryside.

After ten minutes, he found the unmade track that he knew wound its way towards the old pit coking plant, no longer in production since the demise of the mine five years previously. He slewed the car to a halt, the wheels sliding slightly on the rutted and muddied track, threw open the driver's door, jerked his head out and threw up violently into a puddle of oily water.

"You crazy bastard." He heard Carol shout. "You fucking crazy bastard"

He glared across at her. She was pale faced. He studied her features. He had always thought she was pretty and yet now in a surreal way he found her scared look even more attractive. A tingling sensation erupted in his groin.

Snapping himself out of his thoughts he launched himself out of the Fiesta and listened intently. Every sound was distant. They had not been followed. He could now see finger-like wisps of fog drifting over the fields surrounding them and he knew that in an hour or so its blanket would provide cover for him to disappear and for the car to lie undiscovered until at least first light.

Carol joined him. She was shouting at him, swearing and stabbing his chest with her finger.

"Pipe down for Christ's sake." he spat back, wiping his mouth with the sleeve of his sweatshirt.

"You're fucking mad. Did you see what happened to that car you hit? It blew up. Jesus I can't believe this. We are in some serious shit now. You know that don't you?"

He put a finger to his mouth and moved towards her. Then he grabbed hold of her shoulders and fixed her stare. He could see the panic and fear in Carol's eyes. He knew he needed to calm her down. "Everything's gonna be okay. Don't worry."

"Don't worry he says. You've probably killed somebody you stupid bastard."

"Don't call me stupid Carol. I'm not stupid." His features changed. They took on a distinct hardness and his dark eyes became glassy.

"No you are not stupid." she growled, screwing up her eyes. "You're fucking crazy."

He finally snapped. The punch was swift, smashing into her face. He felt her nose give and heard the snap as the bridge broke. He saw the film of tears flood her eyes as she sank to her knees.

Gulping back sobs she glanced up at him, "Now you've fucking done it, I'm going to the cops myself" she choked.

He quickly unfastened the buckle on his belt, whipped it through the loops of his waistband and gripped both ends. It was around Carol's neck in a second and as he tightened it around her throat he saw her big brown eyes bulge.

Just like Bob-Tail's.

A malevolent look masked his face as he pulled her close. The corners of his mouth curled upwards as she thrashed and clawed for survival. Less than a minute later he squeezed out her last breath.

Bob-Tail is staring back. Didn't someone once tell him that the image of their killer was captured in the eyes as they died?

Well mine is the last face she'll ever see and Carol Siddons is not going to identify me to anyone.

- ooOoo -

CHAPTER ONE
DAY ONE OF THE INVESTIGATION: 6th July 2008

She bucked and jerked wildly and he had to bear down all of his twelve stone onto her wiry, yet well toned young body, as her limbs smacked against his.

Every sign she was fighting for her life.

Then the air exploded from her chest for the last time and at last she lay still.

Gasping for breath and drenched in sweat he pushed himself up from her limp figure. He had thought that she was never going to die. He had been amazed at the fight she had put up. He took in several deep breaths and tried to slow his racing heartbeat, watching in fascination as dark viscous blood belched from her eye sockets, joining other rivulets which were already matting her dark bob of hair and forming a pool around her head.

Bending down he scraped the mess from his knife into the dusty earth and then dropped it into his coat pocket and set to work.

He couldn't leave her body here.

Dragging the bloodied corpse by the wrists along the flagstone floor he soon found himself gasping for breath again and he could feel fresh beads of sweat tickling his rib cage as he hauled her towards the barn entrance.

Then a distant unfamiliar noise caught his attention; a noise which didn't belong to the surroundings. He paused and listened. It was coming nearer. He dropped the girl's arms and dashed to an opening slit in the barn wall, threw himself against the damp walls and twisted his head sideway to peer through the gap without being seen. For a split-second the sunlight blurred his vision but as it cleared he spotted a flat-back lorry bouncing along the uneven farm track, coming his way.

He closed his eyes and held his breath. Then he gritted his teeth and cursed. He couldn't believe his bad luck. He had sought out this place especially for its remoteness, regularly visiting the place at different times over the past few weeks to finalise his plan. In all that time no one had come near and now today of all days he had a visitor. For a few seconds he thought about killing the driver, but then realised he didn't know this adversary.

He swung his gaze back along the lane. The truck was now only a few hundred yards away and there was no sign of it stopping.

He took one last look at the lifeless form quickly realising he was left with no other choice but to make his escape; leaving behind this bloodied mess. He couldn't afford to be caught. Not after all this time.

"Damn" he cussed, realising he wouldn't be able to finish off what he had set out to do. He slipped the playing card from his trouser pocket and suit side up placed it over the gaping wound in the middle of her chest. After all he had to let them know this was his handiwork again.

Then he bolted towards the rear of the barn where there was a windowless opening, vaulted through its gap and sprinted towards a thick hawthorn hedgerow that ran the length of the hayfield.

* * * * *

Dennis O'Brian swung the Bedford lorry through the broken entranceway that led to the tumbledown farm and braked sharply, throwing up a cloud of dust. Surveying the old Yorkshire stone buildings in a bad state of repair he smiled to himself. Then making a quick call on his mobile, he shut down the engine, flung open the driver's door and leapt out of the cab. For a good few seconds he scanned the ramshackle buildings, weighing up which portions of stone would reap the most rewards.

Then he froze and his heart skipped a beat as he caught the sound of running feet. He was just about to leap back into his truck when he realised the footfalls were actually growing fainter. Whoever had been here must be fleeing he thought. A grin snaked across his mouth and he chuckled to himself. He bet it was another stone thief who thought he was going to be caught.

As he stepped out of the sunlight into the dimness of the barn's interior he wasn't prepared for what greeted him. Sprawled across the uneven dirt floor was a lifeless and bloody form. Only from the clothing could he tell it was a girl; the injuries inflicted upon the teenager were like nothing he had ever seen.

He began to retch as he fished in his jeans pocket for his mobile.

* * * * *

Pushing the CID car's door to with his hip, Detective Sergeant Hunter Kerr paused for a moment and gathered his thoughts whilst casting his gaze out over the very active crime scene before him. He watched a line of uniformed Officers, regular intervals apart, pushing their way slowly through waist high crops, their white short-sleeved shirts standing out against a backdrop of lush green trees.

Above him the Force helicopter hovered, the drumming noise of its rotor blades disturbing the peacefulness of the surroundings.

He had raced here at breakneck speeds, all the time listening to the up-dates being broadcast over his radio. By the time he had arrived he had gained enough information to enable him to formulate a picture in his mind of what had happened.

Strafing the surroundings with his steel blue eyes he knew that in one of the dilapidated and derelict farm buildings ahead a young girl's battered body had been found, and that her killer had fled the area only about an hour beforehand, and right at this moment, everything was being done as quickly and thoroughly as possible to track down her slayer and secure the site.

Hunter knew this area well. As an amateur artist he had visited this location on many occasions and painted the subjects in the vicinity. In fact, the old farm buildings had been captured many times in his oil sketches. He found it quite disconcerting that suddenly such beautiful surroundings, which featured in paintings back home, were now centre stage in a gruesome discovery.

"Hi Sarge."

Hunter recognised the voice immediately and turned to see his partner DC Grace Marshall tramping towards him at pace. In her smart, pale grey, business suit he couldn't help but think that Grace looked more the confident professional business woman, than a hard working front line murder detective.

As she approached he saw that she was corralling her dark corkscrew curled hair into an elastic scrunchy. Her face was set grim.

"It's bad in there Hunter. You ought to see what he's done to her."

"Tell me what you've learned then Grace."

"We're fairly confident that it's the body of one Rebecca Morris. A fourteen year old girl who was reported missing only a few hours ago. Apparently she didn't turn up for an exam at her school this morning." Grace finished bunching her hair. "She's in a real mess. Her face is hardly recognisable. No one's moved or touched the body yet. First uniform on site could see from the state of her that she was dead and immediately cordoned off the area. The three nine's call came from a guy who had driven here in his flat-back lorry. He's now back at the station being interviewed. His story is that he just happened to be driving up the track to the farm for a quick ten minutes rest, but my guess is that he was going to nick some of the stone or slates from here. Anyway he says he just got out of his cab, heard the sound of someone running from the back of one of the buildings and then a car starting up and screeching away. When he goes round to look he finds the girl dead in the barn."

"And do we believe him?"

"No reason not to at the moment. The local cops know him fairly well. He's got previous for nicking stone and lead from church roofs. He's also got a couple of convictions for drunk and disorderly but those are over fifteen years old, and he's got nothing for violence. And to be fair he did ring it in and stick around until uniform arrived and they say he appeared to be really genuinely shook up over it. I've had him lodged in a cell and he can stew there for a couple of hours til' we're clear from here. I'll get a statement from him and then kick him out. That'll serve him right for coming here to nick stone on my patch. "

"Any description of the person he disturbed?" Hunter asked

"No, unfortunately not. Well gone before he got to the barn. The guy does say he heard a car or van driving off up the dirt track over there." She pointed to a small copse of trees several hundred yards away.

Suddenly realising it was warmer than he anticipated, Hunter found himself tugging at the crisp collar of his blue shirt. Before he had shot away from the station he had slung on his jacket. Now he wished he hadn't and he quickly undid the top button of his shirt and loosened his tie.

"Where does that track go to Grace?" He asked, pointing towards the line of bushes just beyond the old farm buildings.

"It leads up to a B road half a mile away. It brings you out near the village of Harlington. I've just got uniform to seal off that area as well."

"Okay, good job Grace. Are Scenes of Crime here?"

"Just arrived. The Forensic Pathologist and the Senior Investigating Officer are also on route. Everything should be in place in the next hour."

Hunter realised this was an ideal opportunity to slip off his jacket and make the most of the warm breeze drifting across the fields. Going to the rear of his CID car he sprang open the boot and dropped his coat into the back. Then pulling the sides of his shirt from his sticky and clammy skin he reached into one of the storage boxes within the boot and pulled out a white forensic suit and set of shoe covers. He handed these to Grace and then pulled out another set.

"Come on then, show me what we've got," he said as he stepped into one leg of the protective suit.

Having satisfied themselves that all the relevant evidence sites were secured, DS Hunter Kerr and DC Grace Marshall made their way back to the murder scene, carefully following the police cordon tape past the ruined farmhouse building, and into a tumbledown barn. Streams of light burst through gaps between the old roof timbers where slates had become dislodged or broken, and yet despite the sunlight the interior was cool.

The body of the young girl lay unceremoniously on the dirty stone slab floor, a pool of thick congealed blood around the head and shoulders. The battered and swollen face was caked in the same reddish brown deposit. Where the eyes should have been only two dark sockets crusted in dried blood looked back. At first glance, from the facial injuries, if he hadn't already been told it was a young girl, he would never have known. The arms were outstretched above the head and Hunter could see that the hands had already been forensically bagged. He also noticed that the girl's T-shirt had been pulled, along with her padded pink lace bra, up towards the chin, exposing her small pale breasts. A huge gash exposed the breastbone and other less deep cuts covered her abdomen. Her jeans were undone but still around her hips.

In another white forensic suit, bending over the cadaver, he recognised Professor Lizzie McCormack. Slim and petite in her early sixties, with features not dissimilar to the actress Geraldine McEwan she had dutifully earned herself the nickname Miss Marple. She was one of the small number of British forensic experts who had been invited to work with American scientists at the Tennessee body farm studying detection experiments on decomposing murder victims, and had gained national recognition in the location of human remains and the linking of offenders to the scene.

He was pleased that she had been called out. Hunter had first seen her at work a year ago when the remains of a young mother had been found in a muddy ditch just outside town. Being one of only a few forensic botanists in the country she had been able to establish that the pollen found on the shoes of the girl's partner also exactly matched the type found in the ditch. Not only had this evidence broken his story but also such was her presence in the witness box that the jury had no difficulty in reaching its guilty verdict. It had been a good result.

Her light-grey eyes wandered up from the dead girl and from behind a pair of thin gold-framed spectacles, fixed his.

"Detective Sergeant Kerr, long time, no see," she greeted him in her soft Scottish lilt.

The welcome salutation surprised him. "You've remembered me after all this time," he responded.

"With a fine Scottish name like that, how could I forget you?"

"And there's me thinking it was because of my good looks."

She returned a smile, tut-tutted, and gave him a quick dismissive shake of her head. "By the way before I start my examination I think you need this." The Professor handed him a clear plastic exhibit bag. Inside was a playing card, its reverse side facing him.

He turned it over. The seven of hearts. He returned a quizzical frown.

"My sentiments exactly," the pathologist responded. "That card was partially covering the gaping wound you can see in the centre of her chest. She dropped her gaze back to the cadaver.

Hunter watched her move painstakingly around the body, her every move captured on video. The samples she pointed to were quickly photographed and bagged by the Scenes of Crime officers and forensic team who followed in her wake. Pausing momentarily she lifted her head towards Hunter and Grace. Glancing over her spectacles, which had fallen onto the bridge of her nose, she enquired, "Has anyone moved the body?"

Hunter gave Grace a questioning look.

Grace responded with a shrug of her shoulders and shake of head. "Not that we know of. The man who found the body couldn't get away quick enough before he phoned in. Though he has said he heard someone running away from the scene."

"Well the body has definitely been moved. There are scuffmarks in the matted blood on the floor; clearly where she has been dragged. And also we have the arms outstretched above her head which tend to reinforce that theory." She slowly rolled the corpse towards her and examined the purple lividity pattern that covered the back and buttocks.

Looking on, Hunter knew that this was the result of the muscles and organs no longer pumping blood around the body, and gravity taking over.

"The lividity is just starting to blanch. Hypostasis is in the early stages and body temperature readings would indicate she has been here for only a few hours. By the drag marks through the blood I would say that someone has attempted to move this body after death."

"From the bodies general description" interjected Grace, "we're certain it matches that of a fourteen year old girl who was reported missing only a couple of hours ago."

"Well my initial findings would suggest she was most probably murdered less than three hours ago. She has multiple stab and incised wounds to her head and as you can see a sharp instrument has penetrated both eyes. There is also the deep wound to the upper chest. Despite the considerable amount of congealed blood I can't say for sure yet if she was dead before or after the wounds were inflicted because I have also found this." Professor Lizzie McCormack pulled down the neckline of the dead girl's T-shirt a few inches below the throat. With a latex gloved hand she pointed to several red weal marks around the front of the neck.

"There is petechial haemorrhaging on the skin which is consistent with some type of ligature being placed tightly around the anterior neck. In other words she has been strangled with something approximately five centimetres wide. And looking at the nip and graze marks on the side of her upper neck my first thoughts are a belt of some type. The post-mortem will give us a better indication." She snapped off her gloves. "I've finished now if you'd like to bag up this once dear creature and remove her to the mortuary for me."

Lizzie eased herself up gently, her hands clasped around her knee joints. "The arthritis is playing me up today."

*****

The smell of death was something Hunter Kerr could never get used to. Despite the air conditioning in the white tiled mortuary the stench was a nauseating mixture of decaying flesh and stale blood, which enveloped him, and which he knew would be clinging for many hours thereafter to every article of clothing he wore. He popped an extra strong mint into his mouth in an effort to cover the smell. The mortuary also brought back the memories of the time he had dealt with his first cot death. The baby had been roughly the same age as his own first-born and all he had seen throughout the procedure was the face of Jonathan superimposed on the dead child. For days after he had lain awake at night watching the movement of the Moses basket at the side of the bed, and listening to Jonathan's breathing pattern.

The girl on the metal slab had now been cleaned up and he could now see clearly the horrendous wounds, which had been inflicted on the head of the girl. The dark mushy sockets, devoid of eyes, gave the face an almost surreal appearance. Throughout his career he had never been squeamish when it had come to looking at dead bodies, whatever state they were in, though as a young cop he had never actually liked having to physically handle the cold flesh. That was always one job he had always faced with trepidation, and wherever possible avoided.

Now in her green Pathologist's scrubs, Professor Lizzie McCormack moved gracefully around the body, her dexterous hands in an organized routine, measuring and moving limbs, picking up and setting down the many shiny precision instruments, each having its own function to perform, whether it be cracking and cutting bone or slicing through flesh. She probed orifices with swabs and scraped under fingernails, meticulously noting and labelling each sample, whilst speaking with her soft Scottish brogue into a metal microphone hanging from the ceiling, poised above the cadaver.

"The body is that of a normally developed pubescent white female, and appearing generally consistent with the stated age of fourteen years," she began. Moving to the head, she scrutinized, probed and measured the many and numerous wounds. "There is evidence of multiple sharp-force injury," she continued in a steady voice. After spending some considerable time counting and detailing each of the head wounds she moved to the neck. She pointed at several marks to the Scenes of Crime Officer hovering around her and then stepped back whilst close-up photographs were taken. Then, taking a small surgical scalpel, she began the process of incising the yellowing flesh at the base of the neck and peeled the scalp and face completely over the head to reveal a glistening white skull.

Inside fifteen minutes the Professor had removed the brain, measured and weighed it, and sliced off small samples of the grey tissue for further analysis. She then began moving down the body, examining the many cuts and gashes inflicted on the upper torso. Within a minute she gave out an elongated "Mmmm," paused, and caught Hunter's gaze. "You're going to find this very interesting, very interesting indeed."

Hunter's eyebrows cinched together, furrowing his brow.

"That's grabbed your attention hasn't it," she grinned, and began circling an index finger above the cadaver's abdomen. "I thought at first these were minor stab wounds," she continued, dabbing her pointing finger at several regular marks gouged into the flesh. "These cuts are nowhere near as deep as the others. The blade has only penetrated the first subcutaneous layer."

Hunter moved in closer, bending over Rebecca's body, focussing on the area Professor McCormick was pointing to. He stared at the series of consistent slashes above the navel, unable at first to make head-nor-tail of them; that was until he followed the slow deliberate movement of the pathologist's finger; then he did. He could quite clearly make out the letters I I V and a number 3 lined across the stomach. He shot his glance back towards the Professor catching her preoccupied look.

"This is a first for me," she announced. "Well in the flesh anyway, so to speak, but I must say I have seen photographs of similar marking to corpses and read about this some time ago." She paused again before continuing. "What you have here Detective Sergeant is the killer's signature. What you make of it is the same as me at the moment, a series of letters or Roman numerals, and what appears to be the number three." She took a step back whilst the Scenes of Crime officer moved in with his camera and rattled off a sequence of photographs, its flash highlighting the red marks carved into the marble-like flesh.

"Add to this, the playing card which was found lying across her chest and I can say with some confidence that this is definitely the killer letting you know that this is his or her handiwork. Though given the viciousness of the attack, I am more inclined to favour that a man's hand is responsible for this." The pathologist caught Hunter's startled look.

"I would start by contacting other forces, because it's my guess that this young girl here is not his first victim." She returned to her examination of Rebecca and just over an hour later she snapped off her latex gloves and turned to Hunter.

"Many of the wounds to the face and head are regular and suggest a knife of at least ten centimetres in length with an angled blade at its point. Many are stab type wounds, which have penetrated both the facial and muscle tissue of the head, and in places the bone beneath has actually been chipped. The most serious of those are to the eye sockets. Here the knife has actually sliced through into the brain and penetrated to an extent of ten centimetres. The downward slant of these wounds indicates a continued jabbing action. A real frenzied hacking at the face."

Lizzie emphasized by thrusting her arm up and down several times. "My other findings are death by asphyxia due to ligature strangulation. The hyoid bone and the thyroid and cricoid cartilages are fractured, which would indicate tremendous pressure around the throat. The marks suggest a belt of some type and I reinforce this by a buckle mark where it's nipped the upper neck. The mark is so clear that if you find the right belt I will be able to confirm a match. This is a particularly vicious and sustained attack. From the lack of defence injuries I would suggest she was strangled first and then as she lay dead or dying she was stabbed numerous times to the face and head. There is no evidence of any sexual interference, though swabs have been taken for more detailed analysis. It never ceases to amaze me just how cruel the human race is," she finished as she turned towards the shower room.

"Earlier today the body of a teenage girl was found in old farm buildings close to the town of Barnwell. Police have identified her as fourteen year old Rebecca Morris and confirm that she had been brutally murdered."

The hairs at the back of his head bristled and he could feel his face flush. The rest of the news report became just a jumble of words as he stared at his 32" plasma TV screen, which flicked between scenes showing the regional station's newsroom and the reporter who was broadcasting a short distance from the derelict buildings which he recognised as the farm from which earlier he had had to flee.

That had been the closest yet to being caught.

Screwing up his face he shuddered, feeling temporarily light headed. He had held his breath for far too long as he focussed on the news item. He exhaled sharply and took in a much needed gulp of air.

In the depths of his mind he recalled the past two-days' events. The night before last, especially in the early hours, and for most of yesterday morning he had hardly been able to contain his excitement. That fervour had increased ten-fold when he had caught sight of her waiting by the bus stop where he had arranged they should meet. As she had climbed into his car he could feel himself getting an erection. He had to pull the hem of his T-shirt over his lap to hide the bulge.

He could recall the conversation as though it had just happened.

"Didn't think you were going to come."

"I promised I'd be here didn't I?" she'd smiled back at him. "Though I don't know what I'm going to say when mum and dad find out I've skipped an exam."

"That's not going to matter once we get this portfolio done. A modelling agency will soon snap you up and the money you're going to earn will take care of any exam marks," he'd lied.

In the barn he'd watched her change out of her school clothes, blushing with embarrassment, and he'd managed to shoot several frames of her undressing before she had stopped him. She'd placed one hand in front of his lens whilst strapping the other firmly across her chest, covering her pretty pink cotton bra that hid her small yet firm breasts.

He'd laughed and tried to pull her arm away but she'd resisted and got angry.

"I want to go home," she'd demanded. "That's it. I've had enough." And she'd put her blouse back on.

That's when he'd reacted and slapped her across the face. He couldn't believe it when she'd slapped him back. The surprise of it had made him drop his camera.

He had snatched off his belt without thinking and wound it so quickly around her neck that she had hardly registered what was happening. He had pulled it so tightly that the veins at the sides of her temples had swollen to such prominence that he feared they would burst.

The rest had been a blur and it was over as quickly as it had started. All he could remember was the aftermath. Standing over her body, staring at the bloodied mess he had created.

He also could recollect, as he had surveyed his work, the surge of power, which had shot through him, tightening every sinew in his body.

He had tried to recall if the rush had been the same as before. He had thought that this time it had felt better. His erection had still been there, even when she had breathed her last.

The noise in the background brought him back to the present, and as the vision in his mind blurred he felt his chest burst with a sense of urgency and excitement again and could feel the movement in his groin. He was getting erect just thinking about what he had done.

From the kitchen he could hear the domestic sounds of his mother getting their evening meal ready. He pointed the remote at the TV and switched over to the other local news channel to see if the story was being aired there.

- ooOoo -

CHAPTER TWO

DAY TWO: 7th July.

With a spring in his step Hunter breezed into the office, still humming the tune of 'Summer of 69', the last song he had heard on the radio as he'd parked his car in the rear yard. The first thing that greeted him was the strong heady aroma of freshly percolated coffee. Unbuttoning his jacket he saw that most of the squad were in. Barnwell Major Investigation Team office cum incident room was a hive of activity and around the department there was a hubbub of excited chatter.

Nothing like a murder to get the energy levels flowing, he thought to himself as he shrugged off his suit jacket and made for his desk.

Draping his coat over the back of his seat he levelled another look around the room and dropped down into his chair. He knew the Case Teams would be fired up, because for the last four months the majority of the detectives had been working on some of the district's old undetected crime files, often referred to as 'cold case' work. That work had been laborious - poring over old witness statements and cross referencing suspect interviews and alibis, and finally checking old exhibits for DNA traces, the science of which had not been available when the original crime had been committed.

Grace Marshall sidled up to him and handed him his Sheffield United mug.

Hunter looked and sniffed at the freshly brewed tea and mouthed a grateful thank you; he couldn't abide coffee first thing in the morning.

Bathed in the warm sunlight, pouring through the large double-glazed windows, which ran the length of one side of the office, Hunter saw that Grace's tawny complexion glowed more than it normally did, and he couldn't help but notice that her mop of brown curls looked tighter than usual and glistened wetly in places.

"Running late?" he enquired pointing to her hair.

"Don't ask. Mad rush. David's just started his new job this morning and wanted to get in there early to make an impression, so I've had to sort out Robyn and Jade's arrangements for when they finish school this afternoon. They're going to my dad's," she replied turning to a mirror in the office softly patting at her hair. The damp curls were beginning to cascade onto her shoulders. "Do I look a mess?"

He smiled back, thinking of his own similar routine at home, or rather the organisation skills of his wife, Beth, whenever he was working on a murder enquiry. Many had been the time when he had grabbed a quick shower and shave at work when he had worked through back-to-back sixteen hour days, constantly telephoning home and updating Beth with new timescales. She had never complained either when he had finished the day off with a swift beer at the pub with the rest of the team 'just to wind down'. He was always amazed how placid she was about it all, especially when mentally drained he had got home and just sunk into his armchair not wanting to talk about his day. He realised how fortunate he was to have someone so understanding and supportive as Beth for a wife. He'd known of different reactions from spouses in quite a few other police marriages with many ending in divorce.

"Been there, done that, and no you look fine," Hunter smiled back.

He could see that overnight the Home Office Large Major Enquiry System – HOLMES team - had been busy, going through the few reports currently in existence, and drawing up the 'time line' sequence on the white melamine board at the front of the room. A classic school photograph of Rebecca Morris, fresh faced and smiling in her school uniform, was positioned near the start of the line at the time where she had been reported missing. A couple of other pen marks showed where there had been reported sightings and the last indicator showed the time when her badly beaten body had been discovered. Alongside that last mark several gruesome post-mortem images had been affixed, particularly the close-up shots of the curious symbols gouged into her abdomen.

The sudden clatter and scraping of chairs caused him to turn his head. Detective Superintendent Michael Robshaw, whom he knew had been appointed as the Senior Investigating Officer – SIO, for this investigation, was making his way towards the incident board at the front of the room.

Hunter had known Michael Robshaw a long time. At an early stage of his CID career he had become his DI, and had been the one who had first planted the seed in his mind to apply to join Drugs Squad. And he had then supported him for promotion to DS five year ago. Hunter not only liked and respected his boss but he also admired how he still kept his feet on the ground despite his elevation in rank. Especially as to how he had maintained his reputation as being a thinking man's policeman. Whereas some officers who had climbed up the ranks had sold themselves out to Home Office bureaucracy he had kept a common sense and practical approach to today's policing.

Michael Robshaw swelled his broad chest, removed his spectacles, rubbed his handkerchief around the lenses and then replaced them.

"Ladies and Gents," he began in his deep and broad South Yorkshire accent."

A silence registered around the room.

"Rebecca Morris," he pointed to the school photograph. "A fourteen year old girl with everything to live for. According to her mother she left home at a quarter to eight yesterday morning, wearing her school uniform, saying she was going in to school early to hand in some work and to prepare for an exam which she should have sat at ten am."

He pointed to the next time line sequence.

"At five to eight she was seen by a school friend at a bus stop on the main road, five hundred yards from her home. She was still in school uniform. The girl who saw her states this was unusual as Rebecca normally walked to school. She was on the opposite side of the road and she shouted across to her and asked her what she was doing. Rebecca informed her that she had to visit an aunt first to pick up some books for school. We are almost certain from the initial missing-from-home enquiries that this was a lie. She never got to school. The school secretary contacted her mother at ten-fifteen yesterday morning after she failed to turn in for the exam. At eleven, after making several phone calls and finding her daughter's phone switched off her mother contacted the police."

He moved along the board. "The next sighting we have is the discovery of her body at two pm yesterday in the barn of a derelict farm between the villages of Harlington and Adwick-on-Dearne, by a local thief who has admitted being there for the purpose of stealing stone. We are confident as we can be at this time he had nothing to do with this murder."

He broke off a second to lick his dry lips. "She was found wearing a T-shirt and jeans and there was no sign of her school uniform or the school bag she had left home with. A fresh search for those items is to be carried out later this morning."

He paused and straightened himself. At six foot five he had an imposing presence.

"Several avenues have to be gone down today. We need to know if she actually did get on a bus, and if she did so, which bus was it she got on, and where did it drop her off? Are there any other sightings of her, in or out of uniform in the lead up to her body being found? Was she meeting anyone? Did she have a boyfriend?" These are all questions I'd like answering by the end of the day's play."

The Superintendent pointed to the post mortem photos of Rebecca Morris. "And to add a different dimension to this enquiry the pathologist has highlighted a series of marks cut into the body's stomach. Professor McCormack has every confidence that these are the killer's calling card." He tapped the photographs showing the symmetrical incisions 'I I V 3' along Rebecca's abdomen. "Never in my career have I seen or known of anything like this. The professor says she is only aware of similar cases from her past work in America. Quite clearly we are dealing with someone who is very disturbed, and judging by this calling card, we cannot rule out that they haven't struck before."

The SIO paused again, roaming his eyes around the room, scrutinising the faces of the MIT detectives. He continued, "I want to know what the significance of these marks are? What do they mean? Do they have any links to either religion or the occult? What also is the significance of the seven of hearts playing card found placed on the body? Whoever is given that task check the Internet for anything similar. Nothing is ruled in or out."

Superintendent Robshaw placed a hand, palm flat, against the wipe board. "This is a really vicious murder. The extreme violence and sadistic nature of the attack shows we have someone with a very sick mind. We need this person behind bars as soon as possible. I want no stone unturned. Now let's get out there Ladies and Gents and see if we can wrap this enquiry up quickly."

* * * * *

This was one of those moments that Hunter Kerr hated most. He could face angry and violent men without being emotionally disturbed, but facing grief stricken parents, particularly those of young children, had always brought a lump to his throat. Rebecca Morris had become the victim of a crime that haunts the mind of every parent. He and Grace had been given the job of visiting Rebecca's parents to tease out as much background information as possible, whilst also bearing in mind there was always the possibility that one or both of them could be involved in the crime.

Before that they had driven back towards the scene of the murder. Hunter was pleased to see that roadblocks had already been put in place, and he could see that groups of uniformed officers, some with sniffer dogs, were now combing the area around the derelict farm. Specialists were carrying out fingertip searches, and scythes and rakes were being used to hack back the thick undergrowth in the search for clues. A dirt track running from the rear of the farm into the village of Harlington had diversion signs in place, and a white tent protected the area where Rebecca had been found slain.

He noticed several young people had started to arrive with bouquets of flowers, and small teddy bears. He knew very soon there would be a special school assembly in honour of her memory, where the likelihood that both pupils and staff would be reduced to tears, and he felt an involuntary shiver move down his spine, as he drove away from the scene.

This would not be easy, Hunter thought as he pressed the doorbell on the front door of the Morris home. It was a typical semi-detached house in one of the many council estates in the area, though looking at the PVC door he guessed they had been one of the many who had bought their own home during the Thatcher era.

During the next hour or so he knew that both he and Grace would be constantly questioning and cross-questioning, probing those long forgotten secrets and opening up old hidden wounds, at a time when they were at their most vulnerable.

DC Caroline Blake, who had been appointed as the Family Liaison Officer, greeted them at the door.

"Anything?" Hunter enquired. It was typical opening parlance between detectives when visiting the homes of murder victims. What it actually meant was, 'Have they revealed or given anything away;' until Mr and Mrs Morris were 'alibied' they were suspects.

Caroline Blake shook her head. "They're just numb. Still finding it difficult to accept that their daughter is dead." She showed them into the front room and went off into the kitchen to make a fresh pot of tea.

He was pleased Caroline had been given the job as the FLO. He could remember interviewing her for this position only two months ago and guessed this was her first case. Despite her newness to the job he knew from her background that she would cope admirably.

He and Grace could see as soon as they entered the room that Mr and Mrs Morris had suffered a sleepless night, and the redness of their eyes revealed many hours of crying. As soon as the questioning began it was obvious they were trying to be strong despite the intense sadness and pressure that was consuming them. Mrs Morris broke down repeatedly and tears welled in Jack Morris's eyes as he spoke of a very happy daughter and showed off felt-tipped messages on cards from well-wishers that had been pushed through their door.

Hunter and Grace questioned them for almost two hours, going over home and school routines and asking about her closest friends.

"Any boyfriends?" Grace explored.

"There were boys who were friends," Mrs Morris replied "But she had no boyfriends that we are aware of." She always checked her room, she added, glancing at her husband.

They could not give any explanation for Rebecca changing out of her school clothes into the T-shirt and jeans she had been found in.

Hunter could see from their returned looks, that was a mystery, which was tearing at their heartstrings.

"She was a typical teenage girl, loved her boy bands, dressing up and playing around with make-up. She was always so cheerful, the life and soul of the house. Rebecca was a very special person who touched the lives of so many people. We don't know anyone who would want to hurt her like this," ended Jack Morris, a film of tears suddenly washing over his eyes, and as he hooked an arm around his wife's shoulder she began to sob uncontrollably.

"Can you let us see her room?" Hunter asked. "Just in case there's anything which may give us a lead," he added.

Mrs Morris guided them upstairs and to the left of the landing. There was a plaque on the door – 'Rebecca's room' – more than likely put there when she was just a young child. A more up to date one, no doubt added by Rebecca, stated 'KEEP OUT - GENIUS AT WORK'.

"Do you regularly check her room?" chipped in Grace.

"Not exactly check. The odd flick round with a duster and a bit of straightening. Rebecca is a very tidy girl – was," she corrected herself and fresh tears welled into her eyes. Hunter touched her gently on one shoulder. "I'm afraid we need to do a thorough search of her room. If you find this upsetting you can wait downstairs."

"No I'll be okay" she sniffed and dabbed at her eyes "It still doesn't seem real. I feel as though she'll burst through the door at any second."

Hunter couldn't find the right response and chose to shrug his shoulders as he pushed open the bedroom door. He paused for a second, surveying the surroundings. The first thing he thought was how bright and airy the room was. A stream of bright sunshine warmed it. The pink and beige décor of the walls matched the bedding. Two large purple cushions lay against the pine headboard, surrounded by a hoard of fluffy teddy bears and other creatures. Having already gathered from the Morris's that their daughter was still a child at heart. It was these things that reinforced in his mind the innocence of the girl. Posters of several boy bands, whom he had heard of but couldn't name the individual members, adorned the walls, together with photos of A list celebrities snipped out from magazines. Coloured 'post its' and paper arrows, with handwritten personal comments, such as 'gorgeous' and 'luv u' covered some of them: She had stamped her own identity on this room.

Amongst them, in the centre of the wall, opposite the foot of the bed, was a pin board filled with photographs. Many were of Rebecca in different poses and in different periods of her young life. All happy scenes. On the beach. At fun parks. Pulling faces. On rides. With family and with friends. He scanned them for the up to date ones. And they were there. Her brown hair longer, and styled, blue glistening eyes, a nose that was a little prominent. The word cute came to mind. These were more serious poses – more grown up. A smiling face amongst her friends, and he wondered for a second which one of those she had confided in. As he took a last look at them he knew in his mind that these would be the last treasured memories Mr and Mrs Morris had of Rebecca.

He and Grace separated and began to move methodically about the room, checking under the bed, dressing table, wardrobe, and bedside cupboard. Opening drawers, and rifling through her clothing. They picked up books, CDs, DVDs, opening, shaking them and then replacing them. The two detectives had done this many times before and were on autopilot as they went about the task. Hunter caught a glimpse of Mrs Morris, motionless in the doorway, hands clenched together, prayer-like and stifling a sob. He wondered if she could feel the presence of her cherished child as they disturbed Rebecca's things. He fired off several questions about her regular habits and then asked, "Did she have a computer?"

"No she shared the one downstairs," replied Mrs Morris, "so we could keep an eye on her, what with these chat room perverts you read about." Then she checked herself and her voice faltered.

"Did she keep a diary, that you know of?"

"No. Not to my knowledge. If she did it was more than likely in her school bag. She did the odd scribble in her school planner, but I've not checked that for weeks. She recorded most of her stuff on her mobile. Those are with her." She paused. "Who could have done this to her?"

He saw that her face looked tired, care worn, and that dark lines were etched around her eyes from lack of sleep. He wished he had an answer for her.

As he finished he gave the room a final, once over look. He just knew that this would probably remain untouched for many years to come. It would be the Morris's' dedication to Rebecca's memory. A shrine to their beautiful daughter. He felt a cold shudder move down his spine. Someone had walked over his grave.

Hunter finally closed the bedroom door with a sense of foreboding. He had hoped for an early breakthrough. Some sort of discovery. A name, or an indication why such an innocent girl had met a brutal death. But there had been nothing. If she had any secrets, they hadn't found them in that room.

* * * * *

There was a deathly silence about the evening, broken only by the soft squelch of his rubber soled training shoes on the wet garden path as he moved through the fine drizzle. Despite the rain it was still warm. He glanced back up the garden where the lounge window of his home was illuminated in a warm yellow glow, and where he could see the flashes of light coming from the television. Looking at his watch he realised his mother would be fully engrossed in one of her favourite soaps. For at least half an hour he knew he would not be disturbed.

Snapping back the padlock of the old shed he slowly eased open the paint-blistered door. It creaked slightly. The sound cascaded images around in his head from the many horror movies he had watched and he momentarily stiffened, frame upright, and gave another glance over his shoulder. The evening was still. The rain was keeping everyone indoors. He stepped into the wooden hut and secured the door after him. The interior was dingy and he had to strain his eyes whilst surveying the muddle of garden equipment and discarded household items. Finally piercing the darkness and identifying the pile he required he began to pull at several old wooden packing crates, garden tools and old blankets he had placed there several days ago. Lastly he opened one of the plastic sacks that lay in an ordered heap. A pungent musty smell hit his nostrils, and almost simultaneously black and white images of a girl struggling, flashbacked into his mind. He shuddered for a split second and then composed himself.

Item by item he spread out her school shirt, skirt and tie and then removed books, a pencil case and the mobile phone from the pink bag she used for school. He double-checked the battery and SIM card ensuring they were still disconnected. He'd read somewhere that whilst the battery and SIM card were connected that a mobile could still be tracked, even if it wasn't in use.

After yesterday's close shave he couldn't afford to take chances. *Not now, after all this time.*

He picked up her school shirt, white cotton, freshly washed, and he pulled it towards his face, sniffing deeply, picking up the fragrance of her deodorant. His flesh began to go goosey, and a cold sensation tingled up his spine. The muscles of his face twitched involuntary as he caught a final glimpse of her face in his mind. He felt himself getting erect again.

He knew he would have to get rid of all these soon just on the off chance he was questioned.

Folding the clothing carefully and mentally double checking each item's return to its bag, he replaced everything as it had been, and then putting an ear to the door he confidently stepped out into the warm summer rain.

- ooOoo -

CHAPTER THREE
DAY SIX: 11th July.

In contemplative mood Hunter Kerr stared into the bathroom mirror, ran a hand around his freshly shaved jaw line, dabbed water from the bowl onto his head, and then rubbed a wet hand through his brown receding hairline, temples now flecked with grey. He stroked the few mature hairs slowly, for a second thinking about colouring them, then caught himself, and smiled at his vanity.

Stepping back into the bedroom he fastened up his shirt and slung a loose tie around his neck. He saw that Beth was still snug beneath the duvet. He diverted his gaze to the bedside alarm clock and saw that in twenty minutes' time it would be buzzing away. He knew that within five minutes of it sounding Beth would be into her routine, sorting out their two sons for school, whilst at the same time preparing herself for her job at the Doctors' surgery where she worked part time as a nurse practitioner. It always amazed him how she could juggle managing the house, their boys, and still hold down a professional career. He knew he couldn't do it. He bent down and kissed her forehead. She half opened her eyes and smiled.

"Just off love. Don't know what time I'll get in. Got a busy day ahead."

She muttered back something incoherent and rolled over.

In stocking feet he crept downstairs, so as not to wake his two boys, and eased a newspaper from the letterbox of the front door, before creeping through to the kitchen at the rear.

He made tea lazily, dunking a tea bag directly into a mug, at the same time slotting two slices of bread into the toaster. He made the tea strong, adding a heaped teaspoon of sugar to wake himself up. Waiting for the toast he stood before the kitchen sink, mug clutched to his chest, staring dreamily through the window, taking in the sights of the morning freshness stirring his garden. Everywhere was still damp from the overnight rain, and a fine mist was rising as the warmth of the sun slowly appeared over the distant tree tops. He thought for a moment how fortunate he was. His home overlooked farmland that formed part of the old Wentworth estates. A gate at the bottom of his garden opened up onto fields and many a time he had watched his two boys making dens amongst the bushes, or jumping into the stacks of newly cut wheat.

He visualized his own first home as a child. A terraced house with a shared back yard. It was all his parents could afford, but he could still remember being told by his father, that it was far better than the tenement building that he and his wife had left behind in Glasgow.

Both his parents had reminded him many times of how fortunate he should consider himself. They had been born in Scotland and brought up in an era of economic hardship, deciding to move down to Yorkshire to make a better life for themselves in the early nineteen seventies. They had never returned, both choosing to settle when he had been born six months after their arrival.

As he bit into his first slice of fresh toast he opened up Barnwell's weekly paper. The headline 'BRUTAL MURDER' in bold black letters shouted back, and a cherished family photo of Rebecca Morris, a faint smile across her face, filled a good section of the page. There had been hardly anything in the Nationals, but he knew the local paper would make great play on the macabre discovery. He pored over the article to check if the killer's handiwork had been leaked but there were no surprise revelations. Its column inches had used the original police press statement, a brief update by the Senior Investigating Officer, and lastly the usual quotes from friends and neighbours to embellish the misery, anguish and cruelty of this human tragedy report.

He finished reading the article and knew first hand that progress was still in its early stages. Now in the sixth day of the investigation, the finishing touches were just being put around the site of the murder, with exhibit after exhibit being logged and bagged for forensics. There had been no discoveries so far of Rebecca's school clothing, bag or personal mobile. It was painstakingly slow work with no stone being left unturned. And he knew that within the next hour, when he sat in this morning's briefing, the now twenty strong Major Investigation Team – two additional teams of detectives' from district CID had swelled their ranks - would be ready for another day working against the clock.

* * * * *

Hunter and Grace had been allocated the task of interviewing Rebecca's closest friend, Kirsty Evans, who had just returned from holiday to hear the shocking news. As Hunter entered the Wood estate his mind went back to his childhood years when he had roamed these streets with some of his school pals who had lived there. It had once been a model of council planning. Sadly the estate had become like many others – run down. A new generation of people, with legacies of problems, had moved in and had not bothered to change or adopt the same pride as their neighbour's. Consequently, he knew from his previous CID work, that burglaries had increased to fund drug habits, resulting in those tenants with savings moving out for a more peaceful lifestyle.

They pulled into Hawthorne Close, a small cul-de-sac, and Hunter immediately thought that this was not one of those streets that had fallen to the dregs of society. This was how he remembered the look of the estate many years ago. The Evans's had spent money re-furbishing their house, and a garage and extension had changed the appearance of the council house.

Mr Evans greeted them, explaining how dreadful the shock had been, what a pleasant, friendly girl Rebecca was, and finished with the note that Kirsty was still very upset.

Hunter immediately picked up on the tone of how Mr Evans delivered his opening and guessed he had made those comments as a means of expressing hope that they would adopt a softer and sympathetic approach to how they interviewed his daughter. He reassuringly replied, "Don't worry Mr Evans we're just here to get some background about Rebecca."

Mr Evans showed them into the lounge, informed them she was with her mother, and then finished by saying he had some work to do 'out the back'.

It was evident Kirsty had been crying. She was slightly younger than Rebecca by two months, but Hunter thought she looked older. A few years older in fact. She could easily have passed for sixteen. Her hair had obviously been cut and coloured at a good salon. She wore tasteful make up over her newly acquired tanned face, and her slender figure already had womanly curves.

Hunter introduced Grace and himself, but went no further as they had already decided that because Grace's daughter, Robyn, was exactly the same age that she would most likely have the natural affinity to carry out this sensitive interview.

They settled themselves in armchairs beside the settee where Kirsty sat, with her Mother placing a reassuring arm around her daughter's shoulders, and positioned themselves to face her. Hunter, the note taker, sat back pen poised over his daily journal, whilst Grace leant forward hands clasped together on her lap.

"Kirsty, this is important" she began. "We need to catch Rebecca's killer as soon as possible. We need you to tell us everything you know about her. It's also important that you hold no secrets back, even if you think you might get into trouble."

Kirsty's bloodshot eyes shot open and fixed on the detective.

"Trouble, but we haven't done anything wrong. We're not like that"

"I'm not accusing you of anything Kirsty. It's just that in cases like this we can't afford for anything to be held back. We all have things we want to keep hidden, sometimes especially from parents. I have a daughter exactly the same age as you, so I can say that from experience. Trust me Kirsty we're not wanting to get you into any trouble."

"I'm not hiding anything. We don't have anything to hide…" she glanced sideways at her mother, "honest," she finished.

"Fine Kirsty, that's just fine. Now tell us about Rebecca."

For the next ten minutes the girl spoke softly, in warm affectionate tones, about her friend Rebecca. Her likes and dislikes. What they did in their rooms and what they did outside and at school. There was nothing untoward.

It was typical fourteen-year-old girl stuff, thought Hunter as he scribed.

Kirsty appeared to have settled. Grace said, "Did she ever fall out with anyone? Have any enemies?"

"Not Rebecca. She was quiet and friendly. We're all like that, our group. We keep away from the girls we know who are going to cause trouble."

"What about boyfriends?"

"None serious. We knocked about with a couple of lads; walked home with them, saw them at the youth club, that kind of stuff. Just acted around with them."

The replies flowed but Hunter couldn't help but feel that the sentences were somehow so false; so rehearsed. He tried to catch Graces attention, to indicate for her to change tack in her approach to the questions.

Grace said, "Did she ever talk about fancying anyone?"

Hunter smiled to himself. It was almost as if she had read his mind.

Kirsty paused in mid thought, and then glanced across at her mother.

Grace picked up on the hesitation. "Come on Kirsty what is it?"

For a few seconds Kirsty stuttered over the words, until she finally got them out. "Well it was the other way round actually. A couple of weeks ago she just blurted out that this bloke had been coming on to her, pestering her for her mobile number."

"Where did she tell you this?" Grace was edging even further forward, trying to get eye contact with Kirsty.

"Well she told me at the youth club. She just came up to me and said she had something to tell me in secret. Whispered it like. And then we went to a corner and she just said this guy had come up to her when she was on a ride at the fair and told her how nice she looked, and asked her if he could take some photos of her. I told her that was weird. She said it wasn't like that. He wanted to take some nice pictures of her. Rebecca can be a bit naïve when it comes to lads and all that. I think she thought I was making fun of her. She got the hump and said I was only jealous. I didn't want to row with her so I didn't say anything else even though I still thought it was freaky. Anyway I asked her who it was, thinking he was in the youth club, but she said he wasn't there. She'd met him when she'd gone outside the club. I pushed her for a bit more but she clammed up. She said she thought I didn't believe her. I kept telling her I believed her but she wouldn't tell me anymore."

"Do you know which fair this was at, and when?"

"I can only think it must have been the Feast fair, which came a couple of weeks ago. It's the one that comes every year on the fields at the back of the youth club."

Hunter continued to make detailed notes.

"Did she say anything else about him? Mention his name or where he came from?" Grace continued

"Nope. But there was this one time when we were walking home from school and her mobile rang. She looked at the screen and blushed and wouldn't let me see who it was. She never did that, we always told each other everything. Anyway she answered it and I heard her answer that she was with someone. She said it was her friend Kirsty - me. Then she just said 'okay speak with you later,' and cut off her mobile. I asked her if it was her boyfriend, just joking like, and she went bright red. She said if I were taking the mess she wouldn't tell me anything else. I told her I wasn't and then changed it round a bit to try and find out who it was like. She said he was really nice and had his own car. She said he kept telling her how pretty she was, and what a nice figure she had. I didn't say anything but I thought it was really weird stuff to say that to Rebecca. Not that she wasn't pretty or anything like, but I mean she hasn't really developed properly yet. You've seen what she's like. She's stick thin. You know what I mean?"

Grace nodded. "Kirsty you said Rebecca told you he had a car. Which lads do you knock about with who have cars?"

"Well we don't. I mean we know some of the sixth formers have cars but we don't talk to them. But it's not what she said about him having a car, it's how she said it. I just got the impression that when she said guy, that she actually meant someone a lot older."

"A man you mean?" asked Grace taken aback by this sudden answer.

"Well I suppose so, yes."

For the next hour Grace backtracked over everything they had discussed. Kirsty faltered at times, catching a glimpse of her mum, and repeated with a similar answer as previous.

Hunter knew from his policing experience and as a father to two children that she was holding something back. He wanted to jump in and push her for answers but this was Grace's call.

She didn't push. At the end of the talk Grace handed Kirsty one of her batch of small business cards, with the force crest in one corner and the blue block type stating THIS IS NOT A FORM OF IDENTIFICATION running across its length. She took a pen and underlined her work mobile number.

"If you can think of anything else Kirsty," she pressed the card firmly into the girl's palm, catching her gaze, making eye contact. "If you want to talk to me in confidence Kirsty call me on this number," she finished, before nudging Hunter and making for the door.

- ooOoo –

CHAPTER FOUR
DAY SEVEN: 12th July.

Because of the repetitive nature of Dougie Crabtree's work he constantly found his mind wandering, reminiscing and throwing up rose-tinted images of how this dark and stark landscape once looked when it was the site of the former Manvers Colliery. He shifted his nineteen stone bulk from one cheek to the other on the vinyl seat, in time to the swaying motion of his cab on the huge Komatsu track excavator. His thick muscular arms effortlessly and skilfully manoeuvred between transmission and hydraulic gears, as the crane surged over deep rutted tracks, whilst the eighteen foot reach mechanical shovel scooped enormous wedges of cloggy grey earth and slopped them into the waiting caterpillar dumper truck. He was thinking to himself what a coincidence this was. Having started work at the thriving colliery from school and then witnessing its demise and dereliction after the Miner's Strike in 1984, he was back on the site, and involved in its regeneration. Though he hated to admit it, particularly after the struggle, anger and bitterness he had gone through to fight for 'his pit,' it was refreshing to work regularly in the fresh air on a daily basis. The eighty-four acre old colliery and coking plant site was in the throes of a major transformation. The previous infrastructure of winding gear, coal preparation plant, site offices and coking unit had gradually gone, and in its place were plush working industrial units and landscaped environments. And he was toiling on the final phase. Reclaiming the old slurry pits, to make way for a £130 million scheme, which would see retail, leisure and residential units woven into the vista.

The engine growled and his cab vibrated as the huge bucket gouged the lumpy grey surface, scooping out another lump of the toxic earth. The oily surface water bubbled as pockets of methane gas escaped from beneath the mess and Dougie screwed up his face as the rotten 'eggy' smell wafted across his nostrils. He was about to dive the steel fingers of the shovel back into the earth again when he spotted an unusual form poking through the scrape he had just dug. He halted the bucket's dip, and squinting, peered out through the smeared windscreen. He could have sworn that looked like a body. He closed his eyes for a split second, flicked them open again and stared, focusing on the object that he had unearthed, trying to separate the dirt from the shape. "It can't be," he said to himself, as a rush of adrenaline surged through his body and his stomach emptied. "It is though; it's definitely a body."

* * * * *

Detective Constable's Tony Bullars and Mike Sampson, the other half of Hunter's team had been pulled from the Rebecca Morris murder to join the police and forensic team that were foraging amongst the slurry tips on the Manvers site. They took a short-cut to the scene, via a well-used undulating dirt track, which bounced them bruisingly around in the CID car, and found their witness Dougie Crabtree, by the side of a marked police car, talking animatedly to an officer who was attempting to formulate his excited jabberings into hard facts. A hundred yards away a half dozen, white-suited, members of the Forensic Team were on hands and knees probing around in the solid clods of coal dust. A white tent was in the process of being erected. It appeared so bright set against the stark grey backdrop, reminiscent of a lunar landscape.

"That's where our body must be," announced Tony Bullars, moving to the back of the CID car to collect a forensics suit.

Whereas Tony was tall and slim, with a good head of gelled hair, Mike was in complete contrast; small and podgy, unruly dark hair, and a craggy face badly pockmarked from acne in his adolescence. What they did have in common though was a sharpness of mind and a keenness to detect crime, which had elevated them both from uniform into CID, relatively early in their careers. Both had joined the Major Investigation Team at its inception eighteen months ago.

Tony skipped across the rutted site whilst Mike trudged, whingeing and moaning almost with every step.

"Bloody hell 'Bully', just look at the frigging state of me. How come you're not in the same state?" He grimaced, glancing at his mud splattered shoes.

Tony turned and laughed, "You've either got it Mike or you haven't." He turned and then strode away leaving Mike to his predicament amongst the deep ruts.

Both Tony and Mike were glad to see that Professor Lizzie McCormack was in attendance, her latex-gloved hands, already clearing soil around the mummified corpse, still partly entrenched amongst the dingy earth. The remains were curled up in the foetal position and in a bit of a mess. Portions of the body were devoid of flesh, and the skin, which did cover the thin-boned form, was shrivelled and hard as rock. The overall colour of the cadaver matched that of the earth around it.

Lizzie looked up, her glistening grey eyes, appearing over her designer spectacles. "Ha gentlemen so glad you could join us. Two bodies in less than a week, you are keeping me busy." Her sharp eyes spotted Mike Sampson shudder and turn his sight sharply away from the rotted corpse. "I hope you will have the stomach to see this one out officer."

Mike looked at Lizzie and blushed

"You see this is what sets us woman apart from you men," she begun. "We spend months changing smelly nappies without thinking about it. But what you don't realise is all those months of shovelling shit gives us a stronger stomach for the messier side of life."

She gave the detective a wink and forged her mouth into a wry smile. Lizzie continued to move slowly and meticulously around the corpse. Picking at it here and there and removing fragments that were quickly bagged by her young female assistant. After three quarters of an hour she pushed herself up onto her haunches, snapped off a glove, removed her spectacles and shot a glance at the two detectives.

"Gents what we have here is the decomposed yet mummified body of a young female who has obviously been in the ground for some time. There are remains of clothing. What appears to be a shirt or blouse and a pair of jeans. I'm not sure if we are going to be able to get any fingerprints at this time. The body's caked in mud so I'll have to check if we

51

can get into the ridges when the body's back in the mortuary. The head also needs some cleaning up but it does have plenty of hair fragments to enable DNA analysis. There is evidence of massive trauma to the nose and lower jaw area, some teeth are missing, and there are incised wounds around the eye sockets." She bent forward and looked into the dark holes where the eyes should have been, "I will be able to give firm confirmation of my thoughts after the post-mortem, but if I'm not too mistaken here there are some similarities between the injuries inflicted on this corpse and those inflicted on Rebecca Morris."

-ooOoo-

CHAPTER FIVE
DAY EIGHT: 13th July.

By the time Tony Bullars and Mike Sampson arrived at the mortuary the next morning the examination of the mummified corpse was already underway. The dark, shrivelled form lay naked on one of the metallic pathology slabs, having had its clothing cut away, and that now lay separately on another table undergoing photographing by an attendant Scenes of Crime Officer.

Professor McCormack was currently dragging a comb through the dead girl's lank and matted hair, dropping several strands, along with soil fragments, into a clear plastic exhibit bag. She was talking rapidly in post mortem legalese into the overhead microphone. She studied the corpse in a methodical way, observing and touching in timely fashion. Pausing from time to time she pulled at the arms, carefully rotating them, cracking the dried fragile skin, and probed cuts and indentions with a scalpel, before stepping back to allow the SOCO officer to photograph them.

At times she looked carefully at patches of the shrivelled skin under a magnifying glass then instructed a technician, following in her wake, where she wanted incisions on the body, and which parts of the body she wanted chopped away. Finally the hand-held circular saw was switched on and the top of the skull was deftly cut and removed, to reveal a murky brown interior that contained the shrivelled remains of a brain.

"Thankfully because of the toxicity of the soil very few insects have attacked the body, and the internal organs, except one, although badly decomposed, are relatively intact." The Professor stated as she looked up and glanced towards the two detectives.

She continued with the legalese, only halting her speech when she measured and weighed various organs. After the two-hour autopsy she stopped, threw her gloves, and mask into a bin, grabbed a paper towel and mopped her moist brow.

Then wiping her spectacles and replacing then, only on to the bridge of her nose, so she could look over them and turned to Tony and Mike.

"Gentlemen, you have here a girl who is between her early to late teens. The structure of her pelvis and hips tell me she has not yet reached adulthood. She has collar length brown hair and is five feet five inches tall. She would have been very slender prior to her death. She has multiple stab and incised wounds to the head, neck, trunk and upper extremities. Three stab wounds in particular are very nasty indeed. The blade has penetrated the brain through the eyes sockets and part of her upper chest has been sliced open. What is unusual about this is that her heart has been cut out and removed."

Tony and Mike exchanged startled looks.

"You heard me right gents. Her heart has been cut out." She nudged her glasses back into place with her forearm. "And also as per Rebecca Morris's examination I have also found similar markings incised into her abdomen." She paused and studied the corpse's stomach with a critical eye. "I say similar," she continued looking back up. "In fact the first mark is slightly different. It looks more like a reversed letter L. The other marks are the same, an I, and V, and number 3. Could be a combination of Roman numerals; your guess is as good as mine at the moment. I'm going to have to get a scan done of these to confirm this, and I'm also going to re-examine Rebecca Morris just to check if I've missed anything."

Professor McCormick began pulling at the plastic protective apron covering her scrubs. "She also has minor blunt injuries to the head, especially around the nose, left cheek area, and lower jaw. Many of the stab wounds to the head are very irregular, and are located mostly to the left hand side. Her left ear has almost been severed. The majority of the wounds to the trunk and upper extremities have penetrated the subcutaneous skin, and muscle layers, through to the bone. The stab to the sternum has passed into the chest and penetrated the left lung," the Professor continued without catching breath.

"The upper extremities have multiple sharp-force injuries consistent with defensive injuries. Lastly the hyoid bone, the thyroid, and the cricoid cartilages are fractured. The marks on the neck tissue suggest a wide ligature; most probably a belt." The Professor paused, as if to gather her thoughts. "This young lady has suffered a horrendous death. I do have moulds to make from the stab wounds, in order to determine both the type of weapon used and confirm they are a match, but I am confident when I say the weapon used has similar curves to that which was used on Rebecca Morris."

"Do you have any thoughts on the sequence of events?" asked Tony.

"Thoughts, young man. I don't have thoughts. I give out facts based on my forty-two years experience" she cut back at him abruptly.

Despite the tone of her answer Tony Bullars quite liked being called young man, notwithstanding he was twenty-eight years old. Though he guessed to her he must appear quite young and fresh faced. Professor McCormack must be at least retirement age, he thought to himself, and his face creased into a smile.

"Before you arrived gentlemen I carefully removed her clothing. Her blouse had several buttons missing; torn off, and was open to the navel. Her bra had been lifted above her breasts and these would have been exposed. Her jeans were still on and fastened and she was also still wearing her panties. With that in mind and the nature of her injuries it leads me to believe that she was punched first in the nose and jaw area. Her clothing was either disturbed during this, but more than likely after the assault, which, in my opinion would have been violent enough to render her unconscious for a short time. She then came to and struggled, during which time she was stabbed repeatedly. Remember I told you she had defence injuries; like so." The Professor proceeded to raise both her arms and shield her upper body and face. "The angulations of the incisions, and stab wounds, leave me to believe he was above her at the time. More than likely sat astride her. Many of these wounds would not have caused immediate death. What would have killed her without doubt was the stabbing to either of her eyes, or the slicing through of the chest wall to get to the heart, and or the strangulation. At this stage I do not know which was first, and which was final, though I am inclined to think that the removal of the heart was more a defiling act after she was dead."

"How long had she been buried Professor?" Mike Sampson asked, as he tugged the zip of his white forensic suit down over his well-fed stomach.

"There are still quite a few tests to do on that front, but my experience tells me she has lain there for some considerable time. Best guess, ten to fifteen years."

"Anything else I can take back for the briefing Professor?" enquired Tony.

"What I am fairly certain about from my examination of both this body and that of Rebecca Morris is that you are now dealing with two murders and one killer."

- ooOoo -

CHAPTER SIX

DAY NINE: 14th July.

Bright morning sunshine filtered through the blinds, bathing Detective Superintendent Michael Robshaw in a soft warm light. Leaning over the computer keyboard on his desk he entered his password and hit the return key. Then clasping his hands behind his head he leant back in his seat and stared at the screen. Forty-three messages and only two days had lapsed since he had last logged on. He scanned down the list and saw that the majority was In-Force spam, but he knew a few had to be opened up and responded to before his next Command Team briefing.

This was another one of those bugbears that had crept into the job. Though everyone knew the computer highway was a very effective vehicle for today's modern police service, much of the system had been abused and was filled with dross that encroached on time that could be spent better elsewhere. His mind drifted back to his early days when they had relied on the 'yellow message' system for briefings, which were carefully sifted and scrutinized by the morning sergeant before they even came across his desk for actioning. He only wished the computer had its own similar 'gatekeeper' to save him time and energy. He sighed and stretched his well-muscled shoulders. Despite his forty-six years he had still managed to maintain his fifteen stone physique from his rugby playing days.

The previous evening he had spent a restless night fighting the adrenaline rush from the news that the latest discovery of the mummified body, murdered more than ten years ago, was now linked to the murder of Rebecca Morris. The identical marks gouged into each of the body's stomach had confirmed it. No one had come back yet with answers as to what the marks meant. Especially puzzling had been the placing of the playing card on Rebecca's chest. What had been the significance of that he had asked himself time and time again.

He currently had officers combing the site around the latest body-find to see if a card had been left there as well.

He had poured himself a large glass of whisky before retiring to bed, but he had still fidgeted, mulling over the fact that he mustn't allow the latest finding to overshadow Rebecca's slaying, but run the two murder enquiries in tandem. Finally after fighting sleeplessness and seeing the dawn light creep through the fabric of the bedroom curtains he rose early, showered quickly, and drove the eight miles to work hardly noticing what the car radio was playing.

Closing the computer down, he scoured the handwritten sheets he had scribed late last night. They contained detailed notes on each of the murders, featuring all the relevant discoveries from the enquiries already carried out together with a list of fresh tasks that required working on today. There was a lot of work to do and he had to be very focused as he scribbled down further notes for the forthcoming briefing. He glanced up for a moment, and stared at some of his old personal photographs on the wall, particularly at the class photograph of his younger self, standing proudly in the middle row at Detective Training School at Wakefield.

Those had been amongst some of the best days of his career. How he wished he could turn the clock back and be more hands on. He found it so difficult not to get personally involved in a case and accept that his role was no longer operational. He now 'flew a desk'. It was his job to sift and sort the evidence; to identify new leads; pick out suspects, or break down alibis. The greatest personal satisfaction he could hope for was picking out that crucial bit of information from an action or statement through his meticulous reading and careful observation, that others had missed and which would initiate that first step to catching their killer.

Placing the cap back on his Waterman fountain pep he picked up his notes, pushed himself up from his desk and walked out of his office and down the corridor. He could hear the familiar voices of some of his HOLMES team beginning their preparations for the day, and the aroma of freshly brewed coffee teased his nostrils. Entering the MIT office he spotted the new incident white boards that had been erected. There were timelines for each of the victims. The latest one displayed the rotted face of Jane Doe. He knew the immediate task was identifying the unidentified, placing a name to that gruesome form, which had once been a young girl. Without that how could they uncover her lifestyle; her habits; where she hung out and whom she associated with? That valuable information was the crux of the matter right now. He knew how important it was that Jane Doe became a somebody whom he could give back to her family.

He quickly reviewed photos of the scene, looked at the dental x-rays and combed through the post mortem report. He knew behind the scenes that attempts would be being made to obtain finger prints from the corpse, and also that one of the detective's would have the sole task of making the numerous phone calls to track down the orthodontist who did her dental work. At the same time forensic would be working with the clothing and other articles found on the body.

His mind was finalising the day's assignments as members of the team filtered into the briefing room. He fixed his gaze on a few of them and acknowledged their arrival with a firm smile.

Morning briefing began at eight am. He satisfied himself that all who should be here were here, glanced at his watch, and cleared his throat.

"Morning Ladies and Gents, you don't need me to tell you that we have a very busy few days ahead." Referring to his notes he began by re-visiting all the 'actions' so far relating to the murder of Rebecca Morris. He double-checked with detectives on confirmed sightings, revealed that the reconstruction had not brought in any new leads, and finished by bringing in DS Hunter Kerr and DC Grace Marshall to confirm the work they had done with her parents and revealing what her best friend had stated about the man who had been 'coming on to her' to photograph Rebecca. "It is vital we find this man. He is our main TIE suspect."

The detectives around the room didn't need reminding that was the acronym for trace, interview, eliminate. It was given to every major player in an investigation.

He slapped a hand over the blown-up photographs of the symbols gouged into Rebecca's abdomen. "The pathologist has re-examined these marks and now confirms that the first mark should be a reversed L. She'd originally missed it because it appears the knife had not joined the horizontal to the upright. Therefore the marks on Rebecca are identical to those found on Jane Doe." He paused; his hazel eyes peering through his spectacles surveyed the room. He stopped at DC Mike Sampson. "Mike you had the job of making sense of these; any joy?"

"Not yet boss." Mike cleared his throat. "Visited various web-sites, talked to the local priest for any religious link, spoken with some occult specialist that I got off the web, and I've also talked to a forensic psychologist recommended to me by the Met. I sent him a fax of the marks and I also sent him info about the playing card. Other than confirming what Professor McCormick has said about it being the killer's signature, he's not been able to help me further."

The SIO nodded and thanked Mike for his efforts. "Okay everyone back to the job in hand. We are currently widening the search for Rebecca's school bag and other belongings, and the Press Office are putting out a fresh appeal this lunchtime in case our killer has dumped them. I have also got Headquarters monitoring her mobile in case it's switched on at any time. There is still a lot of ground to cover on this murder."

He moved towards the second board and placed a hand over the grotesque photo of the mummified head. "Jane Doe. The only thing we know about her identification so far is that she was of teenage years when she was murdered. She was discovered yesterday in a slurry pit on the site of the old Manvers coking plant." He paused momentarily and pointed to a large map of the Dearne Valley that had been fixed onto another white board "This site is only two miles away from where Rebecca Morris was discovered. What concerns me about this is not the fact that we are now dealing with a double murder, but the time span between the two killings. That body has been in that slurry pit at least ten years and more than likely fifteen. Why the gap between both murders? Was our killer in jail? Was he out of the area? Or worse still has he killed between those years and there are more bodies still waiting to be discovered?"

*　*　*　*　*

Grace couldn't help but notice that without her make-up and now dressed in school uniform Kirsty Evans looked every inch the fourteen-year-old teenager again.

She appeared to be looking around nervously as she crossed the road and Grace guessed she was seeking to avoid drawing attention to herself as she made her way to the unmarked police car.

Grace watched Kirsty's eyes scanning the line of parked cars opposite the school and then saw by her reaction that she had spotted her. Grace raised a hand in acknowledgement.

Taking a final glance around, Kirsty left the footpath and jogged towards the silver grey CID car parked discreetly in the shadow of one of the many trees lining the road.

Grace reached across the front seat and sprang the passenger door open as Kirsty reached the kerb. She stuck her head inside the opening and despite the holiday tan Grace could see that she had coloured up. Grace recognised the sign of nervousness and trepidation. She patted the fabric of the front seat.

"Get in, I won't bite," she invited.

Whipping her school bag off her shoulder Kirsty slid in beside Grace.

"You didn't mind me ringing you did you?" she asked, avoiding eye contact, just staring at the dashboard.

"Course not. I was hoping you would. That's why I gave you my card the other day."

"Only I don't want to get anyone into trouble, or for anyone to think bad of Rebecca." She rattled out her words at pace.

"Kirsty if what you have to tell me will help catch the person who did this to your best friend then people will thank you." Grace rested her hand on Kirsty's forearm causing her to turn and make eye contact. "I have a daughter your age. I know you don't want your parents and especially the police to know what you get up or what you discuss but this is different.

Someone murdered Rebecca and that someone may well have known Rebecca. You may well know that person."

She saw Kirsty shudder. She pulled back her arm.

"I don't know anyone who could be as cruel as that," she responded.

"Maybe not Kirsty, but let me be the judge of that, and from your phone call yesterday it's obvious that something has been playing on your mind. And to be honest I sensed that at your house when we talked the other day."

Kirsty coloured up again. "Yes I suppose so." She took on a sheepish look and started twisting her friendship bracelet around her wrist. "I didn't want my mum and dad to know how Rebecca had changed over the last few months. They might have stopped me knocking about with her if they had."

"Changed? How do you mean changed?"

"Not in a bad way or anything. She was just rebelling you know, because of how her parents were with her."

Grace watched the uneasiness in Kirsty's eyes. "Every teenager goes through a rebellious phase. Just because you probably see me as a level-headed police officer now doesn't mean I didn't go through the same thing. God, I caused all kinds of problems for my parents, in fact I've asked myself many a time how I came to join the police. It's something everyone goes through and Rebecca was no exception." She paused, studying Kirsty's face. "What do you mean by rebelling? What form did it take?"

Kirsty's gaze drifted away, shifting from windscreen to dashboard and back. It was obvious to Grace she was carefully considering her choice of words.

She cleared her throat and went on. "She used to go on about how her mum and dad wouldn't let her grow up. She had asked if she could have her hair streaked like mine but they kept telling her she was too young. Then a couple of months ago apparently her dad caught her wearing make-up when she was coming to our house and she told me he flipped. Told her to wash that muck off and stood over her in the bathroom whilst she did it. She was fuming when she came to our house. In fact she made herself up with my stuff. We went round town and she kept shouting to loads of lads, showing off like. She was a laugh at first but then I got bored and wanted to come back home and listen to some music. She wanted to stay out and we had a bit of a fall-out. I ended up calling her a tart." Her voice trailed off with a hint of sadness, "I wish I hadn't now."

"What's done is done Kirsty. Don't beat yourself up."

She forced a smile and then continued. "It became regular, the putting on make-up thing and going round town. She'd even spent some of her pocket money on a couple of tops and a pair of skinny jeans like mine and left them in my wardrobe for when she came round." Kirsty faltered a second. "She'd started to smoke as well."

"That's all part of growing up," Grace returned, and yet at the same time she suddenly thought of her eldest daughter Robyn; hoping this was an avenue she was not going down. I must have a talk with her, the next time we're alone, she promised herself.

Grace sensed a sudden uneasiness about Kirsty. It was the same feeling she had had during their previous talk at Kirsty's home.

"There's more, isn't there?"

"Well," a slight hesitation in her voice, - "yes. It was when we went to the skate park once, with some lads," her voice tailed off.

"Come on Kirsty you're half way there. It can't be that bad."

"It's a bit awkward," she dropped her head and her cheeks flushed again.

"Please Kirsty this could be important."

"Okay. Well, Rebecca started flirting, really awful like, with these older lads. Fifteen, sixteenish they were. She'd snog a couple of them and then touch them up in the youth shelter, you know what I mean."

Grace guessed what she meant and nodded.

"Then when they tried to touch her back she'd push them away and laugh at them. A few got really angry with her; they started calling her a prick-teaser. I warned her. I tried to tell her to stop it and that someone would take it too far if she wasn't careful. She just said it was a bit of fun. But I knew it wasn't. I saw the lads' faces." She turned and faced Grace square on. "Do you think that might have happened; that someone took it too far. That's why she was killed?"

Grace wondered if that was the case.

- ooOoo -

CHAPTER SEVEN
DAY FOURTEEN: 19th July.

Deep below district headquarters Grace Marshall clenched her pen between her teeth and on tiptoes manoeuvred another manilla folder from the top row of the steel stacking shelves. Turning, she dropped the thick grubby package onto the table below, throwing up more dust particles to add to the dust-motes already floating around the basement room. She jumped off the metal footstool, glad now that she had chosen her flat ballet pumps to wear that morning, and unfastened the securing ribbon before shuffling out the contents along the wooden surface.

Having fed her conversation with Kirsty Evans that previous afternoon into the system it had sparked much debate that morning in briefing, adding another dimension to the enquiry. As a result Hunter and Tony Bullars had the job of tracing and interviewing some of the boys from the skate park, whilst she and Mike Sampson had been given the task of going back over old 'missing from home' reports to determine how many were still outstanding, particularly if they had disappeared in unusual circumstances, and especially where teenage girls loosely fitted the description of their Jane Doe.

Before coming down to the basement Grace had spent the early part of the morning logged onto the UK Police National Missing Persons Bureau computer network, based at New Scotland Yard, feeding in the current details they had of the mummified remains. It had been a frustrating morning with many phone calls to the operators to double-check the information she had entered. She knew the system itself was flawless, providing a cross-matching service by comparing the description of their body, with that of all long term missing persons. It also held a dental index, which was regularly maintained and allowed liaison with Interpol. She had quickly learned that each year 77,000 teenagers went missing, hence the need to double-check everything.

The agitating part was that she quickly uncovered the fact that although the bureau had been operating since 1994, her own force had only joined the network in the last eighteen months. Therefore anything older than that had to be sought in the files, which the Administration Department had stored away in this grimy basement. It now meant that she and Mike had to physically check back over every handwritten record; and there were several thousand, in order to identify those that were marked as still missing. As she began to sift through the latest batch, Grace realised this was a task bigger than she had imagined.

"Nineteen-ninety-six." she announced, a note of frustration in her voice. "How many years have we gone back now?"

Mike Sampson glanced down at the pile near his feet "Three years," he replied, "only ten to go," he retorted with a wry smile.

She scraped back an old wooden chair, which despite its battered and weathered appearance she had found surprisingly comfortable over the last three hours, and seated herself under the long oak table opposite Mike. She let out a long sigh as her eyes roamed around the huge windowless room with its floor to ceiling metal shelves, which appeared to contain just about every paper file which had been generated at the station since it was built in the early 1960s, and it seemed at first sight as though nothing had ever been thrown away. It was one of the many antechambers off the cold windy corridor, which connected the station cells to the nearby courtroom, where prisoners could be escorted to their fate without the need to be dragged in handcuffs through the streets. They were in a cold and drab room, with paint peeling in places as a result of the damp.

From time to time she or Mike had been glad to make a welcome cup of tea, not only to stave off the cold but also clear the dust motes from the back of her throat. During one of these interludes she had discovered a large cardboard box containing the Crown Court files relating to The 'Beast of Barnwell,' an enquiry, which she knew, had occurred well before both their times as detectives. She had attracted Mike as to her finding and the pair had become distracted as they scoured old black and white photographs, and digested parts of the yellowing crime files revealing how during the nineteen sixties the Barnwell man had indecently assaulted, beaten, and raped several women, before being finally captured in the seventies. Back then it had been up there amongst the top of the country's major enquiries, and remembering what the Detective Superintendent had said at morning briefing Grace now wondered if they were also on the verge of something similar.

"On the subject of sex," said Mike as he pushed the box back under the shelving unit, "I once made love to my girlfriend for one hour and five minutes."

Grace caught the smirk creeping across Mike's face and just knew it was going to be another one of his jokes. Since joining the team there had been many times when her sides had ached from his funny stories and at his antics.

"Go on you've got me, when was that?"

"Last March, when the clocks went forward." He started to laugh; a deep belly laugh. It was infectious, sometime funnier than his actual joke.

She joined in the laughter for the best part of a minute, wiping the tears from her eyes, careful not to smudge her mascara. She nudged him eventually. "Stop it now Mike, we've got to get on with this.

It was very rare that Grace worked with Mike Sampson – Hunter was her regular partner, though when she had done, she had found the experience a refreshing change. He was the 'character' in the department. Full of one-liners and jokes and he always had the ability to come up with a witty punch-line to lighten things. Yet she also knew the professional side to his work, and he was dedicated. He was regularly the last person to leave the office at the end of the day. Yet unlike her working relationship with Hunter, where they regularly shared small-talk on a daily basis about their personal lives, she realised she knew very little about Mike's personal life. She knew he was single and spent quite a lot of his time in the pub with mates following a quiz trail around various venues throughout the week and she also knew that he loved to spend his weekends off fishing competitively up and down the country. But that was where her knowledge of him ended. She had never seen him in a relationship and he had never introduced a love of his life. As she dragged her eyes back to her paperwork she made it her objective over the next few weeks to get to know him better.

* * * * *

First Rebecca Morris's smiling face came into view, fading away and followed quickly by a blurry distant shot of her in her school uniform standing by the bus stop, the same one where he had picked her up, and it stopped him in his tracks. The hairs in his nostrils quivered from a sharp intake of breath and he tried to catch up the two beats his heart missed. A cold clammy sensation swelled inside him and the palms of his hands suddenly itched from the beads of sweat, which rolled across his skin. He wavered only slightly but the two cups he was carrying clattered together and a splurge of hot tea splattered his training shoes and the carpet. He felt his heart flutter as he quickly tuned his hearing to the muted conversation that came from the television.

"What on earth are you playing at?" screamed his mother, her head whipping round, peering back over her armchair.

He quickly realised what he had seen was a reconstruction of the last sighting of Rebecca Morris being played out on 'Crimewatch', and that except for her facial photo, what he had witnessed was someone who had only been acting as a body double for Rebecca.

He heaved a sigh of relief but a lump emerged in his throat, which he tried to swallow in order to answer his mother back.

"I don't know," she spluttered. "Nearly thirty years old and I can't even trust you to make me a cup of tea without spilling it."

He plonked the two cups onto the wooden coffee table in front of her, but it was too harsh and more tea slopped out.

"Sorry, I'll just fetch a cloth."

He turned to go back to the kitchen but there was more to the report, which again stopped him from what he was doing. He thought he recognised the scene being shown on their new

HD ready TV. The colourless grey landscape had taken on changes over the years but there was no mistaking the area he was now looking at and he tried to catch what the presenter was saying.

"Police say they are not ruling out the possibility that the recent gruesome findings are linked with the murder of fourteen year old Rebecca Morris whose mutilated body was discovered two weeks ago..."

"Oh just leave it," his Mother snapped. "I'll fetch it. If you want a job doing, then do it yourself."

She pushed passed him slapping at his elbow trying to move him aside, but he was too strong for her now and she wobbled sideways as he flicked out his arm; a reaction to the slap.

He watched his mother, her eyes bulging, glare back at him.

She was getting inside his head again. He could feel the anger welling up inside. Just like all the other times. Sometimes she really messed with his head. Because of her he'd missed the remainder of the broadcast. From what had been said though, he could guess that they had found another one of his girls. He cursed inwardly at his mother's interruptions. Now it meant he would have to go out tomorrow and get the local paper. He'd drive into town and get one from one of the supermarkets. He didn't want to arouse suspicions by getting one from their usual newsagent.

He heard his mother clattering about in the scullery searching out the floor cloth, clucking her tongue against the roof of her mouth, the way she always did when she was annoyed with him.

One of these days he would fucking do for her.

* * * * *

'I feel like a bloody leper' Susan Siddons thought as she drew on the final remnants of her cigarette before flicking it to the ground and grinding it underfoot. As an uncontrollable shiver moved down her back she wished she had put on her cardigan before coming outside. "I'm going to end up with a cold, thanks to this stupid bloody smoking ban," she mumbled to herself, looking at her reflection in one of the pub windows.

She took the breath freshener dispenser from out of her small handbag, squirted it into her mouth and then cupped her hand and blew into it, whilst simultaneously sniffing, to see if her breath still smelt of smoke. Then she replenished her lipstick, flicked a hand through her newly cropped hair and made her entrance back into The White Hart, her local bar, just a five minute walk from her dingy flat. As she entered the snug she tugged at the seams of her short skirt to cover a little more of her still slender legs.

"Another fag break Sue?" her large-chested, generously proportioned friend Debbie quipped, taking a swig of lager.

"My only vice," she responded. "Oh and the occasional drink," she added picking up her own half of beer, before dropping down onto the padded bench beside her best friend.

"And sex," finished Debbie.

They both glanced at each other and gave off a short laugh.

The television was on, mounted high up on a shelf in one corner of the room and despite there being no sound on, the items shown on the screen caught her eye. She immediately stopped drinking, resting the rim of the glass on her bottom lip, as she stared intently at the screen.

"What's this?" she mumbled nodding towards the screen. Debbie looked blank and shrugged her shoulders. Susan spun her head round towards the bar.

"Terry." she shouted to the large bellied manager serving behind the bar "What's this on the telly?"

He took his eyes of the fresh pint he was just pulling for a customer and looked towards the screen. "Crimewatch" he answered and went back to filling the glass.

"Turn it up Terry" she requested sharply, but there was nervousness in her voice.

"What for? You on it?" he shot back.

"Fuck off and just turn up the sound you sarkie twat." She almost slammed down her beer glass onto the round wooden table.

Several heads in the snug turned towards her, but she hadn't noticed. Her eyes were transfixed by the image on TV, focusing on the clothing neatly laid out on a table.

"I wouldn't argue with her if I was you Terry." Debbie said.

The manager aimed the remote handset at the television and held his index finger continuously on the volume switch, watching the numbers rise on the screen until it was audible.

Susan strained her ears, just catching the final bits of conversation between the stocky, grey-haired detective and the fair-haired female presenter. She quickly deciphered that the remains of a young girl had been found on the site of the old Manvers pit and was wearing clothing similar to that on the table. The rest of the conversation became just a jumble as her thoughts began racing. Simultaneously a mist clouded her vision. She clasped a hand to her mouth.

"Oh my god," she gasped.

Debbie spun sideways and saw how the blood had drained from Sue's face. "What's the matter?"

Susan didn't respond. She was moving quickly out of her seat, banging her legs against the side of the table and causing the drinks to slop out of their glasses. She dashed along the corridor by the toilets, her slim figure bouncing off the doorjamb and she had to catch herself before she stumbled outside into the car park. Her fingers groped around the keypad of her mobile. She hadn't dialled this number for a long time but she could still remember it.

"Come on, come on," she muttered with each dialling tone. Finally it was answered. The man's voice seemed a lot steadier since the last time they had spoken several years ago.

"Barry it's Sue" she blurted out. "Susan Siddons. I really need to see you. It's about our Carol. I think they've just found her."

* * * * *

The unexpected phone call from retired detective Barry Newstead later that evening, practically demanding that they meet, took Hunter completely by surprise. But he knew the moment he had replaced the handset that it was a request he dare not refuse. From experience he knew that Barry never rang anyone out of the blue, and therefore it had to be something vitally important.

He turned off the car stereo as soon as he pulled out of the drive and in silence drove the few miles from his home along the unlit country roads to the tranquil picture-postcard village of Wentworth, where Barry had fixed the meet, dwelling on the strangeness of the telephone conversation he had just had with an old colleague whom he had last seen over five years back.

In his head he replayed his first ever meeting with the huge, bullish man. It was the 1st of September 1988 - he had been sixteen years of age. It was one of those dates locked inside his memory bank. That was because it was the day the police told him that his girlfriend, Polly Hayes, had been murdered; her battered body had been found in woodland. Barry had been one of the detectives on the case and had interviewed him.

They had never found her killer, and a year into the enquiry Barry had broken the news to him that the case was being closed until further evidence came to light.

Finding out who had been responsible for his girlfriend's murder had been his incentive for joining the police. And with each murder case since, he had either enquired or examined the similarities of how each victim had met their deaths, but he still hadn't turned up her killer. This recent case was looking no different.

He had stayed in touch with Barry, not just to discuss any fresh information about Polly's murder, but also because a bond of friendship had developed between them, and he had caught up with him again, at the age of twenty-five, when he had achieved detective status, and been posted to district CID.

When he had entered the CID office on that very first day, a nervous knot in his stomach, Barry had been one of the first people to greet him.

He became his mentor. Hunter quickly learned that Barry was one of the figureheads of the department, and also a legend in the office and in the first twelve months he regaled him with his adventures over a many a pint. He soon realised that in spite of his outward appearance he had an incredibly fast and alert mind and he could talk the hind-leg off a donkey. Hunter had learned that Barry had a vast network of informants and that when he 'fingered' someone for a job then without doubt they had done it. Along the way he also became familiar with Barry's interview techniques. Occasionally he had witnessed Barry use violence, out of sight and mind of the custody sergeant, to gain a confession. As he, himself, had become involved in jobs with Barry he became mesmerised by some of his frighteningly unorthodox methods. Methods, which both scared, and yet at the same time, excited him. Hunter soon realised that Barry was so determined to prove that the villains he dealt with were found guilty of their crimes. And he would listen to him continually defend his activities by repeatedly stating "I can put my hand on my heart when I say I have never put an innocent man behind bars." And he would back this up by telling him how many of his miscreants had written letters to him from prison for a visit so that they could 'clear their slate' before release. Hunter soon discovered that his clear up rate for crime was phenomenal.

But then Hunter had transferred to Drugs Squad, and had then achieved promotion and they had lost touch. Whilst in his new post he had picked up gossip which had disturbed him. Sadly, he'd learned that Barry had brought about his own downfall. Barristers and judges had begun to vehemently challenge his breaches of guidelines, in particular of The Police and Criminal Evidence Act, and his 'collars' began to walk away free from court.

Word got back to Hunter that some of the younger managers had labelled him a maverick and a dinosaur, and between them had plotted his downfall. In particular one newly promoted Chief Inspector had removed him from operational CID and sidelined him to a desk job. He'd left numerous messages on Barry's voicemail for him to get in touch. He'd expected him to return the calls and take his advice, but he never had. The next thing he had learned was that Barry had retired. Hunter had caught up with him again at his leaving do. It was one of the biggest he had attended and he saw and heard so many past and present CID bosses praise his efforts. He recalled one retired Detective Superintendent telling everyone 'how sad it was that detectives like him were no longer allowed to operate to the benefit of the victims.'

Hunter had recently watched the TV series 'Life on Mars' and had been amazed how much of Barry's character and working practices fitted into the series. He did wonder at first if he had been an advisor to the programme and found himself scouring the credits for the ex-detective's name.

As he pulled into the rear car park of the village pub Hunter couldn't help think that despite the inconvenience and the fact that he was shattered after another gruelling fourteen hour day it would be nice to catch up with Barry again after all this time.

The George and Dragon, built of Yorkshire stone, was a typical country pub. The interior had a warming ambience and its décor was that of an old farmhouse, with heavy stone flagged floors, timbered ceilings and whitewashed plaster walls. Turn-of-the-century sepia photographs of the pub and the village decorated the walls, and the furniture was a mixture of heavy wooden chairs, high backed benches and many different sized tables. It was one of those pubs he only occasionally visited, particularly on warm summer evenings, though with its range of good quality real ales he quickly acknowledged he should and would pay it more attention in future.

The bar area was a hive of activity and he scoured the sea of faces to see if he could spot Barry. He hoped he would still be able to recognize him after all these years. Then he spotted him, tucked away in the corner on one of the high back seats, just putting a pint of beer to his mouth. 'He hasn't changed one bit', he thought to himself. The same, dark, rumple of hair and red-flushed face, reminiscent of a hill farmer. Hunter was deeply suspicious of the Dorian Grey appearance, especially as he knew that Barry had been retired at least six years and would be in his early fifties. Hunter made eye contact, raised his hand to acknowledge him and then shook it several times towards his face silently mouthing the words 'want another beer'. Barry gave him the thumbs up and Hunter ordered two pints of Timothy Taylor Landlord; one of his favourite real ales, before squeezing between customers towards the seated area where his ex-colleague sat.

Hunter also saw that Barry still had that bushy moustache, which he stroked so frequently and annoyingly, and as he got closer he spied the tell-tale signs that he was dying his hair. As Barry pushed himself up from his seat and thrust out a hand to greet him Hunter couldn't help but notice he was more beer-bellied and rotund than he had last remembered him, but as he gripped and shook his hand he could feel there was still strength in those arms, which he had seen him use piston-like on more than one occasion to pummel an adversary.

"Looking Good Hunter."

"You too Barry."

"Still as diplomatic as ever I see. That's why you got promoted and I didn't. I've put on a few pounds I know, since I retired." He slapped the side of his girth; "but I can still give the young-uns a run for their money."

Hunter had no doubt that he could.

"How are you doing?"

For a good half hour as they sipped their beers Barry quizzed him about the job, tut-tutting and shaking his head as Hunter described the many changes that both the uniform side as well as the CID departments had undergone since Barry's retirement. For a few seconds he wondered if he himself would be as cynical and critical when it became his time to leave. Over the first twenty minutes conversation the chilled smooth tasting beer went down easily and Barry went to the bar to replenish the glasses.

Then as Barry eased himself back into his seat Hunter decided it was time to get to the crux of why he had driven here. "Well I have to say I was intrigued by your call, right out of the blue after all these years."

Barry took the head off his beer. "Have you identified your body from the Manvers site yet?" he enquired not looking up.

"Not yet. We're ploughing our way through hundreds of missing-from-home files going back years and the gaffer went on Crimewatch tonight, but I don't know if anything's come of that."

"That's why I rang you. I got a call just like you, right out of the blue. From a woman I haven't seen or spoken to in years.

It was the mum of a girl who went missing back in the early nineties, a Carol Siddons."

"Should that name mean anything to me? Like I say Barry there are many girls who are still outstanding in our records. What makes her think it's her daughter?"

Barry took another drink of his beer and set his glass down. "I personally worked on that case for a short while, as a favour to the mother. Susan Siddons was a girl I knew from my beat days and she became a snout of mine, a very reliable one. Anyway what I'm getting around to is that she recognized the clothing you showed on the programme tonight as that which her daughter was wearing on the night she disappeared. Let me just give you a bit of background and then I'll give you Susan's address so that you can go and meet her tomorrow."

Hunter eased himself back into his weathered pine chair, cupping his pint, ready to listen. He knew from his early career days that Barry Newstead had a real flair for recounting the many and varied cases he had been involved in.

"Susan Siddons was a young journalist, in her first job straight out of University when I first came across her. She was a real looker. Could fetch ducks off water, but she always seemed to attract the wrong type of bloke. She came from a middle class background; both parents were teachers, and I think she just wanted to experience 'a bit of rough.' Anyway she took up with a guy from a family of villains who was a real bastard to her. She got pregnant and moved in with him. We got called out quite a few times to their house as a result of 'domestics' but she would never press charges even though he'd slapped her around and blacked her eyes on a couple of occasions."

Hunter noticed Barry had started to salivate. He watched him take another swig of his beer and then wipe droplets from his moustache with one of his shovel-like hands.

"Then one night," he continued, "he gave her a real good hiding. Hospitalised her. Broke her nose, an eye socket and a couple of her ribs. I was on evenings and got the call out. He was pissed up when I got to his house and spouting off that she'd not complain about him. I gave him a taste of his own medicine and then took him in. I told the custody sergeant that he'd resisted arrest and that he'd confessed to me about the assault on Sue whilst coming back in the car. He made a complaint, but it was my word against his and the upshot was that he got eighteen months in Armley. When he went down I managed to persuade Sue, who had her daughter Carol by then, to move into her own place. For the first time she took advice from someone in authority. Unfortunately for her, her lifestyle began affecting her job. She started to drink a little too much and they gave her the push. She carried on drinking even more, and in some real dives, but she used to give me some real good info and in return I slipped her the odd tenner, or bought Carol, her daughter, a bit of something from time to time. I later found out she was touting round blokes for beer money, who in return would go home with her at the end of the night. But she wasn't shagging them. She used to give them a large nightcap with some of her sleeping tablets in and they'd go spark out, and then next day she'd spin them a story whilst they nursed their thick heads. That was fine, until one night when one old guy, who'd got angina, took a turn for the worse and was rushed into hospital. Doctors there got a little suspicious and called in the police. A young sergeant went to the house and recovered a whiskey glass, which had the remnants of some of her anti-depressant tablets. I have to confess I tried to intervene in the case, and try and make the sergeant see the job for what it was, but he could only see 'jobs-worth' and she got two years for administering a noxious substance."

"What happened to her daughter?" asked Hunter finishing off his second beer.

"Got taken into care. She was twelve years old. It changed her totally. She could already look after herself. Well she had to because of Sue's lifestyle. But you know how it is. She'd entered a system that was full of young kids who were beyond the control of their parents, who were either on bail from court for violence or thieving, or self-harmers, and she became one of them. A real tearaway. She became promiscuous, regularly went shoplifting, got drunk, fought with kids, fought with staff, even fought with the police. Regularly went missing from home, and so when she went missing in the early nineties no real effort went into looking for her until she had been gone at least ten days. Sue contacted me, and as a favour to her and for old time's sake I put in a fair bit of effort in my own time to try and track her down. But I hit a brick wall. I did have some concerns but the gaffers wouldn't hear any of it. They just thought she'd buggered off to one of the big cities and was working as a teenage prostitute. For years Sue tried to get the police, and the papers interested, but because of her history got nowhere."

"A sad story Barry," sighed Hunter.

"Very," agreed Barry. "When you see Sue tomorrow, a little bit of warning, she'll more than likely be in drink. I contacted you, Hunter because I can trust you to deal with her sympathetically. But I also have to tell you that during the initial enquiries when Carol was first reported missing, Sue told a few lies and I covered for her."

- ooOoo –

CHAPTER EIGHT
DAY SIXTEEN: 21st July.

Before leaving for work that morning, nursing a thumping head, Hunter had telephoned Grace Marshall and given her the 'heads-up' of his meeting with Barry Newstead. When he gingerly sauntered into the MIT office Grace was already in, searching through a huge pile of missing-from-home files. He wasn't surprised, she had already told him on the phone that she and Mike Sampson had decided that they could not spend another day in that dump of a store room and had got the van driver to transfer all the remaining folders to the office.

He found her beside her desk, sat crossed-legged on the floor, amongst foxed and yellowing folders, sliding report after report into separate piles.

Hunter eyed her carefully. He had known Grace a long time. In fact they had both joined the job on the same day and had trained together as new recruits. They had lost touch for a short time because she had chosen to take two career breaks to be with her two daughters' during their pre-school years.

He had first been blessed with working alongside Grace when they had done their CID aide-ship together - she had worked hers at District CID, whilst he had done his at the smaller Barnwell CID department - they had been put together on a rape enquiry. The victim had been a woman with a history of sexual activity with many men in the area, and some of the older detectives on the case, had viewed the complaint as spurious. Yet Hunter had watched Grace approach it with such objectivity. At first, because he had wanted to impress the gaffer, he had tried to compete against her, but she had taught him a valuable lesson. A lesson he would never forget. She matched him for tenacity, flair, and enthusiasm and it had been she who had finally caught the perpetrator. The twenty-one year old offender had initially been a witness in the investigation. He had been drinking in the same pub as the victim. When she had left in a drunken state he had told detectives he had gone home in the opposite direction and used his mother to alibi him. Grace had been the one who had the 'feeling' about him, and she shared her cops' instinct with Hunter. Between them they broke his mother down and she arrested the young man for rape. He was given an eight year sentence.

Since then, he had occasionally enquired of her, and when he had become a DS, covertly monitored her performance. Eighteen months ago, when he had learned he had secured one of the Sergeants posts in the newly formed Major Investigation Team, he hadn't hesitated to call her up and suggest she should apply to join the squad.

She had walked the interview and since then they had been regular partners.

She glanced up from her work and fixed her brown eyes on him. She had a wide grin. She showed no signs of tiredness, unlike him.

The previous evening he'd had far too much to drink and had to get a taxi home. He'd apologised profusely as his wife Beth had driven him to pick up his car from the village pub that morning and he knew he'd overstepped the mark from the stern look she'd given him and the deathly silence throughout the journey. When he'd tried to kiss her she turned only to offer her cheek. 'I'll phone for a table, somewhere nice, this weekend' he thought to himself as he ambled towards the kettle.

"Fancy a brew?" he asked without looking at Grace. "How are you getting on?"

"I'm sure I've seen Carol Siddons' folder amongst this lot it's just a matter of putting my hand on it. Your meeting with Barry has certainly made the job easier. And yes I will have a coffee as you're offering."

"I want to keep where I got the info from just between us two at the moment. It'll only complicate the enquiry. Let's just let them think you found the link, okay?"

He poured the boiling water into two cups, adding a tea bag to his own and coffee granules to Grace's. He slipped two paracetamols into his mouth.

"Feeling under the weather?" asked Grace.

"I feel absolutely shit. I'd forgotten just how much Barry could drink. It was a cracking night and I had a real good laugh with him but I'm paying for it this morning. To add to it, Beth isn't speaking to me. I had to ask her to drop me off for my car this morning, which meant she would be rushing about sorting the boys out before she went into work. I'll have to do some real sucking up for the next few days, but I'll get round her. I always do."

Grace rolled her eyes and raised her eyebrows at him.

She hadn't said anything but that look of hers had said a thousand words.

Hunter returned a schoolboy pout. "Ouch."

Just before nine am Hunter and Grace were driving out of the police station to meet Susan Siddons at her flat.

Hunter had not told the Senior Investigating Officer anything of his previous night's conversation with Barry Newstead, but had given him much of the background about Carol Siddons, who had been reported missing as a fifteen-year-old back in 1993.

Grace had sifted through the pile of reports she had recovered from her spell in the basement and had found a tattered file, containing the paperwork relating to Carol Siddons.

As Hunter drove he saw that she was now speed-reading the contents of the foxed dossier.

Despite a little too much foundation and make-up Hunter couldn't help but notice that Susan Siddons was still quite youthful looking for someone pushing fifty. She was slim and petite and both Hunter and Grace had to glance downwards when she opened the door of her first floor flat. Her hair was bleached blonde and in a choppy, modern style, which softened her thin angular face.

'She can't be more than five foot', thought Hunter and he recalled what Barry had recounted to him the previous night, trying to imagine what type of man would feel the need to batter someone so slight and slender. The prettiness was still there, despite the slight lump on the bridge of her nose, which he guessed was the result of the beating which had hospitalised her and she had a sort of easy smile, which was infectious. He could see why men fell for her, even though it was always the wrong type of men.

"I'll just pop the kettle on," she said softly and moved towards the kitchen on her left. Her South Yorkshire dialect was very broad.

Hunter had already mentioned Sue's drink problem to Grace during the journey and as she spoke he couldn't help but notice the combination of stale beer and fresh mouthwash on Sue's breath.

As Sue disappeared into the kitchen Grace leaned towards Hunter almost planting her mouth on his ear. "Her breath smells like yours," she whispered with a mischievous grin.

"Bollocks," he retorted in a low voice between gritted teeth.

The flat was tidy and clean, but the furniture was old and worn and Hunter guessed it was the landlord's choice rather than Sue's.

Susan Siddons was chattering all the time she prepared the tea, her voice nervous and edgy, just making small talk, enquiring as to what Barry had already told them of her past.

Hunter responded with a small white lie. He didn't want to bring up the incidents of Sue's domestic battering, or anything relating to her term of imprisonment, to avoid any embarrassment or friction. Instead he dwelt mainly on the rose-tinted aspects of her life; her journalistic career, the birth of her daughter and the facts surrounding Carol's disappearance all those years ago.

"You've found my baby now though, haven't you?" She said rhetorically and invited them to sit on a sofa, which sank on its springs a little too much for the detectives' liking, and then placed two cups of strong tea onto a stained coffee table before them. "Sorry it's so strong", she said, looking at the dark brew "I've just run out of milk." She sat opposite them in an armchair, which wasn't a match to the settee, gripping a steaming mug of tea between her slightly shaky hands.

"I know this will be upsetting for you Sue but tell us why you think it's your daughter's body we've found," opened Grace, glancing down at the information penned on the front sheet of the 'missing from home' folder.

"Is that her file?" Sue enquired nodding towards Grace's archived records. "Look I've got to be honest with you, when all that was written back then I wasn't being entirely honest." She sniffed and they noticed tears beginning to form in the corners of her eyes. "Now that you've found her I need to be straight with you and make things right."

"But how do you know it's definitely her?" asked Grace again.

"The clothing you showed on Crimewatch last night. That was what she was wearing."

"How do you know that?" enquired Grace, now scrolling a finger down the report, flicking over pages and speed-reading the handwritten manuscript. "The last time you saw her was three weeks previous to her going missing when you visited her at the care home with Social Services."

"That's just it. That wasn't the last time I saw her." Susan paused and gulped. "It was the night she went missing. And there were several other nights before that as well." She blushed and tried to cover her face by drinking her tea and then shuffled uneasily in her chair

"I think you'd better tell us everything Sue, don't you?" interjected Hunter.

Susan Siddons began by recapping some of the background Barry Newstead had already given Hunter the previous evening. She gave depth and detail to the savage beatings she had suffered at the hands of her partner and they could hear real pain in her voice.

"It wasn't just me he beat. Carol got some real hard slaps from him as well when he was that way out. He bruised her on more than one occasion and I had to keep her off nursery school on many an occasion. One night I came back from bingo and caught him urinating on her whilst she was in the bath. She was only four years old. Bloody hell, I flipped and just went berserk at him, and that's when I got really badly beaten up, which Barry dealt with. You're the only people I've ever told that to. I never even told Barry why Steve gave me that hiding."

"Steve?" quizzed Hunter.

"Steve Paynton. You most probably will know him."

Hunter and Grace looked at one another and nodded together. They knew him. There weren't many local police officers that did not know the Paynton family. Most detectives either knew of, or had dealt with the many members of that brood. Generation after generation of the Paynton's had been jailed at some time during their lifetime. In fact quite a few of them had convictions spanning each decade of their existence.

"That's awful Sue," said Grace. She laid aside the folder and picked up her mug of tea.

"When Steve went to prison Barry found me a place through his contacts and I started afresh. But I got lonely. I was only twenty-four years old. I needed company and I started going out. At first my mum and dad would look after Carol, but when they found out I was seeing different men every few months they lost patience with me and tried to stop me going out by refusing to baby-sit. I started to feel sorry for myself, and I'm not proud of it, but a few times I tucked Carol up in bed and left her alone whilst I went to the pub. A neighbour must have phoned up and Social Services got involved. For years I had to put up with their pious interference for fear of losing Carol."

She took another long sip of her drink. "Then as you probably know I got caught drugging that old guy. I used to get them to pay for my nights out. Many of them were far too old and also married, and although I felt cheap they were good payers. I couldn't stand them to maul me at the end of the night so I'd just slip some of my sleeping pills into a whiskey and they'd go spark out. When they woke up on the sofa the next morning many of them couldn't remember what had happened and didn't give me a hard time in case I told their wives. Anyway I went to prison, by this time my parents had disowned me and so Carol was taken into care. When I got out I was only allowed to see her in the presence of a Social Worker, so she used to sneak out, or run away and stay with me. A couple of the times, after the police found her at my house, I was served with a notice threatening me with arrest for abduction: Abduction of my own child – I ask you. And so we had to be even more secretive. That night she went missing she came to me straight from school. She was wearing that white shirt, which was her school blouse and those jeans you found her in were mine; we were the same size back then. She'd spilt some tomato sauce on her school skirt and she put my jeans on whilst I washed it. At half nine that night she said she'd better leave so that I didn't get into trouble. The skirt was still wet and she said she'd be back the next day to collect it. That's how I know it's her. Those were my jeans."

"Why didn't you tell the police all this when she was reported missing?" asked Grace.

"Because I daren't. I thought I'd get done for abduction. I didn't want to go back to prison and lose Carol completely. I just thought she'd had a row at the home because she had got back late and had done a runner. It wasn't until a few days later when she didn't get in touch that I rung Barry. He covered up for me and did some enquiries without his bosses knowing. I started to pester them. I suppose I was a pain at times, but which mother wouldn't be if their daughter went missing. Finally they agreed for me to make an appeal through the media. The press gave me such a hard time. I reacted badly to their questioning even though I'd been a journalist myself. I came over hard on the telly. They'd edited out much of my emotions and so the public slated me. I couldn't win. For weeks if I cried I was accused of being over dramatic and if I didn't I was a hard-faced bitch. I suppose my past caught up with me over those awful first few months of her going missing."

She put down her cup in order to wipe a tear, which had fallen down her cheek. "Call it a mother's instinct but I just knew something had happened to her. Carol would have contacted me no matter where she was. When I saw on TV last night that a girl's body had been found at the old Manvers site I just knew it was her, because you see I had walked her to the bus stop only a few hundred yards from there." She paused momentarily "Can I ask you something?"

"Sure go ahead," replied Grace.

"Why didn't you show the cardigan she had on? I would have definitely known it was her then."

"Cardigan?" enquired Grace, a puzzled frown on her face.

"Yes a blue and grey striped one, with flowers embroidered on it. I loaned it her because it was so cold that night."

The description of that garment suddenly struck a chord in Hunter's memory and he spluttered loudly as the tea he was drinking momentarily met a sharp intake of breath.

- ooOoo –

CHAPTER NINE
DAY SEVENTEEN: 22nd July 2008.

Linda Morris climbed the stairs to Rebecca's room, carefully draping the freshly ironed T-shirt over her arm. She had found it earlier that morning, still clinging to the insides of the washing machine. She paused for a second at the bedroom door, took in a deep breath, and turned the handle slowly, edging it open like she used to, in case Rebecca was dozing. It entered her head that she would never be able to disturb her daughter ever again. She felt a sickness in the pit of her stomach and she fought back the urge to cry.

The room was exactly as it had been the day Rebecca had left for school. Well that was with the exception that she had to make some minor adjustments herself, after those detectives hadn't replaced everything as exactly as it had been. She folded the T-shirt and put it in its rightful place, in the chest of drawers, beside the wardrobe. She opened up the other drawers and checked Rebecca's socks and underwear. She closed them slowly and then moved to the jewellery box on top of the unit, placing it back into the position where she thought it should have been.

She could hear the sound of children outside, their voices bubbling with excitement and she sidled towards the window. She spotted her husband below on bended knees, doing something with the borders. He'd hardly spoken since the news had been broken to them. He even averted his eyes when she had tried to catch his vacant stare. It just seemed as though the life had been sucked out of him. She knew what he was going through. She felt as though her own life had been destroyed since she had lost Rebecca. She had lain awake night after night, struggling to come to terms with this needless act.

She turned her gaze back into the room, trying to take in every nook and cranny; every aspect of Rebecca's life. She spotted her own dog-eared Enid Blyton Famous Five books on the small bookshelf, beside Rebecca's CDs and DVDs. Mystery stories, which despite being dated, had delighted Rebecca night after night, when they had read together over the years. White flashes hit the back of her eyes and she realised just how drained she had become. An unbearable weight was still pushing down on her shoulders. She flopped onto the bed, falling across the duvet. Reaching across to the bedside cabinet she picked up the framed school photograph of Rebecca and hugged it to her chest. Resting her head on the goose-feather pillow, she breathed in all the smells of Rebecca, curled up in the foetal position, and sobbed uncontrollably.

* * * * *

He stood at the bottom of the stairs in silence, holding his breath, gripping the banister, whilst trying to decipher and make some sense of the moaning which was coming from upstairs. He checked each footfall as he carefully mounted the stairs in his stocking feet. His parent's bedroom door was ajar, and with his senses heightened, he honed onto the sweaty pungent smell, which was wafting towards him through the gap. It was a smell new to him. Silently, pushing the door open further, he began to edge in to see what was happening. There was the almighty crash behind him, followed by shouting, and the form of his mother grabbing at the sheets, attempting to cover up her nakedness, whilst a man, whom he recognised as Mr Carson from across the road, scrambled for his clothing. In a flash his father was rushing past, bundling him against the jamb, causing him to smack his head against the woodwork. He witnessed his father's lean and powerful arms delivering blow after blow to Mr Carson, but he couldn't make sense of why.

Within seconds his dad was snatching off the broad leather belt that he always wore to hold up his work trousers, wrapping the buckle of it into his palm. He watched his father unleash it with such ferociousness across his mother's back, before winding it around her neck. He could see her eyes bulging, fingers trying to pull it away from her flesh, mouth gaping, trying to force out words. Instinctively, he found himself crouching cat-like, before launching at his father, pulling at his hair and ears, and clawing at his face. He couldn't understand why his father's once embracing arms turned against him. He was slung against the wall. The pain was intense, and as the blood trickled down his face, the last thing he could remember was the screams of his mother tearing into his eardrums.

He awoke in a sweat, shooting bolt upright. He was wringing wet and there was a damp patch on his bedding around him. How many times had that dream come back to haunt him. So many nights he had lain awake. Scared to go to sleep because he had to re-live the nightmares of his past.

He leaned back against the wooden headboard, breathing deeply, rubbing the tension out of his neck and shoulders. Then, as always, he closed his eyes and conjured up the images of his childhood.

For the first ten years of his life he didn't have a care in the world. He had a loving, doting mother, and a proud father, who shared his passion for photography. In fact he had built him a dark room, and spent many happy hours helping him to develop his photographs. His father had worked at the local pit, and he could recall the many occasions walking down his street with his mother to meet his dad strolling over the pit pony fields, breaking into a jog for his father to sweep him off his feet and throw him over his shoulders for a 'piggy-back' home.

Then she had spoilt it all.

His mother had screwed that fat and ugly Jimmy Carson, and father had left home.

He remembered how his once so-called mates called his mother a whore, and he had quickly lashed out, venting his anger so deeply on one boy that DC Newstead had come round and told his mother to sort him out, or he'd do it for her.

She had punished him with his father's belt just as severely as she had been beaten with it herself.

But he had been determined not to cry, even as the blood had trickled from the weals on his back.

Father never came back.

He would never forgive her.

He slipped down the bed, curling up, pulling his knees into his chest, and wondering, like he constantly did, if that was the reason why he kept doing these gruesome things.

Fresh images sprang into his mind. The glint of his knife flashed before him. It was so vivid, as though he was still holding it. Then visions of the girl, throwing up her hands, gasping and screaming in terror entered his head. He was plunging the blade down, again and again, burying it in her chest and head. Her blood was everywhere.

He shot bolt upright again, springing open his eyelids, struggling for breath. He had drifted off again, dreaming the nightmares, which were becoming more regular. He hadn't had a good night's sleep for years. Why did he keep doing these things? He couldn't answer his own thoughts, he only knew that whilst doing them the rush of pleasure and the feeling of supreme power overwhelmed him.

* * * * *

Immediately after speaking with Susan Siddons that previous morning, Hunter had set out to trace his old CID buddy Paul Goodright. A quick telephone enquiry revealed he was now attached to the Task Force Firearms Unit and he tracked him down on his second call.

Within minutes of catching up, and without revealing too much, he impressed upon him that it was urgent that they should meet. Between themselves, they arranged their liaison that evening in the snooker room of Hickleton Club, which they had both frequented so regularly when they had worked together, and where Hunter thought the likelihood of bumping into another cop would be highly remote. If in fact they did bump into someone they knew it would merely look as though it was two old partners having a quiet drink together; 'chewing the fat' over old times.

Hunter hadn't recognised Paul at first. His features had taken on such a dramatic change. He was completely bald and he was a lot stockier, virtually all muscle, obviously from intense weight training.

"Long time no see. What's happened to the old barnet?" Hunter quipped as they shook hands.

"This." He ran a hand over his shiny scalp. "I've been going thin on top for years so eighteen months ago I made the decision to shave it off. Makes me look quite macho don't you think?"

"If you say so."

Paul Goodright steadied his cue over the snooker table, scanning his eyes along the green baize to the triangle of red balls at the far end of the table.

There was a loud staccato retort as the frame of balls exploded. The white ball spun quickly away from the sides of the table and returned to the bottom cushion.

There was a glint in Hunter's eye, as chalked his cue and strolled towards his first shot. 'The perfect plant into the top right hand corner pocket', he thought. With cue steady in hands he smashed white into red, causing it to disappear, as he had expected. It had been quite some time since he had last played snooker. During his early district CID days he had played the game on an almost daily basis, and had once been a member of a club. However promotion into a very busy department and the need to spend family time with his two football-playing sons Jonathan and Daniel now ate into the majority of his free time.

Hunter potted the black ball and then glanced around the table for his next shot.

"Still not lost the old touch Hunter," said Paul, swilling the last dregs of his beer around the glass before swallowing it in one gulp.

"Another?" he offered raising the empty glass, and when Hunter nodded he turned towards the bar.

Hunter's break of twenty-five finished, when the white ball miscued into a pocket, and Paul hurriedly put down the freshly pulled beers and snatched it up.

"Thank Christ for that" he announced, plonking it back in the D at the foot of the table, "I thought I wasn't going to get a look in."

Hunter smiled and slid the metal marker along the scoreboard fixed to the wall. "Sorry about the secrecy yesterday Paul, but I never trust works' phones."

"Me neither. When you said you needed to speak with me about finding the body of Carol Siddons, after she had been missing for fifteen years, and then hanging up so quickly, I have to confess I was more than a little puzzled. I was going to ring you at home last night but I've deleted your number from my mobile. I spent most of the night racking my brains over what you did say about her being reported missing back in nineteen-ninety-three. I just can't remember that job at all."

"You won't, because where Carol Siddons was last seen wasn't our area back then. You've heard that we've discovered a mummified body haven't you?"

Paul nodded. "I guessed it had something to do with that."

"Yeah, yesterday morning we found out that the body is that of Carol Siddons."

"So why do you need to speak with me?" Paul quizzed, bending over the green baize, sighting up his shot.

"Remember when the CID car got nicked all those years back?"

"Not much." That night ruined my life and my career. Even though you backed up my story about me radioing in to check up on a suspicious noise which was coming from the back of the shops, and then coming back to find the car had gone, my days in CID were numbered."

"Well it's come back to haunt us again," Hunter responded, a serious note in his tone. "You more than me."

Paul stopped his cueing action and turned to face Hunter.

"Why, what's happened?" he asked, frowning.

"From what I've learned yesterday I'm now certain Carol Siddons was in that CID car on the night she was murdered. Do you recall when we answered the fire brigade shout, because they had found the CID car on fire on that track that used to run at the back of the old coking plant?"

"Yeah, when we got there they had put it out. Although it was only partially burnt it was a write-off as I remember." He'd lost interest in the game now and was resting his hips against the side of the snooker table.

"And can you remember what you picked up from the back seat?"

He thought for moment. "A cardigan."

"That's right a greyish, blue cardigan. What did you do with it?"

"I bagged it and put it in my desk drawer. I can remember thinking it was strange finding that, because as you know back then we didn't have lasses nicking cars in our neck of the woods."

Hunter nodded in agreement. "And do you remember there was front end damage to the car?"

Paul pursed his lips. "On the same night it was nicked there was a hit and run accident in which my sister was seriously injured and her boyfriend was killed. I've always believed that the CID car was involved in that."

Everything about that night, all those years ago, was now being played out in Hunter's head. He could feel his face muscles pinch together in sadness and he nodded again.

Paul continued. "I told traffic what my thoughts were and they got involved in the fatal enquiry. But when I suggested to the DI that I should get involved as well, especially with my sister being one of the victims, he wouldn't have any of it. All he kept whingeing on about was the loss of the department's car. I had a head to head with him because he said that I only had myself to blame. The twat said if I had looked after the car better it wouldn't have got nicked and therefore wouldn't have been involved in the fatal accident. I totally lost it and one of the lads had to stop me from punching his lights out. That virtually signalled the end of my CID days." Paul's face was showing signs of flushing. Hunter could sense the frustration and anger welling inside his old colleague even after all this time.

"I went on a bit of a crusade for a while and showed the cardigan to every villain I nicked," continued Paul. "But no one could place it to any of our female criminals. If you remember the gaffer went off on one when he found out what I was doing and gave me the shittiest jobs for months. That's when I realised my days were numbered, so I decided to go back into uniform. And that's when I joined Traffic division.

To be honest it gave me some freedom to see if I could track down the bastard who crippled my sister." He rubbed his shaven head again. "Do you know Hunter every time I see my sister in her wheelchair I play that night over and over again in my head, wondering if I have missed something or someone and especially regretting my stopping off for a stupid shag."

"Don't beat yourself up Paul. Hindsight is a wonderful thing. We've all done things we regret. Anyway the murder enquiry I'm involved in might now draw a line under who caused your sister's and her boyfriend's accident. That's why I called you. I've mentioned the cardigan because yesterday I found out that our murder victim Carol Siddons was actually wearing the cardigan. Apparently her mother gave it to her to wear on the night she went missing."

Hunter paused, as he saw Paul draw in his breath. He studied his features and saw a look of real perplexity. He was thinking how he could break the next couple of sentences, but there was no other way round it.

"You know what that means don't you Paul," he started. "The cardigan belonged to a victim and not to the person who had nicked the CID car. That's why you didn't get anywhere with your enquiries all those years back. You also know that we're also investigating the murder of a Rebecca Morris don't you?"

Paul nodded.

"Well the discovery of Carol Siddons body is linked to Rebecca Morris. The forensic pathologist has confirmed that the killings are similar. It looks as though the killer picked up Carol Siddons after he'd nicked your CID car that night, drove her around in it, murdered her, and then buried her. Her body was found only about fifty yards from the old track where the car was dumped and set on fire. It had been buried in a shallow grave."

Paul almost dropped into the chair beside the table where they had placed their drinks.

"Fucking hell, I can't believe this," Paul growled beneath his breath, and snatched up his beer and took a swift gulp.

"Do you still have that cardigan, because you know what I'm thinking now don't you?" said Hunter now also seating himself at the table beside his colleague.

"DNA."

Hunter nodded. His head tumbled around the knowledge he had of the scientific processes of matching DNA. Things had changed so radically since its introduction twenty years ago. He knew that forensic scientists were now able to work with the smallest sample of genetic material, such as sweat, or tears on clothing, often referred to as trace evidence, to enable a match.

"Bloody hell Hunter I never actually booked it in as evidence. I've told you what I was doing with it all those years back. It was like treading on eggshells with the gaffer so I kept a low profile with my enquiries. I just kept it in my drawer until I needed it."

"Did you get rid of it then?"

"I'm sure I didn't sling it," Paul retorted. "I can remember taking it with me when I moved. It stayed in my locker for ages." After a moments silence he suddenly blurted out "I do have it. I put it in my garage. It'll still be there. But if I do get it how can we get it into the evidence chain without being disciplined for breaching standards? The gaffer back then, Jameson, died of lung cancer a few years back, so there's no one to back up my story as to why I had to suppress it as evidence."

"Paul this is something you need to sort out. It's not me who breached standards. We need that cardigan for forensic evidence."

"So much for being buddies."

"Look Paul I don't want to fall out over this but I covered up enough for you that night when you were out shagging instead of doing your job, and rightly or wrongly the DI did his best to play down the link of one of his department's cars being involved in a fatal accident, even though it had been stolen. We know there was the death of your sister's boyfriend that night involving the CID car, plus now the murder of Carol Siddons, and the only evidence we've got is that cardigan. You recovered it and it should have been booked in. You know how this job has moved on, especially where it comes to preserving evidence. I don't care how you do it now but we really need that cardigan. It could be our best chance of catching this bastard." He paused and took on a more sympathetic tone. "Look it's like you said, this happened years ago. Things were different back then, and there's no doubt that DI Jameson had some influence on your decision not to book it in. But if you think about this there must be some way you can turn this around. My guess is that the evidence property books will have been destroyed a long time ago, and you'll be able to come up with something to cover your back." Hunter took another sip of his beer, fixing his gaze on Paul, whom he could see was trying to make some sense of this dilemma. "Another thing" he added "And I know this could complicate things further but I also need to know where you were that night. Who were you shagging when the car was nicked, because there might be some vital witnesses to all this."

"I can't do that. You don't need to know this after all this time. What difference will it make? No one will be able to recall anything that far back."

"She was married wasn't she?" He sensed Paul hesitate. "Come on you've got to be straight with me. I need to know what I was covering up all those years ago."

"She was married yes. She still is to the same guy, and that's why it's so messy."

"Come on cough up. You've done the hard part getting this far."

"He's a local councillor."

"Why's that so messy?"

"Because he's now a member of the Police Authority."

"Bloody hell Paul. You certainly pick 'em don't you. Now you've told me that you might as well tell me now who she is."

"Karen Gardner."

"Karen Gardner, married to Jerry Gardner - chair of the Police Authority?"

Paul nodded "One and the same."

"But she must be fifty if she's a day."

"Probably now, yeah. She was in her thirties when we met. I went to a burglary at their flat, and when I caught the kid who'd done it, she sort of rewarded me. After that I used to visit her every so often when her hubby was at his meetings."

"I have to say a few of the lads used to hint that they thought she was a bit of a warm 'un. You dirty bugger."

"Yes she was. In fact she was red hot. Can you see now why I never said anything? And I know that I wasn't the only one doing the rounds with her. I got a whisper she was getting a good seeing to by a local villain and that's when I called it a day."

Hunter's breath hissed through clenched teeth. "That puts a different complexion on things. If you knew about him then he might also have known about you being a cop."

"I have to confess, it's got me thinking now." He paused and screwed up his face, then rubbed a hand across it. "This is a real fucking mess Hunter isn't it?"

Hunter chose not to respond immediately. He was still a colleague even though they had been out of touch for all these years. He bit down on his lip, and then said, "You know who the guy is?"

"No idea. It was just a snippet I picked up in the pub, and so as I say I stayed well clear of her."

"You know what I need to do, don't you?"

"Interview her."

Hunter nodded. "You and I go back a long way. I promise I'll be as discreet as I can be. But it's all fitting into place now. This villain whoever he is, may well have known about you visiting Mrs Gardner and thought of a really good way to get back at a cop. So the possibility is he could have either nicked the car that night, or got someone else to do it to set you up. And then somehow or other Carol Siddons got involved and ended up dead." Hunter pondered for a second, then added, "Most probably because she witnessed the accident, which killed your sister's boyfriend and was going to blab."

- ooOoo –

CHAPTER TEN
DAY EIGHTEEN: 23rd July

On leaving the club Hunter's mood was somewhat deflated. Getting into his car he popped in his 'Bon Jovi's Crossroads' album into the CD player and tried to lose himself in the rock music, but driving home the music slipped into the background as he spent the journey replaying the evening's conversation over and over in his mind and reflecting. Despite everything he and Paul Goodright had done together in the past, he knew that things would never be the same between them again. That trust they once shared had ended with their exchange of words.

He was restless for the remainder of the night as he mulled over his next steps. The saying 'a problem shared' entered his head time and time again, and he knew after several hours of tossing and turning that he had to confide in someone. Under normal circumstances when something troubled him he knew he could always turn to Beth. But this was different. This was a problem within 'the job' and he knew that the one person, apart from his wife, who would not pass judgment, and who would give him good balanced advice would be Grace.

The sleep, which had eluded him for hours, finally caught up with him about four o'clock. When the alarm sounded three hours later he felt thick-headed and completely drained, and he was only able to invigorate himself by staying longer in the shower. Tilting his head backwards, he lingered, feeling the rush of the cool water pour over his face.

As he stood outside on the patio finishing off his toast, taking in all the smells of the fresh morning air, and re-running last night's events, despite the problems ahead he somehow felt himself becoming refreshed and revitalized. He drove to work replaying Bon Jovi, singing along to 'Living on a prayer' and 'Keep the Faith,' before cruising into Barnwell station yard.

When he entered the MIT office Grace Marshall had already arrived, face made up and smartly dressed looking business-like as usual. He noticed she'd scraped her hair back into a tight bunch, accentuating her high cheekbones and showing off the summer freckles.

Grace acknowledged him with a wide smile and as he sidled up to her he could see she was already adding milk to two cups of tea; one for him.

"We need to talk," he said quietly.

Her warm burnt umber eyes widened.

"We certainly do," she responded in quite a formal tone.

Grace's response momentarily took him aback, and he returned her a quizzical look.

"What was the matter with you yesterday? You reacted as though you'd just been shot when Sue Siddons mentioned the cardigan," she said stirring in a spoonful of sugar.

Hunter quickly glanced around, just to make sure no one was in earshot.

"I'll tell you after morning briefing," he replied, picking up the steaming mug and moving to his desk. He set the cup down and began to sift through the pile of papers and files which had accumulated in his tray over the last few days. He hoped he would be able to focus on their content.

The daily briefing centred on the previous day's meeting with Susan Siddons, and Hunter recounted the conversation he and Grace had conducted with her. It had given a new dimension to the investigation. They now had a name for the mummified remains, and with this came the task of uncovering Carol Siddons's past prior to her disappearance all those years ago. It had also thrown up the name of someone who could be considered to be their first major suspect: Steven Paynton, a petty criminal with a hard-man reputation. The police knew that he and his family had terrorised their community for years and many times the cops had met a wall of silence, or court cases had collapsed through fear. True, over the years there had always been enough people willing to tell the police about the family's criminal activities, but to get those people to be witnesses and give a formal statement had been damn near impossible.

Therefore Steve Paynton had very few convictions. Those he had were petty - mainly for theft and burglary. And he had collected those in his early teens, for which, he had spent several months in a young offender's institution. More up-to-date police intelligence revealed him as a minor league drug dealer who used violence to settle debts. Susan Siddons had also given some personal insight into his brutality towards her and her daughter, and this was now supported by information from Social Services who had their own personal file on Paynton. A phone call late the previous afternoon from one of the team leaders at Social Services had revealed that one of Paynton's ex-partners, after numerous beatings, had fled the area just to get away from him.

This had occurred over fifteen years ago, before he had hooked up with Susan Siddons. The paperwork revealed that numerous attempts had been made to persuade the woman to formalise a complaint, but she had point blank refused to speak with the police, choosing instead to change her name and leave her home behind. A member of the team did stay in touch with her for a short time and had helped to re-house her. The last address in Retford, Nottinghamshire, was now five years old and Hunter and Grace were given the job of tracking her down.

Hunter drove the unmarked CID car out of Barnwell Police station following the route towards the A1 for the hour-long journey to Retford. Grace in the passenger seat shuffled uneasily on her seat scanning the file on Steven Paynton.

"Listen to this" she said keeping her eyes on the paperwork, whilst Hunter negotiated the bustling out of town traffic. "He's a real bastard. Social Services have written loads of notes on this woman we're going to see. It seems he started to beat her within a month of moving in. He scalded her with hot tea. He beat her with a dog leash, and he even pissed on her when she was asleep. And listen to this, he held a knife several times to her throat and simulated slicing her open. Now that is interesting. It's making our Mr Paynton seem like a hot prospect in our enquiry. What with this and Sue Siddons's statement it should give us some lever to hold him long enough to rattle his cage."

"We don't know yet if she'll make a complaint. Don't forget this was fifteen years ago. She's got a new identity and a new life now. She probably wants to put all this behind her."

"I'll do everything I can to get a statement from her," said Grace.

Hunter knew that was not an idle threat. Although outwardly Grace came across as being gentle for a detective, from experience he had discovered that there was a sharper and harder edge to Grace, which she could switch on like a light bulb when she needed to. He had personally seen many villains rue the day they had challenged her.

As he swung the car onto the unmarked country lane that led to the trunk road, Hunter knew from the determination in her voice that Grace was on a mission to get Steve Paynton. And he knew that when Grace got something into her head there was no holding her back.

Just before the A1 slip road he pulled the CID car into a lay-by and killed the engine.

"About the other day" he began, and in the next ten minutes he revealed everything from the discussion with Paul Goodright the previous evening. "That's why I reacted like I did when Sue Siddons mentioned the cardigan. I realised it was the one Paul recovered from the back of the nicked CID car."

Grace shook her head. "Bloody hell Hunter, what are you going to do?"

"I don't know yet. I'm hoping Paul can come up trumps and find some way of getting that cardigan into the system. If he can it'll make it easier, but the other problem is Mrs Gardner. At the time she was having her dalliances with Paul she was also seeing someone else - a villain according to Paul, who likewise could have found out about Paul and was trying to stitch him up. As soon as Paul found out he didn't stick around to find out who that person was. If we can find out that was the case, it'd make things very interesting."

"Especially if it was Steven Paynton," interjected Grace.

"Great minds think alike. The problem is Mrs Gardner's respectable status now. What she probably did in her thirties is well behind her now and one thing she won't want is some hairy-arsed cop stirring up her past. Besides that it's going to go down like a lead balloon if the Police Authority gets whiff of this."

"What about a hairy-arsed female cop having a word with her?"

"Grace, one thing I don't want to do is get anyone else involved in this mess, especially you."

"Listen Hunter, no one is any the wiser yet about Paul's and Mrs. Gardner's indiscretions all those years ago, and at this stage we don't even know if they are relevant to this enquiry. If I'm seen going to visit her by a neighbour or a friend it will just look as though I'm seeing her for coffee, or one of her charities she's probably involved with. I'll plan it when her hubby is out and also it will be a lot easier coming from another woman."

"I have to admit I was worried how I was going to approach this, I'm not exactly renowned for being subtle."

"Well then, you've answered the question yourself. And if it looks like we're on to something, then we'll worry how we can feed it into the enquiry system after."

"It would be a help Grace. Thanks. And I promise if this blows up in our faces, I'll just say this was on my orders."

"I'll hold you to that."

"By the way Grace."

"Yes?"

"Have you really got a hairy arse?"

"Wouldn't you like to know."

* * * * *

"What a beautiful house. Victorian by the looks," Grace Marshall commented as she and Hunter strode up the black and white decorative tiled path towards the wide open porch of the semi-detached house. They had already tried two other addresses amongst the terraced rows close to the town centre before being directed to this house on the outskirts of Retford. As they got nearer to the stained glass front door Grace snapped open the folder she was carrying and took a quick look at the photograph pinned inside. It was a dog-eared, discoloured, and dated picture of the woman they were seeking, and she hoped she would be able to recognize her from it. They could hear the sound of a woman singing from within, and Hunter tried to steal a glance through the front bay window only to find that thick curtains prevented his view. Grace pressed the original brass buttoned bell set in the door frame and the singing immediately stopped, quickly followed by a shout of "Just a minute." from somewhere at the back of the house. The clop of footsteps resounded along the hallway before the front door swung open.

Though there were now crows-feet around the hazel eyes, and a slight greying around the temples of her chestnut brown hair, which was dragged back and tied in a ponytail, Margaret Brown, as she now called herself, had changed very little. She was still the fresh-faced, attractive woman, depicted in the photograph, despite now being in her early forties. Switching her gaze quickly from one to the other she snapped off her yellow marigold gloves. "Sorry, I only just heard the bell. It's my cleaning day. Can I help you?"

Grace flashed her police warrant card. She introduced herself and Hunter and smiled reassuringly. "Are you Margaret Brown, used to be Mary Bennett?" she continued.

Hunter saw the colour visibly drain from Margaret's face.

Her eyes glazed over and she went rigid as if paralysed. Then she said, "This is about Steve isn't it?"

"Steve. You mean Steve Paynton?" returned Grace.

She shook, then clasped a hand to her mouth. "Oh my God. He's found me hasn't he?" She shot her gaze past them, searching over their shoulders, staring up and down the street.

"Not that we know of. Look this is about Steve Paynton, but it's to do with his past. That's why we've tracked you down after all this time. Please can we come in? We really need to speak with you," said Hunter

She hesitated, took another nervous glance along the road, and then stepped aside to allow them entrance. Then she pushed the front door shut, turned the key and snapped on the safety chain before pointing to the front room.

Hunter and Grace went in first and seated themselves down on a leather settee without waiting to be asked.

"Sorry I reacted like I did," Margaret said picking up a packet of cigarettes and a lighter from the top of a side unit.

She shuffled one out quickly and put it to her mouth and then offered the packet to the two detectives. They declined and she lit it, taking in a long drag, holding her breath for a several seconds before exhaling the smoke from one corner of her mouth.

"If I appear nervous that's because I am. To be frank I'm shit scared. I've looked over my shoulder for so many years because of that man, and I was just beginning to think I had got him out of my life before you two showed up."

"Please calm yourself down, he hasn't found you. You've covered your tracks well. In fact if it weren't for Social Services we would never have found you. And before you go complaining about them, it's us who forced their hands because of a murder enquiry we're involved in," replied Hunter

"Steve's killed someone," she said so matter-of-fact. "That doesn't surprise me. I always knew it was only a matter of time before he killed someone." Margaret dropped heavily into the only armchair in the room, crossing one slender leg over the other.

"We don't exactly know if he has killed anyone, but he is a suspect."

"Who's been murdered?"

"It's actually two murders we're investigating, both teenage girls, but they're years apart. In fact fourteen years apart. Steve Paynton was in a relationship with the mother of one of them – a Carol Siddons. Carol disappeared all those years ago but we've only just discovered her body and as a result of our enquiries we tracked down her mum. She's told us that at the time Carol disappeared Steve was living with her and was violent to both of them. Then yesterday we found out he was with you prior to being with this woman, and that you'd reported to Social Services that he'd also assaulted you on a number of occasions. That's why we felt it necessary to speak with you."

Margaret drew anxiously on the cigarette again. She blew out the smoke. "Assault is an understatement. He was a real evil bastard." There were nervous inflections in her words.

Hunter could sense the tenseness shackling her and sought to dispel her fears by recounting Susan Siddons story and explaining the measures, which were being put in place to protect her from reprisals, now that she had given a statement against Steve Paynton.

"You don't know what he's like. I had to live with him for two years. I've been in constant fear since that night I ran away. He always said he would track me down and kill me if I ever told the police."

"Things have changed in the last fifteen years," Grace said reassuringly. "We've moved on with how we deal with victims, particularly of domestic violence. The magistrates also have a different approach as well when it comes to punishing offenders. If he's not caught up with you after all these years, then he's not going to do that now. We can protect you and will protect you, but we do need your help to put him away. Susan Siddons has already made a statement and if you also give us a statement about his abuse towards you, it'll give us a real lever and will help us to get him remanded so we can investigate him properly over the murders of the two girls, without him interfering or hindering the enquiry."

Margaret finished the cigarette she had been smoking and stubbed it out in an ashtray beside her. Then she took another and lit it. All this time she said nothing, just stared towards a photograph, which was on the wall above the fireplace. It was an arranged shot of herself flanked by two smiling elderly teenagers – a boy and a girl. Hunter guessed they were her children.

Waiting patiently for Margaret to say something, Hunter suddenly realised what the saying 'the silence was deafening' meant. He was mentally screaming for her to open up and talk about the battering Steve Paynton had exacted upon her.

She seesawed her gaze between Hunter and Grace. A tearful film glazed her eyes.

"Do you know," she began "I've not been able to have a relationship with another man? Since that day I ran for it with both my kids I've not been able to trust another man. Do you know what that's like?" She drew deeply on her cigarette.

Neither Grace nor Hunter responded.

In fact Hunter didn't know how to respond. He'd always been in a loving relationship.

"I've never talked about this. I didn't tell Social Services at the time, and I haven't ever discussed this with Jamie or Samantha – they're my two children. They're twenty and twenty-three now, and I know they wouldn't remember what went on all those years ago, but I'm just so afraid of the damage it would cause them if I brought it all up again. Some might accuse me of burying my head in the sand but that's how I feel I've needed to handle it to get me through all those dark days." A tear fell from the corner of one eye and trickled down the side of her nose. She dabbed at it with her hand.

"I can't imagine for one minute how painful this is but don't you feel now that we're here that it's time to get rid of your demons," said Grace quietly.

"What's really hard about all this, is that some would say I brought it all on myself. You see I knew Steve Paynton from my schooldays. I knew some of the tricks he'd got up to, and yes I also knew about his violence, but he was different around girls. A real charmer in fact. We bumped into each other several years later when I was going through a bad patch with my first marriage and he still had the same rugged good looks and the charm. We used to meet up in the pubs and my mates did try to warn me when we first went out together, but I thought they were just jealous because he was quite a good looking guy. I suppose a real 'Jack the lad' springs to mind. I'd already got Jamie and Samantha from my first marriage but it wasn't working out. Their Dad spent his days at work and his nights at the pub and so I'd already left and moved back in with my parents. Steve was the first bloke after we split up to show me some attention and make me feel wanted, and I just fell head over heels for him. Anyway after we had been seeing each other for the best part of a year he persuaded me to take out my savings and rent a flat with him, and against my Mum and Dad's wishes I did." She paused and took another drag of her cigarette. "Sorry I'm going round the houses with this but I suppose I need you to understand why I ended up with the bastard."

It was the first time Hunter detected real anger in her words.

"After about six months together he started hitting me," she continued. "I kept getting on at him about getting a job. I was out working all day and he was frittering the money I earned down at the pub, so I kept nagging him. They were just slaps at first. But then he would come back from the pub pissed up and wanting sex, and because I said I was tired, he would thump me until I gave in."

"He raped you," interrupted Grace. "You didn't give in."

"It was easier to deal with it that way. The hidings weren't as bad if I gave in to him and I wouldn't have to cover up the bruises so much." More tears ran down her cheeks and she stubbed out the half-smoked cigarette so that she could use the backs of both hands to wipe them away. "Look, what I'm going to tell you now I've never told anyone. Not anyone." She gripped the sides of the armchair, digging her nails into the leather upholstery. "He also abused the children really badly. And the reason I've never told anyone this before is because, for a long time, I didn't do anything about it when I should have done."

"I can see this is hurting you Margaret, but trust us we won't pass judgment on you. We just want enough to put Steve Paynton behind bars so he can't hurt anyone else." Grace said moving forward to hold her gaze with her own probing yet reassuring look.

For the next hour Margaret Brown told them of the terror with which Steve Paynton had held her and her two children over a nine-month time span. "He started by beating Jamie, who was eight at the time, with his belt when he wouldn't eat some of the food Steve had cooked. It wasn't that he didn't like the food," she explained, "but that Steve had burned it because he'd cooked it when he was in drink. At first, he forced Jamie to eat food coated with curry and chilli sauce, depriving him of his pop. And then when he lost control of his bowels Steve would rub the faeces into his face. Then he had began to deprive Jamie of food and would lock him in a cupboard under the stairs. He would keep him there for several days, hungry and thirsty, forced to lie in his own excrement." She tried to hold back her own sobs when she revealed that she would lie awake listening to the cries of her little boy caged under the stairs.

"The last straw," she continued, "was when I came back from shopping one day and found that Steve had totally stripped Samantha of her clothes and was photographing her. She was only five year old for God's sake. I just lost it and I flew at him, but he was stronger than me and he gave me a right thumping. He took his belt off and strangled me with it. I must have passed out and when I came to he had a knife at my throat threatening to cut me up if I so much as whispered this to anyone. That's when I came to my senses and realized just how much danger I was in, and was putting my children under. I knew that I had to get away before he killed one of us. So when he went to the pub that night I gathered together everything I could get in two suitcases and with the help of Social Services got into a woman's refuge. Unfortunately I could only stay for a week because they don't allow males in them, even though Jamie was only eight. So that's when I changed my name and came to Retford. Somewhere where no one knew me. For over a year I didn't even contact my parents, just in case Steve got to them." She sighed. A long sigh, as though a great weight had been lifted off her. "Can you understand now why I've never brought this up with Jamie and Samantha? I feel so guilty. It holds too many bad memories for me, and I blame myself for allowing this to happen to them."

Throughout Margaret's narration of events Hunter had seen the pain, grief and anxiety, etched so visibly on her face, as she had unfolded the horrors, which she and her children had endured at the hands of Steve Paynton.

For the next two hours Grace guided Margaret through the anguish of recounting everything again into a written statement, and as she put her signature to the pages, Grace touched her gently on the back of her hand. "I promise you this Margaret," she said. "Steve Paynton will not be causing you any more pain. After this you can put your nightmares behind you."

- ooOoo -

CHAPTER ELEVEN
DAY NINETEEN: 24th July.

Early that morning, along with a small team of uniformed officers from the day shift, Hunter and Grace sped to Steven Paynton's terraced house, using side streets as cover because they knew how quickly the criminal grapevine worked in his location. They needed the element of surprise on their side.

Before the third knock Hunter put all his force behind a flying kick at the front door. The lock and metal hasp parted company with his first attempt and the door crashed inwards. He and Grace stormed into the hall, followed by the uniformed officers garbed in dark blue 'search' overalls.

The first thing that faced them was the strong pungent stench of cannabis, which immediately overwhelmed their sense of smell. It was the really offensive barbed type that was referred to as 'skunk' on the streets, and caused them to screw up their faces.

The two detectives quickly mounted the stairs whilst the uniform team dashed off to secure the ground floor of the house.

Before Hunter and Grace had even got halfway up the narrow stairway they were confronted by a snarling Steve Paynton on the landing above, wearing only a pair of boxer shorts and wielding a baseball bat.

"What the fuck?" he shouted, glaring down at them.

"Police." shouted back Hunter halting his jog. "Drop that now." he bellowed, pointing towards the wooden bat.

Hunter could see why many feared Steve. Although he wasn't big in terms of his physical proportions, his frame was lean and muscular. The definitions of his well-toned muscles were punctuated here and there by black tattoos of barbed wire and tribal markings. Add to that the shaved head and he realised why to some he could cut such a menacing figure.

"I hope you've got a warrant?" he demanded, lowering the bat to his side.

"Sure have," Hunter responded now continuing back up the narrow stairway, though much slower, wary of how Steve Paynton might react.

"You could have fucking knocked. You didn't need to kick my bastard door in."

"I did knock – repeatedly," he emphasised, "but no one answered...did they Grace?"

Behind Hunter, Grace Marshall nodded.

"Repeatedly" she agreed.

"Bollocks." Steve groused as he backed-off to his bedroom. "I'll get fucking dressed, you fucking morons."

They followed him into his room. It was a pigsty of a mess. Hand rolled cigarette butts, porn magazines, several loose weight training barbells, and an array of clothing in various states of dirtiness littered the floor. It was hard to determine whether the marks on the carpet were design or stains. This room also had a strong smell of cannabis, mixed with the musty stench of body odour, causing Grace to crinkle her nose at the unpleasantness.

"Cleaners day off Steve I see," she said rubbing thumb and forefinger across the bottom of her nose, as though it might wipe away the stench.

Steve Paynton was just fastening the last button on his jeans and he stepped forward to within a foot of Grace.

"You really don't want to be doing this you black bitch," he snarled moving his shaven head forward into her face. A large prominent vein, which threaded its way from the front of his ear to where his hairline should have started was pulsing angrily.

She held his stare. She had heard this type of abuse so many times over the years. "Roll with it girl," her father had told her so many times. "Never let them see they've got to you. You're better than them. Fight back how you know best."

"A bit of a racist as well as a wanker," she curtly replied.

"Me, I'm a signed up member of the Ku Klux Klan," he quipped back.

Hunter rocked onto the balls of his feet, curling his hands into tight fists yet leaving then dangling at his sides – ready.

She pushed a polished red fingernail towards his nose. "Hey, white boy you really don' know who yo' messin' wid," she mimicked her Jamaican father's patois.

"You stupid bitch," he snapped "I'll sort you out."

In that same instant Hunter sprung forwards, swinging a punch from his hip. It smacked into Steve's side, catching the bottom two ribs and the breath exploded from his mouth.

He sank to his knees clutching his side, and for a few seconds his face went bright red, eyes almost bulging from their sockets as he fought for breath. Then he caught it, gasped loudly, and fell to one side.

"You bastard. You fucking bastard." He screamed.

Grace stepped over Steve Paynton's prostrate figure, grabbed the rigid handcuffs from the waistband of her suit trousers and snapped one end onto his right wrist. Then she forced her knee into the small of his back, completely flattening him to the floor and slammed the jaws of the remaining cuff onto his other wrist.

"Fancy that, Steve Paynton being done over by a little black girl. This is really going to damage your street cred," she announced twisting the rigid cuffs until he winced. "You're nicked."

He tried to push himself up, but Grace was now pushing his head into the carpet. "What for?" he mumbled, trying to avoid swallowing the fibres from the pile.

"Assaulting a Susan Siddons, and assaulting and raping a Mary Bennett. Those names ring any bells?"

"Might do, but they wouldn't dare make a statement against me."

"Oh believe me when I tell you they have given two very detailed statements about your activities. And we're adding to that resisting arrest, just in case you feel like complaining about police brutality. Now get up and get down those stairs you insignificant little piece of shit."

As Steve scrambled to his feet, helped by Hunter's hands under his arms, Hunter turned to Grace "My my, we are somewhat tetchy this morning ma'am." He said smiling, before helping her guide the prisoner towards the stairs.

As Steve Paynton was led away by the arrest team Hunter and Grace donned their latex gloves and joined the search team who were already busying themselves in the downstairs room.

Much of the house was squalid, despite some very expensive items of furniture and electrical equipment dotted around. They picked their way amongst dirty crockery, some of which still held days' old remnants of food, strewn across stained seat cushions, which had to be removed in order that they could search down the sides of the suite. They also checked several large screen televisions and DVD players, no doubt stolen, as the serial numbers and markings had been erased, and removed them to the marked police van outside. Behind the washing machine in the kitchen they discovered a stash of cannabis weed, about half a kilo in a plastic bag, amongst hundreds of packets of rolled tobacco, but they knew these day's that this amount wasn't quite enough for CPS to prosecute for supplying, or smuggling, and so they continued. What they really needed was something that could connect him to either of the two murdered girls, and so they methodically and painstakingly moved appliance after appliance, household effect after household effect, and even tore up the carpets in the hope of a breakthrough. And it came; in the bathroom; virtually the last room on the checklist. Working under the strains of a dull glow from the bare electric ceiling bulb, probing the nooks and crannies beneath the bathtub, one of the searching officers spotted a chink of light catching the edge of something metal deep in one corner, and only Grace was small enough to crawl into the space to remove it.

She cursed as she dragged herself back out, her pale grey suit now covered in cobwebs, dirt and other detritus.

The tea caddy she held was probably from the late 1950's and was in poor state. She pulled at the lid and it jerked forward as she prised it open, spilling some of its contents over the bathroom floor. What they stared at took them all by surprise. A collection of black and white, and colour photographs of girls, from pre-pubescent children to young teenagers, in various stages of undress, including nude, lay scattered around their feet. Grace lowered herself onto her knees, and Hunter joined her as she carefully shook out the remaining contents of the caddy. Using only a forefinger she separated the photos and began to sift through the images.

"Bingo." she exclaimed as she dragged away four, single, faded colour photographs. They depicted a young pubescent girl doing what could only be described as posing indecently. In two she was wearing only a pair of white cotton panties, and in two others she was completely naked.

"Recognise her?" Grace enquired catching Hunter's gaze.

"Certainly do," he replied, recollecting the images from the missing from home files. "That's Carol Siddons; a very young Carol Siddons."

* * * * *

"Which one do you want to be: good cop or bad cop?" asked Hunter as he paused at the cell area interview room door, glancing through the folder of paperwork and evidence he was carrying, ensuring it was in correct order for the interrogation.

For a brief moment Grace Marshall returned a look of deep thought. Then, narrowing her eyes, exposing her laughter lines, she said, "bugger it. We'll both be bad cop. We've got enough evidence to send him away for a bloody long time."

"That's my girl," he replied, opening the door and entering the soundproofed room.

Steve Paynton was already seated behind the table, hands clenched together in front of him. He glanced up at them, unclenched his hands and tugged at the front of the all-in-one white forensic suit.

"Why the fuck have you put me in this?" he demanded truculently.

"Your clothes have been seized for forensics," Hunter responded.

"What forensics? You've got fuck all on me."

Grace and Hunter sat down opposite. Hunter slid the file across to Grace. They had already decided, given Steve Paynton's attitude towards women, that it would rattle him more if she was to lead the interview.

Grace opened up the file, being careful not to show the photos they had found, and then she switched on the tape recording machine.

"This interview is being tape recorded," she began, and went through the preliminaries; the opening preamble to any police taped interview, the caution and confirmation that he did not wish the services of a solicitor.

"Don't fucking need one" he asserted.

Grace chided him child-like with a wagging finger, demanding he refrain from swearing for the purposes of the tape, and then continued with her questioning, but in a calm-matter-of-fact manner, in an effort to throw him off.

"We have a statement from a Susan Siddons, whom I believe you were once in a relationship with Steve?"

"No comment"

"Susan says that on a regular basis you would beat her. Is that correct?"

"No comment."

"Are you going to sit there all day saying no comment?"

"No comment." He stared hard into Grace's eyes and smirked.

Grace patiently went through the statement taken from Susan Siddons, outlining every one of the beatings Steve had dealt her. He continued to respond with 'no comment' and then Grace changed tack to discuss the assaults on Carol Siddons, Sue's daughter. His only change in answer came when he was asked about the time he was caught urinating on the girl.

"Look it's her word against mine. Sue is an alkie. If this gets to court she'll be torn apart in the box by my brief."

"She wasn't an alcoholic till she met you," Grace snapped back.

Hunter touched the back of Grace's hand and shot a quick glance at her, raising his eyebrows.

Grace knew that he was silently willing her to not let Paynton get under her skin.

She took a deep breath and then flicked over to the pages of Margaret Brown's statement.

"Do you remember Mary Bennett?" Grace said referring to Margaret's original birth name.

"Should I?" he replied arrogantly and then leaned back in his seat, clasping his hands behind his head.

"You should do. You were in a relationship with her for two years during the nineteen eighties."

"A lot of water under the bridge since then, Constable. Refresh my memory."

Grace again patiently read over Mary's statement, careful to detail every incident of assault and introducing the numerous times he had raped her whilst being in fear of being beaten.

"Rape you say." He rocked forwards and stroked his chin. "Definitely not rape. I would say it was consensual sex. She liked it rough if I recall. Don't all women?"

Grace took another deep breath, exhaled slowly.

"Mary says she came home from bingo one night and found you had stripped her five year old daughter Samantha and were photographing her," she said calmly.

Grace saw an immediate reaction to his look. His face had lost that cockiness.

He said after a long pause "No comment."

Then Grace took out some of the photographs they had recovered from the tin under the bath. They were in two separate evidence bags, each one containing a number of images.

She slid out five photos from one of the bags.

"For the tape" she continued, "I am now showing the defendant exhibit one - five colour photos of a pre-pubescent girl. She is naked in each one and two of them focus on her genitalia."

The colour drained from Paynton's face. Grace knew that she had him.

She continued. "These have been identified by Mary Bennett as being those of her daughter Samantha, then aged five, and corroborate her statement. Can you tell me why we found these hidden in your house?"

He remained silent.

Grace opened up the second exhibit bag and removed four faded photographs. She slid them across the desk directly in front of his face.

"I am showing the defendant four colour photographs of a pre-pubescent girl." She paused staring into Steve Paynton's ashen face. "Two of these are naked, and two show the girl wearing just a pair of white panties," she continued. "This girl has been identified as being the daughter of Susan Siddons - Carol Siddons, - whose body was recently discovered buried on the site of the old Manvers Colliery."

"Whoa. Whoa." he shouted. "Just a minute, where's this fucking going? You're trying to pin her murder on me aren't you?"

"Never mind you shouting the odds saying we're trying to pin the murder of Carol Siddons on you," Grace retorted her own voice now raised a pitch higher. "We know you lived with Carol and her mum for some time. We also know that you were violent towards them, and you have a history of violence, and now we have found these nude photographs of Carol when she was only a child hidden in your bathroom. Join the dots Steve."

He dropped his head into his hands, and then rubbed his forehead feverishly.

After about thirty seconds he stopped, snapped bolt upright and banged his hands on the table. "All right you've got me," he snarled. "But I ain't done no murder. I had nothing to do with killing Carol or any other girl. Yes I photographed them, but it was fun like, I'm no pervert. And yes I'll admit that I slapped Sue and Mary about but that's it. Okay? That's it."

"Come on now Steve, you've made a start now. That's the hardest part over. Now just get it off your chest and tell us the rest. Shall I make it easier for you." Grace reached forward fixing his gaze with her own.

A mixture of fear and hate played across Paynton's face.

Grace continued. "I think as Carol got older she got the courage to tell you what you had done was wrong and that she was either going to tell her mother or the police. You couldn't afford that to happen and you realized you had to silence her once and for all."

"No." he shouted and banged a fist on the table "You're twisting this. Yes I photographed her, but that's it. I didn't harm her like you're saying. I didn't fucking kill her."

Hunter 'high fived' Grace and punched the air as they left the interview room an hour later. The interview hadn't ended entirely as they had wanted, but they had made a pretty good start to one of many questioning sessions that would be conducted over the next thirty-six hours. Steven Paynton had fully confessed to the brutal beatings against both women and went some way to admitting he had forced Mary Bennett to have sex against her will.

Hunter knew that at least would give CPS enough evidence to consider a charge of rape.

Finally Paynton admitted taking indecent photographs of Samantha Bennett and Carol Siddons when he had been living with their mothers. But no matter how hard they had pressed they couldn't move him on Carol's murder. Hunter hoped that would be only a matter of time.

- ooOoo –

CHAPTER TWELVE
DAY TWENTY: 25th July

The headline 'DEARNE MURDERS – SUSPECT HELD' brought a smile to his lips. He'd read the storyline in the local Barnwell Chronicle several times and the thought that someone else was taking the rap for him only boosted his confidence.

He knew it would mean that those around him would be more relaxed and less suspicious, enabling him to go about his activities again without raising so much as an eyebrow.

He rested the compact digital camera on the sill of the open car window, monitoring the crowd through the two inch screen. The camera had been a marvellous buy for the price. Small and discreet enough to hide in the palm of his hand and yet powerful enough with its 10X zoom to pick out the finest detail at fifty yards.

He checked and double checked his rear view mirror again, and then scoured the faces of the bustle of parents hovering outside the school, attentive to any suspicious reaction, especially as he had now parked in the same spot for the past week whilst he waited and watched out for her. He took a fleeting glance at his watch again. She was late today. Or had he already missed her. He hoped not. He especially liked to see her in her school uniform. And he also knew that this would be his last opportunity to catch her in her uniform for some time; the school's were breaking up today for the annual six-week summer hols.

At the edge of his peripheral vision he caught sight of her, coming his way from a different part of the school. A shaft of sunlight broke through the clouds just as she emerged from a row of trees close to the boundary fence. For a second it cast a halo effect on her mane of blonde highlighted hair, and he snapped off a shot. He wasn't too concerned about the composition of the shot because he knew he could play with the image later on his computer to get the effect he wanted. He wondered why she had been so late for him. He zoomed in and caught the frown creasing her pretty face. Something or someone was troubling her. He snapped another shot of her chewing at a finger. She looked particularly attractive today. Was that a hint of mascara around her beautiful brown eyes?

He took another picture of her climbing into her mother's car, catching more thigh than normal as her short, grey school skirt rode up her legs, before she went partially out of his sight as she slammed the passenger door shut. There was a brief exchange of words between her and her mother before they pulled away from the kerb. He wondered what that was about.

Dropping the camera onto the seat beside him he took another glance around. He let out a deep breath as soon as he was satisfied he had not attracted any unwarranted attention, and then he put his car in gear and slowly crept away.

He drove the three miles to his usual quiet spot and veered off the road onto the dirt track to the woods. He edged slowly along the tree line until he was on the long stretch where he knew he would have a good view of anyone approaching from a distance, and then he turned off the ignition.

He wound down both front windows to listen to the sounds around and picked up his camera and started to go back through the images he had captured. He was particularly interested in the ones he had caught of her two nights ago when he had crawled to the bottom of her garden, waiting for her to go to her room. It had reminded him of his teenage years when he had sneaked around his neighbours' properties with the camera his father had left him, snapping away as they emerged from their bathrooms.

When she had come from the shower he had set the camera to video mode, watching her as she gently rubbed the moistness from that long mane of hair. He particularly liked the way the light glistened on her face and neck and shoulders. He had captured her petite, slender form perfectly.

Viewing this was almost as good as being in the room itself with her.

He found himself getting excited again. He felt the rush of desire as a burst of testosterone surged through him. He set the camera on the dashboard of his car, switched to playback mode, cranked back his seat, unbuttoned his jeans and began to masturbate.

* * * *

"Harder, faster." barked Jock Kerr, setting all his weight behind the leather punch-bag. "C'mon son, thirty more seconds, put it in."

Hunter's gloved hands pummelled the sand-filled bag in piston-like fashion. Every muscle in his arms felt as though it was on fire and beads of sweat ran from his forehead, down the sides of his face and neck, adding to the already soaked patch on the front of his gym vest.

"Okay son, that's it. Good work, call it a day," ordered his father in his strong Glaswegian lilt.

Hunter punched the bag twice, hard for luck, then dropped his guard and rested his chin on his upper chest taking in great gulps of air. He felt physically drained almost to the point of sickness, and yet he was mentally alert, pleased that he had managed an hour of his father's training. Hunter loved his boxing sessions in his father's gym. His passion for them was almost on a par with his painting, but unlike finding enough time for his art, he knew he could always squeeze in an hour or two at the gym several times a week. It also gave him quality time with his dad, and it had the added bonus of sharing a well-earned pint or two with him after in his local working-men's club. Inevitably conversation revolved around Hunter's job or the distant memories of his father's boxing days.

On a repeated basis he found himself listening to the potted version of his father's life changing experiences. The same story, over and over again, of how he had boxed since he was a young boy back in his native Scotland. Explaining in detail how he had been introduced to it by his father, Hunter's grandfather, so that he 'could stand up for himself.' He had very quickly discovered he had a natural flair for the pugilistic art, and so as a teenager he had been taken on by an ex-professional at one of Glasgow's leading clubs and had been coached to a high level. Then he would re-run some of the fights in animated fashion, especially when he had got to the part where he told Hunter he found himself selected to compete in the Commonwealth games. And especially how, at seventeen, he had won a Bronze medal and that had carved the way for a professional career. His story tailed off when he told him about the bout which ended his career. He picked up a nasty cut just above his eye, where the flesh is at its thinnest, and despite several skin grafts, the scar opened with every fight and so at twenty-two years old his career was over.

Then with immense pride he would pick up the story again, telling him, that rather than turn his back on the sport he was good at he had worked even harder and immersed himself fully in the training side of the game. His father's story always ended on a note of sadness as he explained how he had soon come up against the seedier side of the fight game, finding himself constantly warding off some of the undesirables, especially those involved with the Glasgow gangs.

Hunter always wondered why he would go quiet at this point of the story and would find something else to say or do. Though his father would return to the story later, telling him that when he discovered that he had a child on the way, he decided he had had enough of Scotland, and moved down to Yorkshire with his pregnant wife, where he began a new phase in his life, setting up one of the best boxing gym's in the area, which earned him a very good living. He always ended his life tale by putting an arm around his shoulders and telling Hunter that his birth six months later changed his life.

Hunter leaned against the tiled wall of the shower area rolling his neck slowly whilst the warm jet of water swept away the sweat from his head, along the curve of his back, and away down his legs. That felt really good, he said to himself as he shut off the shower and padded into the changing area. As he dried himself he switched back into work mode, recalling the previous night's telephone conversation with Barry Newstead.

He had kept in daily touch with Barry since the interview with Susan Siddons, updating him as to the latest developments in the investigation into the two murders. He had also shared the predicament of Paul Goodright, particularly raising the issue of how he could legitimately introduce the cardigan as evidence without it being subject to too much scrutiny, especially if it proved to be a vital piece of evidence to the enquiry. If anyone could resolve this, he had told himself, it would be Barry. After all he had employed so many unorthodox methods in his past; Hunter had no doubt that he would have been involved in something pretty similar over the years, especially the era which Barry had moved in during his career. The phone call yesterday evening had proved him right.

"I'm your guardian angel," Barry had begun. "Meet me in the pub after work tomorrow, and bring that young Goodright with you. He can keep me in beer all night whilst I reveal all and keep him out of the proverbial shite."

As he had pressed the phone to his ear Hunter could almost visualize the smug grin on Barry's face as they discussed details of when and where they should meet.

He dressed hurriedly, slinging on a T-shirt over a pair of jeans, and then stuffed his sweaty training gear into his bag. As he left the gym he could hear his father turning off the lights and closing doors behind him throughout the building.

Hunter popped the locks of his car and was about to open the driver's door when the shuffle of feet resounded behind him. Before he had time to turn his head he felt a sharp blow to his back, directly over the region of his right kidney. The sickening stab of pain was instantaneous and his knees buckled beneath him. A sea of stars blurred his vision as he reached out to stop himself falling further. Another blow caught the side of his head, sending him crashing against his car door and throwing him onto his back. He let out a groan as he slumped to the pavement, but instinctively snapped open his eyes to see who his attacker was. There were three men towering over him and he instantly recognised two of them; Steve Paynton's younger brothers; David and Terry. David, the younger of the two, was grinding his fist into the palm of his other hand. A menacing grin ripped across his face.

"Our Steve's asked us to pay you a little visit. He just wants you to know that thanks to you and that fucking black tart of yours he's on the Nonce's wing at prison and we're here to pass on his regards." He sneered. "Oh and when we've finished with you we're off to see to that black bitch as well."

Hunter tried to scramble to his feet but quickly found himself reeling back against his car as a boot caught him mid-chest knocking the wind from his lungs. The three figures became shadows as a film of tears washed across his eyes, and expecting further blows he pulled his knees into his body. In that same instant, in the distance, he heard raised voices and the running of feet coming towards him. Scuffles broke out around him and as his vision cleared he saw his father and Barry Newstead grappling with his assailants. Feeling instantly buoyed by their presence he took on an inner strength and sprang to his feet.

He dodged another blow from David, twisted and lashed out with a tightly clenched fist. The punch he swung came from the hip and arced into his foe's head. He knew he had connected well when he felt the crunch of gristle and bone. For a second Hunter stared into a young man's face that was frenzied and distorted. The eyes were bulging and menacing. Hunter was hurting and he was also mad. Jumping instinctively to boxing stance he let fly again, raining punch after punch upon David Paynton. He could hear the cries and squeals flowing from David's busted mouth, but he never let up until the man had slumped to the ground. As he pushed himself upright Hunter could see that in spite of his father's and Barry's age, neither had forgotten how to channel their aggression nor had they lost their touch. Barry had quickly overcome his foe and was standing over the man Hunter hadn't recognised. The prostrate man was holding his chest and moaning.

The fate and suffering of Terry Paynton was still ongoing. It was only as Hunter took stock of the situation that he realised Terry was out of it. The only thing that kept him upright was the grip his dad had on the front of Terry's sweatshirt, yet the viciousness with which his father still pummelled him was unrelenting.

A knot formed in Hunter's stomach and he lurched forward grabbing hold of his dad's swinging fist.

"Dad he's had enough." He caught his father's stare and for a split-second he witnessed something in his dad's eyes, which he had seen on many occasions during drunken street fights he had attended over the years doing his job, but never before seen in his own father. It was the look of sheer hatred and evil.

For a second his father tried to resist his son's grip.

Hunter clenched his dad's wrist tighter. "Dad, I said he's had enough."

Hunter saw the look in his father change dramatically. His command had registered.

Terry Paynton's bloodied head was flopping around like a rag dolls.' He let go of the sweatshirt and there was a sickening thump as Terry's skull whacked the pavement.

Hunter saw the colour drain from his father's face as though it had just registered what he had done.

Hunter reached for his mobile.

"What are you doing?" snapped Barry.

"Ringing for an ambulance," Hunter replied.

"What on earth for?"

"So that we're covered for the mess they're in and they can be nicked later."

"Don't be so fucking daft. There's no way they're going to complain when they started it. If you were them with a reputation to keep up would you admit to be being beaten up by two old men? We've given them a bloody good hiding. They'll lick their wounds and keep their heads down if they've any sense. Trust me I used to be a policeman." A wide grin creased Barry's face. "Come on there's a well earned cold beer waiting for us."

"Do you know I haven't had so much fun since I gave Tam Watson a good thumping back in nineteen-ninety-one for taking my wee dram," his father added in his broad Scottish brogue. "I've not lost my touch have I son?"

That comment disturbed Hunter.

It continued to play on his mind during the journey to the club. He kept glancing across at his dad who was staring out through the windscreen, eyes fixed daze-like. It was as if he was unmoved by the whole event and yet Hunter had to continually grip the steering wheel to stop himself shaking.

He swung into the club car park, pulled into a space and killed the engine.

"You seem a little quiet son." His dad was still staring out through the windscreen, the gaze nowhere in particular.

Hunter took a deep breath. The image of his father pummelling Terry Paynton flooded back into his mind. That look in his father's face. It was as though he was 'getting off' hurting the man. His stomach was churning.

"I've never seen you like that dad. I thought you were going to kill him." He wanted to say more but it was his dad he was talking to.

"Nae chance son. He's made of stronger stuff than that. Anyway the little scumbag deserved what he got. Anyone who goes toe-to-toe with my son goes toe-to-toe with me."

"But Dad..."

His father held up his hand, giving him the stop sign. "Listen to me now son you need to understand where that came from. I had a hard life in Glasgow. I had to fight for everything I got – literally. I had to learn how to take a punch and come back stronger. That's all I want to say about it. I don't want to talk about it again. And I don't want you saying anything about this to your mother." Then a smile creased across his face. "Come on, mines a pint of heavy and a wee dram."

Before Hunter could say anything further his dad was pushing open the passenger door.

* * * * *

Without exception, whenever a group of policemen get together conversation always turns to one thing – the job. Earlier that day whilst working out at the gym it had been a spur of the moment decision for Hunter to take his father to meet Barry and Paul Goodright, especially as he knew what the conversation was going to expose him to. However, having just dished out a good beating to three nefarious characters with the help of his dad and then agreeing to hide the fact with Barry had made him realise it had not been too difficult a call to make.

125

Hunter shot a glance at his father's smiling face. He was still disturbed by his dad's actions and he knew at some stage he would have to discuss the earlier events again with him, though this wasn't the time or the place.

Barry was on his soapbox and in full flow, chattering excitedly, recounting the fight. He paused as he finished the story, took a swill of beer and wiped the froth and saliva from his hairy upper lip and then leaned forward facing Paul Goodright.

"Now then young Paul, the reason why we're all here." He took a sideways glance towards Hunter's dad. "Jock, we have some quite dodgy business to discuss. Not that we don't like your company but it might be a good time to get the beers in." Barry tapped his nose as a signal of secrecy.

Hunter could see the disappointment and yet acceptance on his father's face as he collected the empty glasses and moved from the table. "Need some help dad?" he felt it necessary to ask.

"No son. You get your business done. It's okay" his dad replied and winked as he loped off towards the bar.

Barry dragged a bulky supermarket carrier bag from beneath the table, which he had been gripping tightly between his legs. Hunter had seen him tugging it from the boot of the car after they had pulled into the pub car park and had wondered what was in it.

"In my early CID days it was always acknowledged that somewhere along the line you were always going to drop a bollock. Whether it was a small one or a big one was not in question, but how you were going to get out of it was another matter." Barry began. "So each office had their own contingency plans. Before the days of numbering pocket books or other admin items we kept spares for the inevitable 'faux pas' usually in a locked drawer or cupboard. I also had my own spares just for back up." He dropped the bag onto the table and pulled it open. "Ta dah." he announced. He slid out its contents just like a poker dealer would do a pack of cards. There were two old Police 'property other than found' books, which Hunter and Paul could recall using early on in their careers to record seized items of property which would be required as evidence.

"I forgot I'd kept these, and it's fortunate for you young Paul that I did. You'll find one of these books is from the nineteen eighties and the other, which you will need, is from the nineties. All you have to do is fill out one of the carbon exhibit labels, date it the day you seized that cardigan and put it into the bag with it."

"Barry, you're a Godsend," Paul responded excitedly and then paused. "Just one thing though, how am I going to get it submitted properly as evidence without having to admit I've kept it in my locker and then my garage for all these years'. The last thing we need is for some smart arsed barrister to knock it back especially if it has good forensic on it."

"I don't know. Have I got to wet-nurse you as well? I've even thought of that. These days' civilian admin staff have taken over the role of looking after property and my guess is none of them will have been around in the nineties when the cardigan was seized. All you have to do is go to the station with the bagged and labelled cardigan inside your coat. Tell one of the admin staff you need to get some property from one of the stores, and when you go into them, pretend to have a rummage amongst the shelves, distract the admin person and Bob's your uncle, or in this case Barry's your saviour. When they try to check out the number on the card they'll just think that the relevant property book has been destroyed after all these years."

Hunter had sat transfixed throughout this, and now that Barry had finished he leaned back in his seat in reflective mood. On the one hand he knew that what he had been a party to was completely unorthodox, and yet on the other, if this would help catch their killer he knew it was something he could live with.

Then as he slid the books back into the carrier bag Barry glanced at both of them and spoke slowly. What he said was as if he had read Hunter's mind.

"Something my old Sergeant once said to me when I was a young CID officer and the words remained with me throughout my service. Sometimes we have to use as much trickery as the villains do. You match lie for lie and make sure yours are better than theirs. At the end of the day you've got to protect the public and pay back the bad guys. Always remember the pen is mightier than the sword. And one last piece of advice. When you've worked them one, don't get a conscience about it."

- ooOoo -

CHAPTER THIRTEEN
DAY TWENTY-ONE: 26th July

Grace Marshall had arrived early at the tea room, ordered a strong black coffee and sat down as close to the rear of the shop as she could. She was uneasy and experiencing butterflies in the pit of her stomach. It wasn't every day that a possible main witness had links to the police authority, even if it was only through marriage. This was going to be an uncomfortable meeting and needed a delicate approach. Grace had rehearsed over and over in her head what she was going to say and deep down she wished now she hadn't suggested this to Hunter.

If this goes wrong she thought to herself, and the gaffer got to hear of it I'm going to get a right dressing down. She stared at the glassed front entrance wondering what Mrs Gardner looked like. It was just after ten-thirty am and the world outside the glass was bathed in strong sunlight. For a second she tried to recall the women's soft tones without a hint of local dialect when she had called her yesterday afternoon. The voice had been very calming, very reassuring, and yet quite concerned about why there was a need to meet in such secrecy.

Whilst she waited for the coffee her eyes strayed around the room. It was the first time she had taken notice of the contemporary décor despite having used this tea room as a place to meet friends on many an occasion whilst out shopping. There were only another couple of people in there; a young mum with a toddler in a buggy and an older woman whom she guessed was the child's grandmother.

When she had agreed the arrangements over the phone she knew from her previous visits that generally very few people would be in at this time. The other customers were just out of earshot; their conversation was just a muted jumble of words. That also meant they would not be able to overhear her speaking with Karen Gardner.

Five minutes after ordering the waitress appeared with her coffee. Grace thanked her with a smile and picked up the cup, holding it in front of her with both hands and turning her attention back to the entrance. The coffee was stronger and hotter than she had anticipated and caused her to jolt. It also wasn't the best she had, but it would do; after all she wasn't here to do a coffee morning.

The door opened with a pinging noise as it caught the bell fastened to the lintel. The slim, attractive, faired-haired woman in a dark, well-tailored suit met her own gaze, smiled, raised a hand and moved towards her.

"Detective Marshall - Grace?" she asked standing before her.

Grace nodded and pointed out a chair opposite. It was a natural reaction, for she knew Mrs Gardner was going to sit anyway.

Within seconds the same young waitress returned, pen poised over a small notepad.

Karen glanced at Grace's drink. "Another coffee please," she said softly. "Cappuccino."

As the waitress walked away Grace leaned forward holding out her hand, carefully clasping the slender hand of Karen Gardner. Grace couldn't help but spot the well-manicured French-polished nails. "Grace Marshall," she introduced herself."

"Karen Gardner," replied Karen, taking back her hand.

The voice sounded nervous.

"Sorry I was so vague on the phone, but I didn't want to give too much away."

"I gathered that," Karen replied.

Grace saw her swallow hard. She had visually examined Mrs Gardner as soon as she walked through the door and she could instantly see why Paul Goodright had visited her all those years ago. At forty-eight, she was still a very attractive woman and very tastefully made-up and dressed. She guessed she was a woman who could afford to spend lots of time at the gym judging by her slim figure and sunbed tan. Grace waited a few minutes whilst Karen's coffee order came, making small talk about the weather and asking questions about Mrs

Gardner's fundraising events, hoping to put her more at ease. The cappuccino soon arrived. Grace waited whilst Karen took a sip, and then continued. "Mrs Gardner – do you mind if I call you Karen?"

She saw Karen finish the last dregs of the coffee, set the cup down and indicate with a faint smile and slight nod for her to continue.

"I asked to meet you here away from your home because what I want to talk to you about is a bit sensitive, but I won't beat about the bush Karen. We're trying to tie up some loose ends on one of our enquiries, and well basically it's about an affair you had with a young detective, Paul Goodright, a good few years' back."

"Oh God is that all this is. I've been fretting ever since you called. I thought it was something more sinister." She started to laugh. "It wasn't an affair, we just went to bed together a few times."

The response surprised Grace, but at the same time she knew from the reply this was now going to be easier than she had expected.

"How is Paul? He must be early thirties now. Is he married? Kids?" Karen Gardner was now firing off her own questions.

Grace responded with a series of nods.

"Please don't beat about the bush any more, as you put it. About five years ago my husband discovered I was seeing someone, not Paul, another guy, and he confronted me about it. I never denied it. I told him a few home truths about all the meetings he went to, leaving me alone at night only to be wheeled out and be the dutiful wife when he needed me at his do or other. We had a big clear the air session, and to be honest it was well overdue. I suppose I was a little wild in my late twenties, early thirties. I saw a few guys, just for the attention which I wasn't getting from my marriage, but for the last five years I've been the faithful councillor's wife." Grace saw her pause for a second glancing towards her. "I can see by your expression you're surprised at how forthright I'm being."

"I am a little taken aback," replied Grace. She took another sip of her cappuccino. It was cold now, and she set it back down on the saucer.

"Look, as I say we sorted our marriage out. Oh by the way I only confessed to the one, he doesn't know about the other couple, which includes Paul. My husband forgave me and its all water under the bridge now. Jerry's not daft. He's a politician at heart and he still sees me as his bit of 'eye candy' I think the term is. I'm by his side when he needs me, flutter my eyelids and say all the right things to his colleagues, and he allows me my freedom to shop and meet my friends down at the gym, and get my beauty treatments; it's a happy compromise." Mrs Gardner broke off, signalled to the waitress and ordered two more coffees, and then continued. "Now I've bared my soul officer Marshall can you give me a clue what this is about. The investigation?"

"Well it might not actually have anything to do with our investigation, but as I've said, it is a loose end that we need to tie up. I want you to try and cast your mind back to nineteen-ninety-three when you were seeing Paul."

"Good God. I can't remember what I did last week without my diary."

"I think you might remember this Karen, he had the CID car stolen whilst he was with you one evening."

"Oh yes I do remember that," she started to laugh. "He was in a right flap. I was laughing when he came back and told me what had happened and he had to make the call back to his office. He told me it wasn't funny. He said he had to come up with a story to cover up being with me. I wasn't very helpful to him I'm afraid. I couldn't take it seriously and to be honest that signalled the end of our short relationship." Karen Gardner paused again and Grace saw her looking towards the waitress as the girl returned with the second order and cleared away their cups.

After she had gone Mrs Gardner continued. "Wasn't the CID car involved in some kind of serious accident with another car; ran it off the road or something?" Karen stopped for a second, gazed up at the ceiling and tapped her chin. "Yes, that was it," she continued, and Grace fixed eyes with her again. "I'm sure Paul told me that his sister and her boyfriend had been in the other car and that she had been seriously injured and her boyfriend had been killed. I think he also mentioned there was some kind of internal enquiry and if I was ever interviewed about Paul being with me I was to deny everything. That's when he also told me he mustn't see me again until things died down. But he never did get in touch again." Mrs Gardner picked up her cup, took a sip, set it back down again. "Is that what this is about? Have you found out who took the car?"

"I'm afraid not," replied Grace. "We're looking into the possibility it was taken out of spite. A revenge sort of thing, which went wrong." Grace knew she wasn't being entirely honest with her answers because there was still the cover up she had got herself embroiled in. She continued. "Paul heard on the grapevine that you were also seeing someone else. Someone with a bit of character shall we say, who wasn't too friendly with cops, and so we're looking into the possibility he found out about Paul visiting you and took the car."

Grace saw the perturbed look creep across Karen's face.

"Hmm I can see your dilemma. Grace, can I just ask if all this is going to come out?"

"Not if I have anything to do with it. If you were seeing another guy, and you choose to give us that name, he will have no idea it came from you. We'll make him believe his name cropped up through our informants, because if he did do this as some kind of perverted joke he will have told someone."

Grace lost eye contact again as Karen dropped her gaze to the steaming cup of coffee. Then she looked up. "Paul isn't wrong. I was seeing another young man at the time. And I suppose he was a bit of a character, as you put it. I met him through my husband's dealing with licences. Jerry used to be involved in the issuing of the licence for the local fairground 'feast' when it came to this area a couple of times a year. The fairground owner brought his son to our apartment one day and I got chatting to him whilst they did their business. We met a few times over about a six-month period and then it fizzled out, sadly. He had a hell of a body I'll tell you for someone in their early twenties." She suddenly had a sparkle in her eyes. "He told me he was some kind of fighter, bare knuckle stuff, illegal. He told me he regularly fought with the gypsies for money."

"What's his name Karen?"

"You sure, he's not going to find out I told you?"

Grace crossed her chest. "Cross my heart."

"Okay it's Billy. Billy Smith. His family own a plot of land near the canal where they have some static caravans. He's still around, when he's not travelling with the fair."

"Thank you Karen you've been very helpful."

Karen picked up her coffee cup, wiped the base on the edge of the saucer and took a sip. "If you haven't already tried it, you should you know." Karen Gardner said, pulling away the cup and smiling at her.

"Try what?"

"Having sex with another guy. It does wonders for your self-confidence and it keeps your hubby on his toes. Life's not always Mills and Boon you know." Grace was sure she spotted a mischievous smile stretch across her face as she finished off her drink.

- ooOoo –

CHAPTER FOURTEEN
DAY TWENTY-TWO: 28th July.

The intermittent trill from the alarm clock pounded Hunter's ears. Grunting he rolled over and swung out an arm to smack it off, pulling back quickly as the pain registered in his ribs. It was a sharp and tender reminder of the fight with the Paynton's.

The strong coruscating light of early morning sunshine filtering through the curtains should have given him the vigour to leap out of bed and yet somehow he felt totally drained. Dropping his head back onto the pillow he shut his eyes. In that instance the images of the melee flashed inside his head. Especially that look in his father's eyes. Not one of anger, but actually of pleasure. He snapped open his eyelids again hoping to dismiss the mental pictures in his imagination, but they were still there, haunting him. He eased himself up into the sitting position, letting off a low moan. Seeing Beth's face screw up as he disturbed her he kissed her gently on the forehead, rolled out of bed and made for the bathroom.

Stepping out of the shower he delicately dabbed the towel over his wet torso. He hurt like hell this morning. In the mirror he examined his well-defined stomach and ribcage. The bruising had already taken on an intense purple shade. Thank god he'd been able to cover his face.

It took an eternity to dress and he had to skip breakfast to get to work on time. As he pulled his Audi out of the drive Simple Minds, 'Alive and kicking' played out from the radio and he laughed to himself, and then winced as it caused him much discomfort.

Turning onto the bypass he wound down the driver's window to let in the fresh morning air. It was already warm and not yet seven-thirty am. The road ahead was clear and ELO's, 'Mr Blue Sky' had just started. He turned up the sound and forced down the accelerator.

Half a mile from the station the wail of two-tone horns approaching from the rear and at speed tore his attention away from the pounding music. Glancing in the rear view mirror he picked up the ambulance screaming towards him and he pulled in and hugged the kerb as it shot past. As he picked his speed back up he hoped to God it wasn't going to be another call requiring his team to attend. They didn't need another murder at this time - they were fast running out of detectives.

* * * * *

Following morning briefing and the de-camping of the teams from the MIT department to carry out their daily tasks the Detective Superintendent had called together Hunter, DS Mark Gamble, the two supervisors of the MIT teams, Detective Inspector Gerald Scaife, the office manager who coordinated all the actions, and Isobel Stevens, the supervisor of the HOLMES team, to review the investigation.

They had all been told to meet in the conference room and they were now seated around the large table. In front of them they all had several A4 size computer generated replications of the timelines relating to Carol Siddons and Rebecca Morris, and a summary of the important issues taken from key statements of witnesses, which had been supplied by Isobel's team.

The Detective Superintendent had already mentioned that he wanted to discuss the status of the investigation and by the end of the meeting confirm the strategy for the next phase of the enquiry.

"Heard the latest?" said Detective Superintendent Robshaw, leaning forward, resting his chin on cupped hands and roaming his eyes around the table. "Seems somebody gave Steve Paynton's two brothers, and one of his cousins a good hiding. One of the brothers has got two broken ribs and a punctured lung, another has a broken nose and cheekbone and several teeth missing, and the cousin has a broken jaw and a badly gashed eye. Rumour has it that a police officer was involved."

Hunter saw the SIO land his gaze upon him. Defensively, he shrugged his shoulders and gave him a 'why are you looking at me' expression.

"Anyway it seems none of them want to make a complaint, and we've got too much on our plate to have to follow up on malicious gossip."

As the Superintendent leaned back in his chair, folding his arms, Hunter saw that his eyes were still fixed upon him. Seeing that look, he knew in his mind that Michael Robshaw was letting him know that he was fully aware of what had gone on, and more than likely realised what lay behind it, and that he wanted him to know that nothing 'on the shop floor' slipped past him despite his managerial position. Equally Hunter knew that the Superintendent was making it quite clear that given the circumstances he was prepared to not make a great fuss about it.'

A bright shaft of sunshine pierced the gap between the partly closed blinds covering the many large windows which spanned one side of the conference room and reflected off the surface of the well polished oak veneered table giving additional warmth to the already stuffy room. Michael Robshaw unfolded his arms and, using a hand held remote control switched on the air conditioner. A low hum came from the unit high up against the ceiling and an almost instant coolness drifted down.

Michael Robshaw said. "Okay, I'm going to open things up. Firstly, have we got anywhere yet with the playing card found with Rebecca Morris, or these markings carved into the bodies stomachs?"

Hunter looked up from his papers and diverted his eyes towards the white melamine boards lined up at the front of the room. He particularly focussed on the blown-up photos of the killer's signature on Rebecca's and Carol Siddons' abdomen. He couldn't help but notice the contrast between the pale waxen flesh of Rebecca and the wrinkled parchment-like skin of Carol's mummified body. It made the marks appear so different. He thought that Professor McCormack had done a magnificent job spotting them.

"I've been thinking," said Isobel Stevens, an experienced detective with twenty-two years' service behind her and who had joined the HOLMES team following the Home Office review arising from the mistakes of The Ripper Enquiry. She had been elevated to the role of Supervisor within a short space of time. She was generally the first to be called out whenever a new investigation required the HOLMES network to be set up.

She continued. "We know from all the enquiries that DC Sampson has made that they are not religious markings or anything to do with the occult. So could they be a code of some kind?"

Hunter tilted his head as he stared at the images, recalling what Isobel had just said. The puzzle the killer had left behind had been playing on his mind ever since the pathologist had highlighted it.

He swayed his head the other way to get a different view. Then it hit him. The flashback to earlier that morning when the ambulance appeared at his rear was the trigger. He recalled how that in his interior mirror he had been able to pick out the wording on the front of the vehicle because it was written in reverse.

"I've got it," he couldn't help but blurt out. Pushing himself out of his seat he made his way to the feature boards. He tapped the shots taken of Caroline Siddons torso. The marks were clearer on these.

"It's a word, don't you see?" He moved his finger right to left underlining the marks. The last digit is not a number three, it's a letter E. It's written facing backwards. And they're not roman numerals they're all letters. Look," he continued tapping excitedly. "He's carved the word EVIL backwards into these girls' stomachs."

Hunter saw that he had grabbed all their attentions.

"Bloody hell Hunter," interjected Det Supt Robshaw, "I think you're right."

A silence ensued around the table.

It lasted a good ten seconds then Isobel piped up. "So is the killer saying he's evil, or the girls are evil?"

Hunter tapped his chin; pondering. "I think he's saying the girls are evil. That's why he did to them what he did. Just think about it, Carol Siddons was taken into care and within a month or two had completely changed character. Her background statement describes her as a drunken, violent and promiscuous girl. She had become known as a girl with a bit of a reputation. And then Rebecca," he aimed a quick glance at the school photo of her. "We know from her best friend Kirsty Evans that Rebecca wasn't the sweet innocent girl we have pictured here. She'd become a bit of a rebel the few weeks prior to her death. In particular she'd started flirting with older lads to an extent she'd get them worked up to expect sex and then she'd push them away and embarrass them. If we surmise that the killer got to know that side of their characters then maybe in his twisted little mind he saw them both as evil and needed to be punished."

Hunter returned to his seat.

"Okay," said the Detective Superintendent rubbing his hands together. "Well done Hunter, you've convinced me with that explanation, unless anyone has another interpretation."

The detectives around the tables all looked at one another. A few shrugged.

The SIO looked along the sea of faces. "So what's the significance of the playing card? The seven of hearts found on Rebecca Morris's body, yet none found with Carol Siddons."

Blank stares faced him back.

"We don't actually know there was no card with Carol's body," returned Hunter. "Quite a lot of earth had been removed around her before the digger uncovered her remains. It could still be amongst the waste we're sorting through."

The team nodded in acceptance of Hunter's response.

There was further silence for a good thirty seconds then Detective Superintendent Robshaw said, "Right, the playing card issue is one we need to think about for future briefings." He leaned forward, clasping his hands together into a ball "And I don't need to remind you all that what we discuss here doesn't get to the press. The playing card and the markings on the body we keep to ourselves, okay?"

There was a nod of acknowledgment from the team.

The SIO unclasped his hands. "Right let's move on. Isobel give us a rundown of what we have so far."

Isobel dropped her paperwork onto the desk and lifted a pair of reading glasses, hanging from a cord around her neck, onto the bridge of her nose.

As Hunter listened and watched Isobel he couldn't help but notice that over the years, at every new investigation, she seemed to have put on extra pounds, and he couldn't help but think that her pudgy features made her appearance look older than her forty years. He guessed it was down to all the constant deskwork and long hours, only able to grab fast food and in-between snacks, to fuel her working day.

She cleared her throat and began to read slowly through the pages of summary, occasionally pausing to cross reference with the two timelines to confirm sightings and evidence. She began with Carol Siddons affirming that her mother Susan had last seen the fourteen-year-old schoolgirl, on the twelfth of October 1993, after making an unofficial visit from school to her mother's house, instead of going back to the residential care home where she had been placed by the courts.

"Carol spilled tomato sauce on her school clothes and so her Mum loaned her a pair of jeans and a cardigan and saw her to the bus stop at half past nine. She left her at the bus stop and that is our last sighting until her body is discovered on the old Manvers Coking plant site ten days ago. Now this is where we have had a real breakthrough. A PC Paul Goodright, who used to work here in Barnwell CID back in nineteen-ninety-three, has come forward following the Crimewatch appeal. It appears that on that night he had his CID car nicked whilst he was out on enquiries and that was found by a passing dog walker on fire on the dirt track behind the Coking Plant. The Fire brigade put out the fire and PC Goodright recovered a cardigan from the back seat of the CID car."

"I remember that." interjected Hunter feigning amazement, as though this was all fresh news to him. "I was working that night. I went out with Paul after the Fire Brigade called in with the news. Scenes of Crime were called but the car was badly smoke damaged and they didn't manage to lift prints or anything unfortunately. The car had also got some front-end damage and there had been a fatal hit and run that same night. We're certain it hit a car being driven by the boyfriend of Paul Goodright's sister. The boyfriend was killed and she was badly injured in that crash. In fact it confined her to a wheelchair. He was trapped inside when it burst into flames. The gaffer at that time, DI Jameson, encouraged the Traffic Officers, who were investigating the accident, not to make the link with the CID car. I think he was going for promotion at the time and he thought it might affect his chances. Back then having the embarrassment of one of his department's cars being nicked and linked with a fatal was not a sign of good leadership."

"Well," continued Isobel, "It seems PC Goodright recovered a cardigan from the back of that car and booked it in as evidence. He's taken the trouble to search through old property at Headquarters and found the cardigan. It's still sealed in its original bag and labelled and it's been identified by Susan Siddons as the same cardigan she loaned her daughter Carol on the night she went missing. That's on its way to Forensics as we speak."

"That is good news" said the Superintendent elatedly. "This could be the breakthrough we've been looking for."

Hunter lowered his head and smiled. Paul and Barry Newstead had come good.

"Now to Rebecca Morris," continued Isobel. "As we know she was last seen walking towards a bus stop five hundred yards from her home, in school uniform. That sighting was at five to eight on the morning of the sixth of July – three weeks ago. Her body was discovered the next day in the barn of a derelict farm near to Harlington, four miles from her home. There are no sightings during this time and we are as happy as we can be that the man who discovered Rebecca's mutilated body was not involved in her murder. The man who found her states he thought he heard someone running from the back of the farm and then a van or car driving away. We have no description of a person or vehicle."

Isobel followed the line of her finger down the summary, glancing up from time to time as she spoke to see if the others were following. "When Rebecca's body was discovered she had on jeans and a T-shirt. We have not found her school uniform, or the school bag she was seen with, or her mobile phone. A close friend of Rebecca's, Kirsty Evans, states that Rebecca hinted that someone older had been chatting her up, phoning her, and asking if he could photograph her. Kirsty says the impression she got from Rebecca was that this guy was older, more than likely a young man as opposed to a teenager."

She paused again and looked over her glasses at everyone studying her paperwork "And finally our only suspect at this time, Steve Paynton. Steve was the partner of Carol's Mother, Susan, and we know from what she has said that Steve was physically abusing the pair of them and when he was arrested he had in his possession indecent images of Carol when she was very young. He also had almost a hundred other indecent photographs of children, none of which were of Rebecca. So although we can link him to Carol, we cannot link him to Rebecca at this time. As we know both Carol and Rebecca were killed by the same weapon and the moulding taken from the wounds, which has come back from the Forensic team is pointing us to a Bowie type knife. Extensive searches have now been carried out at all the locations where we know Steve Paynton has lived over the past thirteen years and we have not found anything similar, or anything relating to Rebecca." Isobel paused again removed her spectacles and sat back. "That brings us up to the present," she said picking up her paperwork and tapping it neatly together on the tabletop.

The Detective Superintendent looked up from his copies of the documents and leaned forward. "Okay, thanks for that Isobel," he began. "Next steps." He raised his eyes to the ceiling for a second and then returned his gaze. "The matter playing on my mind is the time gap between the killings. So whilst we have teams going over the background stuff of the two girls, we now need to concentrate on some of our old cold casework. Are there any other unsolved murders out there, which could be connected to ours? We also need to focus on the killer or killers. What have they been doing or where have they been during the past fourteen years. We need to make enquiries with prisons and the probation service, to see if we can come up with any likely candidates. We have a lot of tasks to be getting on with and with limited resources so Headquarters have approved me taking on more staff to help."

Hunter's ears pricked up and immediately seized on the opportunity. "Can I make a suggestion Boss?"

The Superintendent nodded.

"You're probably aware that Barry Newstead, ex-CID, was instrumental in pointing us in the direction of Carol Siddons, when her body was discovered."

Michael Robshaw nodded again.

"Well what you might not be aware of is that when she was originally reported missing, Barry was the only person who believed what Carol's mum was saying, and worked against the wishes of the then DI to try and trace her. Knowing Barry like I do I'm sure he will still have all his notes, and seeing as we're allowed to take on ex-detectives to help us on these enquiries he would be a great asset."

The Superintendent pulled a face.

Hunter spotted the look of angst. "Look I know what you're thinking. Yes he was a bit of a maverick in his day, but I've been using his knowledge to good advantage just lately, and I'll vouch for him. I'll supervise his work and if it looks as though he's going out on a limb I'll draw him back, or get shut. Is that OK?"

Before Michael Robshaw had time to respond they were all taken back by the hurried opening of the conference room door, as it swung back and thudded against the flimsy stud wall. A red faced, perspiring DC Mike Sampson, filled the doorframe.

"Sorry to disturb you gaffer," he gasped, "but another body's been found."

* * * * *

On their hands and knees, in their blue boiler suits, the Task Force search team were working shoulder-to-shoulder carrying out fingertip searches around the site where Carol Siddons' mummified remains had been unearthed two weeks previously.

Search grids had been taped off on the old colliery site and white suited forensic officers, some with metal detectors were combing the murky topsoil for exhibits. They had also brought in a specially trained sniffer dog.

Police dog handler Peter Broughton and his Springer spaniel Lady were currently outside the roped off area, scrambling around in scrubland at the edge of the old pit site. Here the undergrowth was thick and dense in places and it was proving difficult for them to keep on a straight course. This was a first for Peter and Lady. Generally they only got called out when there had been a disaster, where the likelihood was that someone had been buried alive. But this is what they had both trained for. Lady had a nose for finding bodies even if they had been dead for some time.

On a long rope the Springer darted in and out of sparse bushes and amongst clods of long grasses. They had been doing this for just under two hours and were due a break when Lady stopped longer than normal, sniffing and pawing at a mound of overgrown gorse. Peter increased his pace, taking in the slack of the rope until he was beside his dog.

"What we found here then girl?" he said patting the Spaniel's back. He pushed Lady to one side and on bended knees delved into the gorse, parting fronds carefully and slowly. Some of the ferns and grasses split easily from the soil; far easier than he had anticipated and he found himself tugging at a huge clump, taking away a good two inches of top soil. He wondered if Lady had found a badger set and for the next couple of minutes he scraped around an area where the clay was softer and strangely discoloured. He had never seen soil stained in this way before. He was considering calling for a member of the forensic team to join him when he exposed a piece of hemp sacking. Scraping more loose soil away he spotted the NCB black lettering stamped across the old decaying sack. The dog handler muttered to himself and tugged at one corner. It resisted more than he had conjectured and he pulled harder. Quite unexpectedly, it freed itself from the earth and sent him rolling backwards. Cursing and disgusted with himself he pushed himself up onto his knees, brushing dust from the backs of his thighs. He looked into the crevice, which the sacking had covered. What faced him rocked him back on his heels for a few seconds. It was then that he knew he definitely should shout for the forensic team.

* * * * *

It was with a feeling of déjà vu that Hunter, Grace, Tony Bullars and Mike Sampson pulled up before the cordoned off area on the Manvers site. Whilst travelling there they had learned that the second body was in fact a skeleton and that what appeared to be girl's school clothing was still clung to the defleshed bones.

The team could see that Scenes of Crime, working with the forensic team, were already erecting a second white tent around the site of the decomposed body.

The MIT team viewed the activity before them. The one good thing about this recent discovery was that the majority of the resources they required were already on site.

Hunter was duly briefed by the uniformed officer at the entrance to the scene that the other experts who were required to scrutinize this discovery of skeletal remains were already on their way. He knew from that information that Professor Lizzie McCormack and the body recovery team would be soon joining them.

Hunter realised that for the next few hours very little evidence would be gathered but things would be frantic. The Recovery team would need to excavate and remove the cadaver to a climate-controlled Pathology lab as soon as possible because he knew that now the body had been exposed there would be further acceleration in its decomposition. At the same time the body recovery team would be ensuring that the chain of evidence remained intact for the remaining forensic team.

He stood, hands on hips surveying the scene. His instinct was telling him that this was now a serial murder enquiry. He saw that Tony, Grace and Mike had already passed through the 'Police line do not cross' tape, and were busy organizing and briefing officers as to their respective roles in this investigation.

Within twenty minutes Professor McCormack had landed at the site. Hunter spotted her by the open boot of her car, stepping into her forensic suit.

Within five minutes he saw her heading towards him, bouncing on the balls of her feet, and he was sure that a perverse grin was stretching across her face, as though she took great pleasure in probing around dead bodies.

"My my, we are busy little bees," she said in her soft Scottish voice as she drew ever closer.

Soon she was easing herself down over the disturbed earth around the grisly corpse. It was devoid of any flesh, a perfect set of white teeth grinned back from the dirty brown skull, and hanks of course and matted dark brown hair still adhered to it. It was dressed in a white blouse and dark blue skirt, and although the upper parts were exposed most of the legs still remained covered in the surrounding red clay soil.

The Professor probed around the skeleton with a scalpel, leaning forwards occasionally, raising the flimsy cotton blouse and skirt and examining some of the bones. She tutted and clucked as she moved around the makeshift grave on her knees. Then she looked up at Hunter, eye raised above spectacles.

"This is a difficult one for me," she announced. "This body, unlike the other one you found a couple of weeks ago is completely devoid of any tissue whatsoever. This is not my skill area I'm afraid. What I can tell you is that this is the body of a young teenage girl."

"How's that?" Hunter asked.

The pathologist hovered her scalpel above the pelvic area of the skeleton and began to rotate it. "These flared bones on the hips are a dead giveaway. This is called the sciatic notch. It spreads as a young woman. Nature's way of accommodating a foetus. Also look at the forehead." Still using the scalpel as a pointer she aimed it towards the skull. "The frontal lobe is flat. In a man's there is more of a slope." Lizzie McCormack studied the body a little longer, before giving off a long winded "hmm."

She turned to Hunter. "What I can also tell you is that injuries to the bones in her neck suggest she has been strangled again just like the others." She paused a second, "And I can also tell you that this looks very much like the handiwork of our killer again." She pointed to a clear plastic bag poking upwards through loosened soil, its transparency masked here and there by clinging detritus. "If I'm not mistaken that's another one of those playing cards. Looks like the three of hearts to me."

She pushed herself up from the ground. "That's as far as I can take things for you I'm afraid. I'll put in a call to check how long the forensic anthropologist will be before he can get here. It's a colleague of mine so I can speed things up for you. He'll collect and examine the bones and tell you how long the body has been buried here and hopefully help identify her for you."

As the Professor edged away from the site, Hunter saw over her shoulder that the forensic recovery team had just arrived and were taking out the Ground Penetrating Radar, which would determine if there were even more bodies buried in the vicinity.

* * * * *

Josh: Hi Kirsty.
Kirsty: Hi Josh, howa yoo?
Josh: yeah im gud thanx.
Kirsty: wot u doin?
Josh: listenin to sum artic monkeys, jus chillin.
Kirsty: that's cool.

He had been trawling the social network sites on the Internet for weeks, tracking the profiles of a number of people, picking up the language and learning how to develop a character from a mixture of the various sites. It had been time consuming but all too easy.

He'd made copious notes at first in his attempt to create a believable character with substance. To step inside the head of a typical seventeen year old boy he had searched the music sites for hours on end, selecting the most popular bands and solo artists, and then he had followed up with a little research about each one to enable him to convince his audience. He had also done 'dummy runs' to 'test drive' Josh, developing convincingly his use of the teenage text language on the websites. It had been a worthwhile exercise and he had hooked several unsuspecting teenage girls in the three weeks he had been socialising across the networks. One thirteen year old had even exposed her cute little breasts to him, which he had captured on his web-cam.

By the time he had 'hooked up' on Kirsty's site he was an accomplished player. She had been wary at first and tested him on several occasions, but his research had stood him in good stead and within a week he knew that she firmly believed she was conversing with seventeen year old 'Josh'.

Josh: saw u at skwl the othr day. u lukd sad.

Kirsty: wot wer u doin nr my skwl.

Josh: jus passin lukin 4 a pretty face.

Kirsty: u r makin me blush. No serious wot wer u doin nr my skwl.

Josh: jus passin. Goin 2 the park for a game of footie. Why wer u sad.

Kirsty: I wantd 2 stay over at my friends wiv sum mates cos of skool brake up but mum wudnt let me cos of wat append to Rebecca. We ad a row she freakd out.

Josh: do u want me 2 cheer u up?

Kirsty: wat do u mean?

Josh: u r cute u kno. Do u want to meet up.

Kirsty: r u askin me out?

Josh: Of cors.

Kirsty: but I hardli kno u.

Josh: u do wev talkd for ages on this chat room. Uv seen my foto. Don't u like me.

Selecting the right photograph and then altering it in his Adobe Photoshop programme had been another worthwhile project. He was quite proud of how physically good-looking he had made his character.

Kirsty: u luk nice. u sound nice.

Josh: well then lets meet.

Kirsty: ok but I can't 4 a few days. ive been grounded. in fact im supposed 2 b doin mi bedroom now instead of chattin wiv u. mum wil freak again if she catchs me.

Josh: wen can u get out then?

Kirsty: next satrday evenin. mums out wiv dad wiv frends. Wot about the park?

Josh: souns gud. c u then pretty face.

As he exited the chat room site he leaned back on his swivel chair, clasped his hands behind his head and grinned widely.

Another lamb to the slaughter.

- ooOoo -

CHAPTER FIFTEEN
DAY TWENTY-FOUR: 30th July.

The ringing of Grace Marshall's desk phone disturbed the unusual concentrated silence in the MIT office. She answered it without looking up from her paperwork, clamping the handset between her neck and shoulder. But the nature of the call changed her demeanour. She lifted her eyes as she listened intently to the voice on the other end of the line. Picking up a pen she scribbled notes in her own form of shorthand, only answering occasionally with a one word clipped response. Two minutes later she set down the receiver.

Solemn faced, her eyes swept across four desks that had been recently fixed together into a square format.

The two opposite were occupied. Hunter and Barry Newstead were picking through the piles of documents spread across their surfaces.

"Do you want the good news or the bad news?" she said.

Hunter looked up from his desk and pushed aside notes he had been making on the recent body find. For the last half hour he had been trying his best to make sense of it all. True he had worked on body count murders before, but it had been where members of the same family had been killed in one single event. He had never worked on multiple victim deaths, which were now being dubbed as the actions of a serial killer. His head felt woolly. A mixture of long hours of intense work, and a lack of sleep, from his lying awake night after night, mulling over the recent events, were taking their toll.

"Hit me with the good news first," Hunter responded, placing an already well-chewed pen back into one corner of his mouth.

Barry Newstead dog-eared the page he had been perusing and peered over his reading spectacles at Grace. It was his first day with the Case Team, joining as a civilian investigator and he had been given the job of sending the profiles of the murdered girls, and the descriptions of how they had met their deaths, to Headquarters Public Protection Unit. In return they had faxed him the backgrounds and histories of the districts most violent and dangerous sex offenders. He had already said to Hunter 'that he thought nothing could surprise him anymore, that was until he had ploughed through this lot' and he had confessed 'he was astonished at just how many paedophiles there were living in his area.'

"That was the forensics lab," continued Grace. "They have found some traces on that grey cardigan belonging to Carol Siddons. But the bad news is none of it is human DNA. All they have found are lots of dog hairs, and some black woollen fibres which appear to have come from a duffel coat of some type."

"Dog hairs?" interjected Barry. "Carol never had a dog, and neither Susan."

"Sure about that Barry?" enquired Hunter, eyebrows raised, teeth clenching harder on the end of his pen.

"I'm positive. I can give Sue a quick ring, but all the time I was investigating Carol's disappearance there was never any dog around. And I would have definitely known because I hate the bloody things, I've been bitten three times in my career, one of those times by a bloody police dog would you believe."

Grace let out a chuckle, then clamped her lips firmly together, when she saw Barry's not too impressed reaction.

"And she was living at a children's home, where pets were not allowed. So more than likely those dog hairs will have come from her killer." Barry paused, his eyes lighting up. "Just a minute," he continued, "Steve Paynton used to have a couple of dogs; Staffordshire bull terriers if my memory serves me right. He used to keep them in the old outhouse at the bottom of his mum and dad's garden. Rumours were that he trained them for fighting. That was a good few years' back, they'll more than likely be dead now. Knowing him though, they'll probably be buried on his dad's allotment, or somewhere like that. Can they tell the breed of dog if we find them?"

"I asked the same question," returned Grace. "They can. They'll be able to confirm a match if we find the correct dog. Well done Barry," Grace continued excitedly. "I'll feed in to the HOLMES team what forensics have told me, and what you've just said and get a search team round to the Paynton's. They are going to be thoroughly pissed off by the time we've finished."

"That family's had it coming for a long time," added Hunter. "You set that in motion and muster up a search team, we've more officers joining us now that we have a serial killer on our hands."

As Grace raced out of the room Hunter pulled the pen from his mouth and leaned back in his seat thinking about the sheer volume of ongoing enquiries. They now had three separate crime scenes running, the most recent of which, was a hive of activity. Forensic Anthropologists were picking over every inch of ground, digging in several areas around the scrubland, following the path of the radar. In addition there was Peter Broughton and his dog Lady who had identified further 'hot spots' where other human remains might well be. He was just thankful that there hadn't been anymore body finds.

Elsewhere house-to-house enquiries were being conducted around the area where Rebecca Morris had last been seen, and the HOLMES team were fully engaged in linking all this together. The work was slow and laborious, but it was necessary.

Thankfully Barry had already been a big help in the Carol Siddons case and Hunter was hoping that with his lifelong knowledge of villains and their families, together with his previous casework as a detective, he might be able to point them in the direction of their killer. Barry's immediate task was to determine if the 'modus operandi' of the murders fitted the profiles of any of the district's sex attackers. And to add to his workload he had also picked up where Grace had left off sifting through the dozens of 'missing from home' case files, which had been removed from the basement at Police Headquarters. Earlier that morning he had set to work on those and had already been able to dismiss a good quantity of those reports quite promptly. Many of the files still had photographs of the 'missing' girls stapled to the front sheets, and although they were now yellowing with age, by carefully studying the images, Barry had found that either because of hair colour, size of the individual, or clothing description, they could not possibly be the latest victim

"And how are the missing from home checks going Barry?" Hunter enquired returning back to his own mound of paperwork.

"Painful and tedious," Barry responded, pushing his spectacles back onto the crown of his head. "I've managed to get a rough height and age of the bones together with colour of hair from the anthropologist, and the exhibits officer has managed to clean up the labels from the clothing to give me their size and original colour, for comparison with the reports. What is interesting however is the exhibit Professor McCormack found. Remember? The playing card inside the plastic bag. I can confirm it's the three of hearts by the way. Well this was also inside the bag." Barry held up a small section of paper. It appeared to have been torn from the top heading section of a newspaper and although yellowing and cracked at the edges the black print was still decipherable.

"Not all the headline print is there but it looks like it's from our local weekly paper and it shows the date the sixth of October nineteen-ninety-nine. On a hunch I went through the 'misper' files, and using that date as guidance it's helped me separate one girl's folder - a Claire Fisher - but we're slightly out of sync. She was reported missing on the first of October that year – five days before the newspaper cutting. She's roughly the same height as the skeleton and had the same colour hair, but no clothing has been listed on her report."

"Was the torn newspaper actually inside that plastic bag with the playing card?" asked Hunter, becoming alert to Barry's information.

Barry nodded.

Hunter's eyebrows raised and his blue eyes engaged with Barry's. "This killer is one really twisted evil bastard Barry. He wants us to know this is his work. He placed that with the body so that we would know when she was killed, and I'm guessing that part of the paper will lead us in the direction of who she is." Hunter pushed aside his notes. This find had his fullest attention. "We've been making enquiries and wondering why such a gap between the murder of Carol

Siddons and Rebecca Morris, well it's my bet that this will go some way to fill in those gaps. Contact the local paper and see what's in the copy, and then get that exhibit to forensics and see if he's left any DNA or prints. Let's just hope he's slipped up somewhere along the line."

* * * * *

At the same time as Grace Marshall was organising the warrant, and search team with the local Task Force, to raid Steve Paynton's old family home and allotment, Barry Newstead was entering the local history room at Barnwell library. Following a
phone call to the local weekly newspaper, The Barnwell Chronicle, he had discovered that old archive editions were no longer kept at the newspaper office, but had in fact been put onto microfiche and were held in trust by the local history group.

Within ten minutes of entering the small history room Barry was seated before a large microfiche reader, receiving instructions in its use by the female supervisor, who was at the same time loading the roll of microfiche containing all 1999's editions of the weekly local newspaper onto the machine's spool. As she leaned over him he couldn't help but take in the alluring smell of her perfume. Quite an expensive one he thought, as he sneaked his gaze to her face only a few inches from his. It made him realise how much he had missed the smell of a woman since the sudden death of his wife from a stroke three years ago. Although heavily made-up he guessed she was in her mid fifties, roughly the same age as he, and he found himself being distracted from the task in hand.

"Right Mr Newstead," she said straightening up.

She had taken him by surprise. He hoped she hadn't caught him staring at her. He could feel his cheeks flushing.

"You just turn those handles at the side of the machine until you find the edition you want, then when you've found what you want you hit the print button, which will copy what you see on the screen. Understand all that?" she checked with him and smiled.

A very attractive smile he thought.

"If you need anything else just give me a call" she finished, then turned on her low heels and clicked her way back towards her desk.

He turned the spool slowly at first, watching the blown up images of the past editions of his local paper float across the screen. He was soon getting a feel for the movement, which he quickened as he became used to the momentum of the apparatus, and in less than a minute he was soon spinning past the editions until he hit mid-September's pages and then began to slow until he settled on the 6th October's front sheet. He took out the torn section, now secured inside a police exhibit bag, which had been discovered beside the female skeleton. He manoeuvred it around and held it in front of the reading screen for comparison. Confirming it was from the same paper he set it down to begin scanning the newssheet. He didn't need to go far down the page. Within seconds he knew that what he had been looking for was contained in the front-page headlines. He began to pore over the print.

POLICE SEARCH FOR MISSING TEENAGER

Detectives leading the enquiry into the surprise disappearance of 15 year old Claire Louise Fisher from Barnwell are urging the public to help them with information.

Claire was reported missing five days ago on October 1st.

The last reported sighting of Claire was by her boyfriend at 9.30pm that night.

There was more to the report. The journalist had filled the remainder of the story with Claire's background, plus interviews with her parents and friends, which he quickly scanned. And he recognised the photograph of Claire that the paper had used. It was a clear replica of the one from the front of her missing from home file back on his desk.

He slapped the table excitedly. He knew in his mind that having read this that Claire Louise Fisher was their latest corpse.

He looked for the print key on the microfiche reader, hovered his index finger over and stabbed at it. Almost instantaneously the copier below the microfiche reader spurred into action and within seconds a facsimile of the front page of the 6th October 1999 edition had been printed onto an A4 sheet.

Barry sat back in his chair and perused the story again. He found himself shaking his head and muttering to himself as he read it a second time, whilst thinking of the ramifications of what he had just uncovered.

Claire Fisher went missing on the first of October ninety-ninety-nine, he said to himself, and the edition of this newspaper didn't go on sale until the sixth. That means the killer didn't bury her straightaway. Claire was either alive and held somewhere, or killed and kept somewhere for the best part of a week until the paper came out, and then she was finally buried.

"This is one twisted bastard." He said. From the corner of his eye he caught movement from the desk, and he glanced up to see the faired-haired local history Supervisor looking in his direction.

"Sorry about that" he whispered loudly towards her, and apologetically raised a hand. "Talking to myself. A sign of age eh?"

She smiled back.

Quite a nice smile; a welcoming smile, he thought. There was something about it, which conjured up the image of Susan Siddons. It seemed perverse that such a painful event as this should bring them back together again after all these years. It made him realise just how much he had missed her. This has to be fate he thought. And he was a great believer in fate. He wondered about giving her a call.

-ooOoo-

CHAPTER SIXTEEN
DAY TWENTY-FIVE: 31st July.

Thunder growled and rumbled overhead, and a split second later the rain fell in streams, pelting the earth like spears. Grace Marshall cowered beneath the canopy of the rear entrance of Barnwell Police station. She had been petrified of thunder since a child and for some reason it still scared her. She would rather tackle a violent man than face thunder. Her eyes darted back and forth across the car park searching for Hunter who she knew was waiting for her in an unmarked police car. She spotted a dark blue Vauxhall whose windscreen wipers appeared to be working overtime to cope with the sudden downpour, and although she couldn't see who was driving she guessed it would be him.

She glanced up at the thick mass of storm clouds, placed her working clip file over the top of her head and in the same instant made the decision to dash to the car. Despite the fact it had only been seconds, as she bounced into the passenger seat of the CID car, the rain was already beginning to soak through her Italian linen trousers. She shook her work folder into the footwell and then pulled down the passenger side visor and stared into the mirror. She flicked a comb of fingers through her hair in a vain attempt to stop it frizzing like it usually did, and then brushed several stray droplets of rain from her cheeks.

Hunter stared at her shaking his head.

She looked back.

"What?" She returned her eyes to the mirror. "Image is everything Hunter, and if you were a woman you'd know that," she finished, slapping the visor back in place.

"A little rain never did anyone any harm," he retorted.

"It does when it takes me half an hour to put my make-up on, and another half an hour to do my hair each morning. Bloody British weather."

Shaking his head he said. "Anyway, I understand you had a good day yesterday."

"The Paynton's you mean?"

Hunter nodded and then turned the demister on the dashboard full-on to clear the fogged front windscreen.

Grace gave back a mischievously wicked smile. "They were really pissed off by the time we'd finished. In fact old man Paynton almost got locked up for breach of the peace when we dug up his allotment. We found the bodies of the dogs though, just like Barry suggested. Forensic have got those and we should know if we have a match with the hairs on Carol Siddons's cardigan in a day or two. Oh, and by the way, did you know that some of the locals have graffited Steve's house. *Paedo's* been sprayed all over the front of it. The family are going ballistic," she chuckled.

"Serves them all right. That family have plagued that estate for far too long. It's nice to see them get a taste of their own medicine for a change."

"Anyway where are we off to today?"

Hunter dropped the Claire Fisher file onto Grace's lap. He wound down the misted over driver's door window a fraction.

The burst of rain had halted but the skies were still rumbling and threatening overhead.

He pointed at the folder as he accelerated slowly out of the station car park. "We're off to see a Mr and Mrs Fisher. Barry also had some success yesterday."

As he drove, Hunter recounted Barry's newspaper discovery and how he'd managed to confirm his findings with a dental match from Claire Fisher's records.

"It looks as though the killer had Claire for five days at least before she was buried with that newspaper report. Is that sick or what? I find it hard to believe this has been going on in my own district for all these years. Now I know what the detectives were going through when they were dealing with Fred and Rosemary West." Hunter slowly shook his head.

Grace felt her skin go goosey.

"This twisted bastard seems to be taunting us Grace. He doesn't mind us finding out who his victims are. It's as if he knew we'd eventually find this one and he's actually helping us to identify her. It's almost as though he thinks he's never going to be caught. That he's cleverer than us. We really are up against it at the moment. I just hope we can get a breakthrough before he kills again." He slowed the car as he met the rush hour crawl. "And another thing Barry's unearthed. He did some further digging yesterday, going back across old local newspaper reports and then made a few phone calls to other police stations in the District. As a result of what he's uncovered there's at least another three local teenage girls who have disappeared without trace over the past thirteen years."

"What." exclaimed Grace looking up sharply from the Claire Fisher file.

"Yes, Barry's found that there are three other cases of girls missing from this area since nineteen-ninety-three when Carol Siddons was first reported. He's pulled all their files and found that they all disappeared with no apparent reason and more disturbingly that they all fit the same profile, especially as to age and physical appearance as our present three victims."

* * * * *

The Fisher house was a sumptuous, four bedroom detached residence on a small exclusive estate on the edge of Barnwell. Hunter had learned that the family's engineering business had flourished over recent years and that Mr and Mrs Fisher had moved home on two occasions since nineteen ninety nine when Claire had gone missing.

The woman who answered their knock at the door took Hunter by surprise. She appeared a lot younger than the details on file. In fact she looked not much older than him.

As if reading his puzzled expression as Hunter introduced himself and Grace, the slim raven-haired lady responded. "I'm Julia. Mrs Fisher number two. Derek's new wife. Well not really his new wife. We've been married nearly three years now. Beverley, Claire's Mum, died in two thousand and one from cancer."

"There's no need to explain," replied Hunter showing his police badge.

"Derek keeps telling me the same but I could tell by the look on your face that you were surprised that I was a lot younger than you were expecting. I'm used to greeting people like this even after three years. I suppose I don't want people to think bad of me. As though I'm jumping into a dead woman's shoes if you know what I mean. I was his secretary you see, at the firm, and got very close to both Derek and Beverley when Claire went missing. Then of course when Beverley was diagnosed with breast cancer I took on a lot of the responsibility of the business and of course got even closer to Derek especially when Beverley died. I know there are some people who think I was having an affair with Derek whilst his wife was dying, but that's so far from the truth."

"You really don't have to explain all this to us," Hunter responded.

"But I feel better now that I have done. Anyway Derek's expecting you. He's in the lounge. Come through."

Hunter and Grace followed Julia Fisher along a bright and airy hallway into a large, tastefully furnished lounge. The room was filled with sunlight; its brightness enhanced by magnolia painted walls and highly polished oak flooring. Leather furniture and bespoke light oak units containing antique 'blue' pottery added to its expensive look.

Hunter noticed in particular a number of impressionistic style paintings hanging around the room, which looked original and under different circumstances he would have loved to have sauntered around to view them.

French doors at the end opened up into a large hardwood orangery, which gave view over a garden festooned with a wide variety of plant colour.

Derek Fisher was standing in the centre of the room waiting to greet them and he energetically moved forward upon their entrance offering his hand to shake. Hunter immediately recognised the Masonic signal and responded accordingly.

"Which Lodge are you in?" Derek Fisher asked, pointing to a tan-coloured leather settee, one of three in the large room, inviting Hunter and Grace to be seated.

"Knights Templar," Hunter replied. "But I don't get so much now. To be honest it's not really my thing. I joined

160

because of my father. He's from Glasgow and as you know it's quite a Scottish tradition to be involved in The Masons. When he came down here to live he joined the Knights Templar Lodge at Barnwell and then of course sponsored me just like his Father had done for him."

"I must invite you to mine some time. In fact I'm in the chair next year, so I'll send you an invite." He paused and smiled at Grace "Enough of the funny handshake stuff eh, and down to real matters. You're here about Claire you said on the phone."

Grace took over. "We are Mr Fisher. We believe we've found her. But I'm sorry to say it's not good news."

"Don't apologise dear. I guess I knew all along it would come down to this. Is this visit because of the bodies you've dug up on the old pit site? It's been all over the news."

Grace nodded. "The dental records point us towards it being your daughter and a simple DNA sample from you would make it conclusive."

"I'm guessing you won't be allowing me to see her. Although I suppose I won't be able to recognise Claire after all this time."

"I'm afraid not. She's been buried a long time."

Derek Fisher gave off a long sigh "The one good thing I've got now after all this time is closure. It's such a shame her mum's not around to know that you've found her, even though Claire is dead. She grieved right to the end you know," he gulped and pursed his lips. "I'll get the opportunity to lay her to rest?" he asked.

"You will, but not just yet. I'm afraid we'll need to hang on to Claire for some time yet until the Coroner gives permission."

"I hope you don't find that me being not so upset about the news that Claire is dead reflects on my relationship with my daughter. I can assure you we were very close as a family. But I'm also a realist. I suppose I've known that Claire has been dead for a long time. Even though I never said it openly to Beverley when she was alive, I've always felt that Claire was lying somewhere in a grave where she shouldn't be. She's always been in my thoughts. Every time I saw or heard of a body being found, no matter where, I waited for the call. I've been waiting over ten years. The Police came back to us on many occasions at first, and her disappearance was re-investigated on a couple of occasions, and both me and Beverley used to get so excited. But then when Beverley died and there was no fresh news I just accepted the reality of it all." Derek Fisher raised himself from his seat and went to a nearby wall unit. From the cupboard he brought out a bulging photograph album and handed it to Grace.

She opened it to find the folder crammed with yellowing newspaper cuttings and scraps of paper filled with copious notes. She leafed through the folder quickly. It had been meticulously maintained. Every milestone had been recorded from day one to the present time and was interspersed here and there with happy family photographs of the Fishers. Their past was in this book.

"I don't know if that will be of any help to you. It's everything we collected over the years relating to Claire. Every newspaper report. The possible leads. Every glimmer of hope. Keep it as long as you need. I hope it'll help."

"It'll certainly help us. Thanks, I'll make sure it gets back to you safely."

"Before we leave you in peace Mr Fisher" interposed Hunter, "can you just remind us of Claire's movements the evening she went missing."

Derek Fisher stroked the line of his jaw and chin, cleared his throat and seesawed his eyes between Hunter and Grace.

"Do you know I don't even need to think about what I'm going to tell you. I've said the same thing so many times over the years. Claire left home at just gone six. She told us she was going to her friend's Stacy's and would be back to finish her homework about eight o'clock. At quarter to eight she phoned us from a payphone to say she was at the youth club and asked if she could stay whilst nine. We were a bit concerned because it was dark, but at the same time we were going through a bit of a rough patch with Claire and we wanted to allow her a bit more freedom, so we told her no later than nine. That was the last time we spoke. What we subsequently found out is that she was in fact seeing a fifteen-year-old boy called Gary

Martin and that they were at the fair together. She had been dating him for two months without us knowing. Police told us that the pair rowed that night because he found out she had been just stringing him along as cover. It appears she had been seeing someone older. She confessed it to him and he apparently stormed off in a huff and left her. That was about half past nine. You'll see from our own file that Gary was interviewed many times and was a suspect on several occasions but he was alibied by quite a number of people that night. I've spoken with him myself many times over the years and I'm confident he wasn't involved in Claire's disappearance." He shifted in his chair and cleared his throat. "I'm guessing you'll no doubt want to speak with him again. Gary's married now with a family of his own. We still keep in touch. He'll tell you things that are not in those folders I've given you." He stared at Hunter and then Grace through unblinking eyes. "In the few months before Claire disappeared we went through some bad times with her. She seemed to have changed, and it wasn't for the good." He paused. "Do you have children?"

Both Hunter and Grace nodded.

"Oh I know all teenagers go through a phase, but Claire really put us through it. She came in drunk, smashed up her room once when we tried to keep her in, and we even found out from Gary that she was seeing other lads behind his back. She'd become a real rebel in her last days, and that's what's so sad about it. My last memories of Claire are not nice ones."

Now where had he heard all this before, Hunter thought. A pattern's emerging here.

"Let me just check this with you Mr Fisher," enquired Grace. "Just back-tracking a little you said Claire was last seen at the fair by her then boyfriend Gary Martin?"

Derek Fisher nodded, "Yes, that's right. He told me that when he left her he got the impression she was hanging about to meet up with an older guy"

"Which fair was that?"

"The local Feast Fair, that's held on the Common Field every year. It still is."

Alarm bells were ringing in Hunter's head. This was the second time The Feast Fair had featured in their enquiries. Hadn't Rebecca Morris's best friend Kirsty Evans told them that someone older had been fancying Rebecca when she had been at that fair? This was their first real link.

* * * * *

"I've just had a very interesting conversation with Derek Fisher" said Hunter strolling into the office and spotting Barry Newstead hunched over a pile of paperwork. He dropped the Claire Fisher file onto his desk jotter, then slipped off his jacket and hooked it over the back of his chair.

Barry looked up from the sheaf of papers he had been reading, pushed himself back into his seat and rubbed the back of his neck. "Oh yes and what was that, as if you didn't want me to ask?"

"He told us that his daughter Claire was last seen at the local Feast fairground by her then boyfriend Gary Martin on the evening she went missing back in ninety-nine. The boyfriend apparently left her in 'a strop' after she told him that an older guy was fancying her. I don't know if you've managed to get up to date with the investigation yet Barry but that's very similar to something which Rebecca Morris told her friend Kirsty Evans, after they had also visited the Feast fair a couple of months ago – that someone older was fancying her. Added to that do you remember what Karen Gardner told us about the guy she was seeing at the same time as she was seeing Paul Goodright, way back in ninety-three?"

"Crikey yes." interjected Grace, teasing off her own jacket which was stuck to her blouse, a consequence of the muggy heat from the earlier thunderstorm. "She told me that she was being visited by a Billy Smith who travelled with the local fair. I checked his name against the database in the Intelligence Unit and although there was very little on him, an old conviction for drunk and disorderly, I did, however, discover from one of the beat officers that he didn't just travel with the fair but his parents actually own it. He currently lives in a static caravan in a compound next to the canal." She paused and her eyes widened. "Bloody hell. The compound where he lives is only about a mile from the Manvers site, where we found Carol and Claire's bodies."

"This is just too much of a coincidence" Hunter said. "Barry does that name ring any bells with you – Billy Smith?"

Barry pushed his reading glasses up onto his mop of tousled dark hair and fixed his gaze upon the ceiling as though the answer lay somewhere up there. He muttered the name 'Billy Smith' under his breath several times then shot his gaze back towards Hunter, slamming the flat of his hand on top of his pile of papers and jabbed an index finger towards him. "Billy Smith – Fairground Billy Smith, Of course, I've got him. He's someone I came across way back in my really young CID days. It was from a job in the late eighties. We got a call to a shooting at the Barnwell Hotel – 'The Drum' as everyone referred to it. It's been knocked down now but back then it was a real dive. One of our problem pubs. If a fight broke out there you knew you had to go in mob handed to sort it out. Anyway I can remember being radioed up one Friday night to attend there. Uniform had responded to an ambulance call and found a man in the back yard of the pub with shotgun wounds to the stomach. He wasn't dead, but half his guts were hanging out and he was in a real bad way." Barry paused for a moment taking in Hunter and Grace's expressions. "The guy wouldn't say a thing about what had gone on and the whole place had emptied by the time we had arrived. The pub was locked up at first but we eventually managed to rouse the Landlord. You could see he didn't want us inside the place, and no wonder. When we got in the poolroom had been virtually demolished. Chairs, tables, and pool cues smashed up, glass everywhere, and someone had tried to clean up the blood. At first the landlord refused to say anything but after we threatened to lock him up for attempted murder he spilled the beans. He told us that earlier that night there had been a load of gipsy travellers in from a local site and that they had been playing pool for money. After squeezing him a bit more, particularly with the threat of losing his licence for allowing illegal gambling on the premises, he told us that there had been a thousand pound bet on the pool table and that one Billy Smith from the fairground had won the game, but then the gipsy who he'd been playing wouldn't pay up. There'd been a bit of a scrap between him and Billy. Apparently Billy was very handy. We later found out that Billy was a bare-knuckle fighter who earned quite a bit of money from his illegal activities. Anyway Billy was getting topside of the gipsy and a few of his pals joined in so Billy had to get away quick. The landlord told us that whilst he was trying to get the gipsies out of his pub, because he was scared some of his locals might call the police, Billy Smith suddenly appeared back, and armed with a shotgun, demanding his money. There was a standoff at first and then some of the gipsies started goading Billy that it wasn't loaded. So Billy shot off one barrel into the ceiling and again demanded his money. The guy who owed him the money responded by mouthing off and that's when Billy shot the gipsy in the guts. Then he followed that up by smacking another couple of the guy's mates with the butt of the gun, and then legged it."

"Did you get Billy?" Grace asked.

"We did actually. I was so hyped-up I can tell you. It was early in my career and it was the first time I had actually seen armed police. We surrounded the fairground compound where Billy lived with his parents and he came out meek as anything telling us he'd been at home all night, and his father backed him up. We arrested him of course and carried out a search as best as we could but there was no sign of any gun. The gipsy who'd been shot was operated on and they stitched his guts back in and we finally managed to speak to him three days later but he refused to say anything. He wouldn't even confirm his name. At the travellers' site we couldn't find anyone who wanted to talk to us so without witnesses and vital evidence the enquiry went nowhere. We found out later that the elders from the traveller site settled things with Billy's father, whatever that meant." He paused and smiled, "How's that for someone who's supposedly past it?" then in a hammy Poirot accent he added, "Hastings the little grey cells they do not desert me."

"That was a crap attempt at a French accent. It sounded more Welsh" goaded Grace.

"You Philistine," sneered back Barry, "Hercule Poirot, the greatest detective in the world – even greater than you, is Belgian not French." He finished by giving Grace a quick wink.

Hunter couldn't help but smile. It hadn't taken Barry long to settle in, and just has he had thought he had not lost any of his recall. His storage of information on villains, their cohorts and their networks, plus all the jobs he had attended over his thirty years was far better than any local Intelligence Unit computer system.

"Right you two I'm going to get this to the HOLMES people and then get Tony and Mike. Meanwhile, I think it's time to shake Billy Smith's tree a little. I want you Grace to sort out the paperwork and get a magistrate's warrant. "

* * * * *

Hunter's team sped into the open entranceway of the Smith's fairground compound in two unmarked cars only to find themselves being greeted by two snapping and snarling Alsatians acting as sentries. The surprise element was long gone. The cars swerved around the slavering animals, churning up the ground of loose shale, and they slewed to a halt in front of a thirty-six foot static caravan where Barry Newstead had earlier indicated Billy Smith should still be living.

Before jumping from the car Hunter whipped his head around in the direction they had just come from, focussing on the vicious hounds that were frantically jerking and leaping against the chain which was holding them. He quickly scanned its length, and only averted his gaze when he judged those brutes couldn't reach him. At that same instant a single facing door shot open, crashing against the aluminium side of the caravan with a resounding clatter. A tall, stocky built, man confronted them.

Hunter could see that the man was well over six feet tall and judging by the broad shoulders, expansive chest and bulging arms, which strained the white T-shirt he was wearing, he was someone who regularly trained and maintained his physique.

His facial features were quite striking. Overall he had a tanned weather-beaten appearance framed by a head of thick, naturally curly, almost black hair.

His ice blue eyes, wide and alert, strafed the compound. "What the fuck's going on?"

Hunter leaped from the driver's seat. Mike Sampson and Tony Bullars were also pulling themselves out of their CID car and Hunter signalled towards them with a raised hand. "You and Bully hang back five," he ordered and turned to the thick-set man framed in the doorway of the caravan. "Billy Smith?" He shouted, raising his voice over the now hysterical dogs, wishing he could silence them – permanently.

As if reading his mind the man suddenly ordered loudly "Quiet! Sit! Sabre, Spike!" Then with a smug grin turned towards the detectives as the two dogs immediately stopped barking and settled back on their haunches. "What do so many cops want me for? You'd think I'd murdered someone."

"Funny you should say that," Grace mumbled under her breath.

Hunter caught the comment and nudged her arm. "We could do with a word with you Billy. You got a few moments?"

"Sure come in, but wipe your feet," he replied and disappeared back inside the van.

As Hunter stepped up into Billy Smith's home, he couldn't help but be impressed by the vision, which met him. The plushness of the interior took him completely by surprise. Thick pile carpets, lush furnishings and soft pine cabinets ran from its entranceway into the open lounge. Expensive pieces of Crown Derby were much in evidence, both on the windowsills and in the glass units. The smell of fresh polish hung in the air. The mobile home was immaculate with everything neatly in place.

"My next question is," said Billy Smith as he eased himself into an armchair, "What is so important that it needs two car loads of detectives to turn up at my door?"

Strong sunlight shone through slatted blinds behind him throwing his form into silhouette.

Hunter narrowed his eyelids to catch a glimpse of Billy's face.

"How did you know we were cops? We haven't introduced ourselves yet," Hunter responded.

"Dogs can smell you a mile off" he retorted. "Now get to the point and tell me what's going on?"

"We're here making enquiries into the murder of Rebecca Morris." Hunter replied.

Prior to setting off from the station Hunter had briefed his team and decided against introducing the parallel investigation of the slaying of Claire Louise Fisher which provided the fairground link to at least two of the three murder victims, and only he and Grace knew the tenuous link to Carol Siddons through the Billy, Karen Gardner, Paul Goodright ménage a trois.

"I've seen that on the telly. Why do you want to talk to me about that? I don't even know the girl. I've never met her."

"We believe there's a link to your fair, in as much as she was at the Feast fair shortly before she died." He lied in order to get a reaction from Billy, which might indicate guilt.

"I hope this is not leading where I think it is. I swear on my mother's death I had nothing to do with that girl. If she was at the fair I never saw her."

"In order to satisfy ourselves, is it all right if we do a search of your home?" Grace interjected.

Billy thought for a moment. "What if I say no?"

"Well we have got a search warrant," Grace responded waving the magistrates' document in her hand.

"Looks like I've got no choice does it? But please don't wreck things. I've heard about police and searches."

Hunter called in Tony and Mike and the four of them split up to begin a methodical high and low exploration of the caravan.

Hunter ensured Billy remained in view throughout his search, continually glancing towards him through the corner of an eye, at the same time chatting in general terms endeavouring to relax him with a view to throwing him off guard when it was time for the more probing investigation-based questions.

Then after about twenty minutes Mike Sampson shouted from one of the bedrooms at the back of the static.

"Got something," he announced and appeared in the doorway holding aloft a small item in a latex gloved hand. He strode purposefully through to the lounge followed by Grace and Tony. He showed the item to Hunter and then held it in front of Billy Smith.

"Whose is this?" he requested sharply.

"Mine, why?" Billy responded.

"Not with these markings on it," returned Mike. "This is Rebecca Morris's mobile phone.

* * * * *

"I've told you a dozen times I found the damn thing," Billy Smith replied, an agitated note in Billy Smith's reply to Grace's question.

"And so you keep saying" she responded, "But you're not convincing me."

Hunter watched Billy's face beginning to flush across the desk. Grace had pressed Billy hard to the extent that sweat was now staining the front of his T-shirt.

"All right, all right, I might well have not been straight with you but I thought you were just trying to pull a fast one on me with that Rebecca Morris business."

"Believe me Billy we do not lie about murder. Especially of a fourteen year old girl." Grace said calmly leaning across setting her stare upon him.

"I thought the phone was nicked that's why I've not exactly been straight okay. But I really did find that phone."

"Tell us where then, and stop messing us about or you're back in that cell and on remand," Grace snapped back.

Billy dropped his head into his hands, but only for a second. He wiped the beads of sweat from his forehead and pushed himself back in his seat. "It was partially buried in the woods over by the canal - honest, you've got to believe me. I walk Spike and Sabre there every morning. I go over the canal bridge near the Low Lock and then let them loose in the woods. A couple of days ago they were digging round a hole just above a dyke and when I shouted to them they wouldn't come away. I thought they'd found a badger set or a foxhole with cubs in so I went to drag them away. When I got to them they'd dug out a black bin liner and started to shred it. Inside it there was some clothing, a backpack and that mobile phone. I thought it was gear from a burglary that someone had buried to come back for later. The bag was only filled with what looked like schoolbooks and so I just took the mobile. It was the only thing worth anything."

Grace turned her gaze away from Billy and looked towards Hunter.

If he was to be believed then this meant that the investigation was taking another twist.

Hunter had been carefully watching Billy throughout the last half hour of the questioning, studying every aspect of his body language. Looking for those tell-tale signs that spelt guilt. To put a finger on what those signs were was never easy and certainly not something Hunter could define. It was built on years of experience, gained with every arrest and interview. And he'd also learned from others – others like Barry Newstead. He had heard his colleagues refer to it as a sixth sense. Whatever it was he knew he had it. As he had observed Billy he had noticed that the man had always held Grace's stare. He had never shifted nervously, or gulped when he had responded to her probing questions. Hunter somehow sensed that on this occasion Billy was telling the truth.

Hunter said. "Billy it's getting late now, we're going to terminate this interview, lodge you in the cells overnight and then tomorrow go and see if you're telling us the truth. First thing in the morning, I want you to show us where you found the mobile."

- ooOoo –

CHAPTER SEVENTEEN
DAY TWENTY-SIX: 1st August.

As soon as he had made contact with Kirsty over the Internet and hooked her with 'Josh' he had begun the same process as he had done with all the others. For over three weeks he had been following, watching and hiding from her, learning her life. And he had collected hundreds of photographs along the way. He had placed the digital images in an album and brought them out nightly from their hiding place to run his hands over her pretty face, imagining he was touching that smooth unblemished skin.

Two days ago, after all his hard work, he had pulled it off. He had finally managed to entice Kirsty into meeting his seventeen year old creation, and as he stood very still beside the bushes of The Barnwell Countryside park he knew that very soon he would be meeting and physically touching the girl who had so far only been a two dimensional vision in his fantasies.

He took another glance at his watch and scanned the area around him. There had been a couple of dog walkers earlier but he knew from previous visits to this location that around this time the majority of people who used it would be at work. It was the perfect meeting place. He knew as soon as he had suggested the venue to Kirsty that it would lure her into a false sense of security. She didn't know the area as well as he did. He had done his homework.

He had made attempts to disguise his appearance, to make himself look old enough to be the father of a seventeen year old. He had waxed down his hair, put on a pair of unfashionable spectacles from a charity shop and had donned his father's old pit duffel jacket, which had been left behind all those years back. When he had looked himself over in the mirror before leaving home he had thought he had got the effect about right. After all he didn't want to scare her off because he looked weird. And he had rehearsed his lines so many times.

Spotting movement by the stile, which he had under surveillance, he caught his breath. When he had done an earlier recce of the park he had identified it as being the entranceway nearest to the woodland.

He squinted at the moving figure, bringing it into focus. He could tell by the outline it was her. He double-checked that the area was clear, slipped on his gloves and slid out of from the bushes.

* * * * *

"Hi I'm Josh's Dad."

The man had suddenly appeared from nowhere and had made Kirsty jump.

"I'm sorry I didn't mean to scare you like that. Josh was delayed at his football training and he asked me if I'd come and meet you and run you back to the house."

Kirsty's mind was racing. She hadn't expected Josh's Dad to turn up. She looked him up and down. He looked silly in that coat – it was too big for him. Although a good eighteen inches taller than her she could tell he was only slightly built. There were signs that his hair was thinning despite covering it with a layer of wax and he had the kind of facial growth that looks like a perpetual five o'clock shadow. The heavy rimmed glasses hid his eyes, but she did notice they seemed to be darting around, not really focussed on her.

In that instant she thought his face was familiar, and yet somehow different. It puzzled her.

"You okay with that?" He asked.

Now where had she had heard that voice before. She hesitated for a second, trying to remember where she had seen this man.

"Well I'm not too sure," she replied.

Then the man pulled his mobile phone from his pocket. "You can give him a ring if you want." He slid the screen up to reveal the keypad, and edging closer proffered it to her.

This didn't feel right one bit Kirsty thought to herself.

"I'll just ring my mum and tell her what's happening." She could feel her voice burbling nervously, the words almost sticking in her throat. She reached into her own pocket for her phone, but the man took hold of her arm gently.

"Josh will be so sad if he doesn't meet you. I can assure you everything's fine, you've no need to worry."

She tried to act normally and not to freeze. She knew what she should do – what her parents had always told her to do, but her legs wouldn't let her. A panicky fear enveloped her.

Then the man turned sharply. Kirsty saw his eyes in those too big spectacles widen revealing a look of real evil and she opened her mouth to scream.

He swung back his hand and she felt the sharp slap on her cheek, which rocked her head sideways. It was less painful than expected; the terror inside was more frightening. She choked back her scream as he grabbed at her jacket.

"I'll fucking kill you if you fucking scream."

His voice had taken on a deep and menacing tone and she could feel his breath hot on her face, and it smelt stale.

"You're coming with me and if you fucking struggle I'll kill you right here and now."

For a split second it entered her head that this must be the killer who had murdered her best friend Rebecca. She made an attempt to pull free from his grip. She never saw the fist, just felt the searing pain around her right eye. There was a crunching noise from the bridge of her nose and a series of flashes and stars clouded her vision. Then came the pain – a sharp and hot pain that made her feel sick.

The man grabbed at her hair, but she twisted away from him and she felt strands being ripped from her skull. Instinct to survive was now taking over and Kirsty was thrashing and kicking out, screaming for all she was worth.

Another blow to her face momentarily stopped her from fighting back. She felt something trickle into the back of her throat and it sent another wave of panic through her body. Then something tightened around her neck closing off her ability to breathe. She clawed at her throat. She felt herself slumping forward and there was a painful thump in between her shoulders. There was the strange sensation, which felt like a warm trickle of fluid running down her spine. Then it was as if someone had thrown a bucket of water onto her back. Darkness seemed to drift over her. The dark became thick, cloying and sticky, throttling and choking her senses. The darkness became black; black as pitch.

* * * * *

"See I told you I was telling the truth," Billy Smith said, delving his handcuffed hands into a muddy hole and dragging out a dirtied and battered bin liner which had seen better days.

"You wouldn't believe how many times we've heard that," Grace replied dryly, slipping on her latex gloves to preserve the evidence. "I'll take over now Billy," she continued, jumping across the dried up dyke.

"And I'm guessing you want me to take those cuffs off you now?" Hunter asked, following Grace's lead across the dyke.

Billy offered his encased wrists, prayer like, and Hunter snapped off the police bracelets.

"Thank Christ for that," Billy said rubbing the red weal marks on his wrists. "You had me sweating back there in the nick. I really thought you were going to stitch me up for murder you know. Even when I'd offered to show you where I found that mobile."

"We don't do things like that Billy," Hunter responded. "Anyway that's for all the times you've got away with it. And you're not exactly in the clear yet we've still got your alibi to check out."

Billy coloured up and returned a sheepish look.

In one respect Hunter was disappointed. He had thought that the finding of Rebecca's mobile in Billy's caravan was the breakthrough they had been waiting for. Finding this lot buried as Billy had said took the enquiry into another dimension. It also meant that if Billy's alibi did check out, and he now firmly believed it would do, it would mean he was also in the clear over the Carol Siddons murder, and therefore his link with Karen Gardner and Paul Goodright wouldn't need to come out. He couldn't wait to ring Paul up later and put his mind at ease.

Grace eased the black bin liner further out of the hole. Looking back over her shoulder she said "Whoever's hidden this certainly didn't want it to be found." She clawed around the entrance way, scooping away debris and depositing it behind her mole-like.

Slowly she picked out the contents from the liner, examining each item carefully before placing them on the ground beside her. Rebecca Morris's pink schoolbag, her school uniform and books were all here.

"Is it that murdered girl's stuff?" Billy asked.

Hunter watched his face. Billy looked to be fascinated by the events unfolding before him. Hunter guessed that he'd be recounting all this later in the pub, telling his cronies how he had been helping police with their enquiries. It almost brought a smile to his lips.

"It certainly is Billy. How much of this did you actually handle before you put it back into the black bag?" asked Grace.

"I just opened the bin liner and looked inside. The mobile was virtually on top of everything. I had a quick rummage around inside but didn't pull anything else out. Why is that bad for me?" he replied, concern now etched on his face.

"It just means forensics will have to separate your DNA from any other we find on these." Before she could say anything else the ringing of her own mobile disturbed her. She flipped up its top, slipped the unit under her thick curly hair and slotted it to her ear. Crooking her head she trapped the mobile between the top of her shoulder, listening to the call as she carried on examining the contents of the black plastic sack.

Hunter watched on as lines appeared on her forehead, slowly creasing into furrows as she listened intently. He attempted to catch her gaze, wondering what was being said over the other end of that phone which was causing her to be so concerned. He tried to grasp her mumblings but only caught, "We'll be there inside the hour," before Grace dropped the phone from her ear and snapped it shut.

"That was Bullars," she announced anxiously. "He's at the District General hospital. It looks as though our killer's just struck again. And get this; it's Kirsty Evans, Rebecca Morris's best friend. She's in a critical condition but she is alive."

* * * * *

Hunter and Grace had tried their best to avoid the press who were now swarming all over Barnwell District General hospital, but after finding every entrance way barricaded by the gauntlet of reporters, they had ended up resorting to storm-trooper tactics in order to get into the hospital. In one case Hunter had actually smacked shut the entrance door of the Intensive Care Unit in a camera-man's face. Hunter mouthed the words 'sorry,' trying to not break into a grin and jammed his foot against the bottom of the door until a uniformed officer rushed to his aide and took over the department's security.

The surgeon who had operated on Kirsty Evans met Hunter and Grace in the reception area of ITU. He was still in his green surgical scrubs.

"She is one extremely lucky girl," he began, removing the green cotton cap to reveal a thinning head of ginger hair. "She's been stabbed repeatedly in the upper back area, but none of the knife wounds have penetrated her vital organs. There was also an attempt to strangle her with a leather belt but luckily her attacker was disturbed and the guy who saved her managed to get it off before any serious harm was done. I'm told that the Good Samaritan was an off duty paramedic who was out jogging, chased off the girl's attacker and then administered first aid before the ambulance and police arrived. She has lost a lot of blood and in fact we've had to put ten units into her during the operation. There's no doubt she would have died had it not been for him. We've stitched her back together for now and later she will need plastic surgery to some of the wounds. She's not exactly out of the woods just yet but she is off the critical list."

"Thanks for that," replied Grace. "Will we able to speak with her at all?" she asked.

"Certainly not today I'm afraid. In fact it might not even be tomorrow. She has come round since the operation but as you can imagine she is in a lot of pain, so we've had to sedate her with quite a strong dosage."

Hunter spotted Tony Bullars hovering at the end of the corridor trying to catch his attention. With a raised hand he acknowledged him, shook hands with the surgeon thanking him and left Grace to finish off the conversation.

He saw that Tony was clutching an abundance of brown forensic evidence bags. He had already bagged up Kirsty Evans's clothing.

"What have you got for me Bully?" Hunter enquired.

"These are just her clothes," he replied tapping the forensic bags, "but I can tell you that we've recovered the belt he used. The guy who found her had loosened it but it was still around her neck when uniform got to the scene. I've had a quick word with Mike Sampson who's down at the park and bagged it up for forensics. He tells me that from the width of the belt and the buckle shape and size that it looks like the same one our killer used on Rebecca. The surgeon who operated on Kirsty allowed forensic into theatre and they've recovered blood and fibres from underneath her fingernails. She put up a hell of a fight and it means we should be able to get his DNA for the first time."

This is one of those Eureka moments Hunter thought as Grace sidled up beside him.

He was pleased to see that a uniformed officer had been stationed outside Kirsty's side room. At least for the time being the killer wouldn't be able to get to her.

Hunter flashed his warrant card and he and Grace entered.

The beeping noise from the heart monitor was the first sound, which greeted them. Kirsty was hooked up to an IV and a nasogastric tube. Her head was covered in a turban style bandage and under the bright fluorescent lighting they couldn't help but notice the signs of a real battering around her face. Both eyes were heavily bruised and her nose was disjointed and twice the size it should have been. Mr and Mrs Evans were at her bedside, faces creased with anguish, her Mother tightly gripping Kirsty's left hand and gently stroking the back of it with her other. They acknowledged the officers' arrival with a solemn nod and Mr Evans rose from his high-backed seat. "Have you caught him yet?" There was a sharp edge to it, his question almost a demand.

They understood the tone. The anger was inevitable.

"Not yet, but don't worry we will do," Hunter responded.

Grace moved closer to the bed. Kirsty's breathing was laboured; the sedative, which had been administered, was playing its part in relaxing her system. The girl's eyes fluttered for a second and then stopped.

"The doctor said she's going to be okay." Mrs Evans caught Grace's gaze.

She returned a sympathetic smile. "She is Mrs Evans. Kirsty will pull through. You watch in another couple of weeks she'll be her old self. Young people are extremely resilient"

"Was she -?" Mr Evans paused and gulped.

Hunter knew what he was trying to say, but was afraid of the answer. He offered, "There are no signs she was attacked like that. The man who did this was scared off before he had time to do anything else. He wouldn't have had time to do anything like that." Like Mr Evans, he avoided using the word rape."

"Is it the same man who killed Rebecca?" Mr Evans asked.

"We don't know for definite. That's something we're working on. We'll know better when we get Kirsty's clothing and the samples from under her fingernails up to our forensics lab. Your daughter was very brave, she put up a hell of a fight and it saved her life."

"Do you think Kirsty was hiding something about Rebecca's murder and that's why he's tried to silence her?"

Hunter recalled what Grace had told him following her clandestine meeting with Kirsty, less than a fortnight ago. It brought to the fore the secrets about Rebecca which she had revealed, and which Kirsty had kept from her parents; the drinking of alcohol and the meetings with older boys.

Hunter decided that no one would benefit by revealing what Kirsty had told Grace. Especially he knew it was something that her parents wouldn't want to hear at this time.

"That's something we'll have to ask her when she comes round." Hunter stared down at Kirsty's damaged body. A cold sensation shot down his spine and caused him to shudder.

"When you catch the bastard who did this, I hope you hang him," Mr Evans snarled.

- ooOoo -

CHAPTER EIGHTEEN
DAY TWENTY-NINE: 4th August.

The local and national tabloids together with the international press had now joined the hunt for the serial killer. They were crawling all over the district; tramping around every cordoned-off crime scene and laying siege to the District General hospital where Kirsty Evans lay sedated. It had meant bringing in extra uniform resources just to fend off the press. Every witness the police had visited received a follow up call from the media vigilantes. At night locals shared their stories in exchange for pints from journalists. Every hotel and Travel Lodge around Barnwell had been booked up. It was great for the local economy but it wasn't good for allaying the fears of the community. The hacks were making a thorough nuisance of themselves.

The Major Investigation Team had adopted a siege mentality to all this and only Detective Superintendent Michael Robshaw dealt with the daily press conferences.

However amongst the chaos the good thing that had come from the high profile status of the investigation was the drafting in of extra staffing. Hundreds of actions were now being tasked to detectives and there was a real resurgence to the enquiry.

Hunter's team had processed the fresh exhibits from the serial killer's latest attack on Kirsty Evans and those were now being 'fast tracked' by forensics. The hope was that within days they would have a name for their murderer.

* * * *

He had been to six separate newsagents to collect different editions of papers to read what they were saying about him. It had taken him a whole morning to digest the contents, going back over many of the paragraphs time and time again, picking over the key words, and he was at boiling point.

Speculation about his background and the press's portrayal of him was making him angrier and angrier. They had continually described him as being pure evil and that the victims in all this were so innocent.

He wanted to scream. The stupid bastards have got it so wrong. It was those girls they should look at and blame for all of this. He was the one ridding society of its evil. After all what had his mother told him repeatedly when he had been so young; that he was the Angel sent by God to deliver his message. And the press were liars as well: So much of each article had given detail of how close the police were to catching him.

What a load of rubbish, he said to himself. This drivel isn't going to help them catch me.

What did worry him though were the paragraphs about his latest attack on Kirsty. Sooner or later she was going to come round and give police a description. Despite the fact he had disguised himself he couldn't help but think – remembering that strange look on her face when he had spoken to her - that she had registered something about him. He hoped that what he had already done about that would throw the police completely off his scent.

In the past few days he had run the attack through and through in his head. How could he have missed that jogger?

I don't make mistakes – not like that anyway.

He'd even had to leave his father's old belt behind on Kirsty's neck.

How could I have been so stupid? I never make mistakes. That's why I've never been caught.

But on reflection he'd realised why that had happened. He'd panicked when he'd heard that guy shouting and seen him running towards him.

That was twice in short succession now, when for years he'd gone without being disturbed.

Is someone up there trying to tell me something?

Thank goodness the man had stopped to help Kirsty, instead of chasing after him, otherwise he'd more than likely be in prison now.

As soon as he had got out onto the road he had checked himself, told himself that this action could get him caught and so he had changed his pace to a gentle stroll and taken stock of who was around. There had been no one and so he had slipped off his disguise and dropped his coat and glasses inside the boot of his car. He had started the engine and waited; listening for the sound of the police cars and the ambulance, which he knew, would soon be arriving. When he had been satisfied they were going in the opposite direction he had driven slowly away from the parking lay-by.

He took in a deep breath, and composed himself and continued about his business, carefully snipping out the newspaper articles to place in his files; adding them to the other cuttings and to his own personal photographs of the girls; the ones he taken when he sneaked around their homes, and when he had dealt with them. He smoothed a hand over the images.

He still couldn't believe the thrill he got from tightening the belt around their throats.

Watching the fear in the slags' eyes as he'd squeezed out their lives.

The same fear he had seen in his mother's face when his father had done the same.

* * * * *

Catching her image in the hallway mirror as she made her way into the kitchen, she took a long look at herself. Seeing the large number of deep worry lines etched into her face made her realise that the years had not been kind to her. Continuing on, picking up pace, she lugged the wicker basket towards the washing machine and dumped it in front of the open circular door. As she bent down to scoop out the dirty clothing wisps of frizzy grey hair fell across her face. She swept them back over her ears and continued with the chore of separating the colours into piles. "Dark wash, whites," she mumbled to herself, like she always did when doing the washing. She stopped abruptly as she caught sight of the stained blue and white striped shirt, which had been stuffed to the bottom of the basket. Using only her thumb and forefinger she picked out the shirt slowly, holding it up to the light streaming through the kitchen window. The dark spots and splashes on the cuffs and sleeves were unmistakeable. She had seen them so many times. Automatically she reached for the bottle of stain remover kept below the sink. As she gripped the bottle in front of the shirt, ready to spray, the news bulletin, which had been broadcast that morning, sprang into her mind.

'A fresh plea for witnesses to an assault on a teenage girl three days ago. Links to the murder of Rebecca Morris.' The words from the female newscaster were all coming back to her.

The noise of her son shuffling about in his bedroom above disturbed her thoughts and she raised her eyes to the ceiling. They became fixed as though attempting to penetrate the plaster.

At that same moment the vision of her ex-husband surged into her mind. How he'd cursed and berated her over the years. Blaming her for their son's condition.

"You've given birth to a psycho." she remembered him blasting at her, the stench of chewing tobacco on his breath only inches from her face.

And as he'd grown older her boy had given her as much grief. Saying it was also her fault that his father had left. If he had only known the truth. He'd never seen the beatings, which had been dished out to her. She had always taken great care to hide the bruising. She had always wondered if the damage had been caused when her husband had kicked her in the stomach when she was carrying her boy.

Her neighbour, Jimmy Carson, had caught her crying so many times after arguments and had been the only one to comfort her. She had thought that taking a beating for being caught in bed with him might have been a good thing; might have changed the way her husband had treated her all these years. But it had only made things worse. He had punished her even more by leaving.

Her son had got worse after he'd left.

She hadn't even heard of the condition, which the psychiatrist had diagnosed. Paraphilia he'd called it. She could see the Professor now, leaning towards her, solemn faced, elbows resting on desk, fingers fixed as a pyramid and pointed towards her. He'd spoken so softly, choosing such carefully phrased words.

"The condition mean that your son needs to do something extreme or dangerous in order to get a buzz," had been the gist of it.

And he'd rightly concluded that he would get worse as he got older.

How ironic that the son she had named after an angel had turned out to be the devil himself. She knew he should be locked up, as much for his own sake as for others, but she couldn't bring herself to betray him any further than she had already done.

She shook herself out of her daydream and glanced back down to the shirt she was holding. Tears welled into her sad grey eyes. She wondered if it was time to bring all this to a halt.

* * * * *

The double set of doors burst open, one of them crashing against the wall. Grace was bristling with excitement as she bounced into the MIT office holding aloft a bundle of papers.

"I've just got off the phone with our Sex Offender Officer in The Public Protection Unit. I've got a cracker of a suspect."

Grace's sudden arrival and announcement caused Hunter to jump. He was the only person left in the office; everyone else was out on 'the ground.' Only a minute earlier he had looked at his watch wondering what was taking Grace so long. First thing after morning briefing he had given her the task of contacting the forensics lab to see if they had got a result yet from the Kirsty Evans's samples, and he couldn't help but wonder why one phone call had taken her the best part of an hour.

Grace almost missed seating herself on her chair. She spun it out from under her desk with one foot and just managed to catch the edge of it as she plonked herself down. She adjusted her posture quickly and slid the sheets of foolscap towards Hunter.

"Firstly we've got a positive result from forensics," she began, almost out of breath "The fibres from under Kirsty's fingernails match the fibres from the cardigan found on Carol Siddon's body. The killer is still wearing the same clothing after all these years. And the belt, which was recovered from Kirsty's neck, fits the marks found on Rebecca's neck. That's the good news."

"What's the bad news?" asked Hunter. "And take some deep breaths I don't want you keeling over on me."

She laughed, "Sorry but I'm so giddy. I've got loads to tell you." She took in a deep intake of air. "The bad news is not that bad actually. Although there is a match for the DNA found under Kirsty's nails with that from Rebecca's body and the property Billy Smith found - and it's not his by the way – it's not on the national database at present. However all is not lost. Remember you gave Barry the task of going through Rebecca's school stuff. Well I've just had a cuppa with him in the exhibits room and he's shown me some very interesting snippets from her school journal. I've photocopied them to show you. Just look at pages six, seven and eight. There's nearly three weeks between the first entry and the last extract which was written the day before she went missing."

Hunter shuffled through the sheets and found the ones Grace had mentioned. He scoured the excerpts from Rebecca Morris's daily school diary.

Met up with G after school. He showed me the photos he had taken of me. He said I looked very pretty and should consider taking up modeling. He made me blush. We talked for ages. He said I was a lot more mature than my age. Asked if he could meet up again, and I agreed.

Went early to the fair today to see G again. I went early because I had arranged to meet Kirsty but G told me he didn't want her to be around. He said she would be jealous of me meeting him, because he said she had been txting him because she fancied him. He took my photograph again and *said he was going to make a professional portfolio for me. After G had gone me and Kirsty went to the youth club. I told Kirsty about someone older fancying me and wanting to take modeling photos of me. She just laughed and said it was weird. G is right she is jealous.*

Arranged to meet G tomorrow. He told me to miss school for once. He was going to start my portfolio so I could take it to a modeling agency. He told me not to tell anyone just yet as it would be a big surprise. I can't wait to see him again. He treats me just like a grown up.

Hunter whistled through his teeth. "Bloody hell Grace, I bet this is how our killer has been luring the girls. He's a groomer."

"He certainly is and there's more. I got back on to the technicians at Headquarters this morning. Do you remember Tony and Mike were given the job of searching the Evans's house and they seized the computer?"

Hunter nodded.

"Well they've pulled off a number of chat room extracts, which Kirsty's been having, with someone called Josh who says he's seventeen. Well they've managed to trace the IP address and it comes back to one Geoffrey Collins." She dropped several printed sheets in front of Hunter adding to the pile already on his desk.

Hunter knew from previous dealings that Grace was referring to the Internet provider service, where addresses could be tracked back to an individual computer.

"And get this, Geoffrey Collins is actually a thirty-seven year old man, and Public Protection Unit have confirmed he's on our sex offenders' register. If you look at pages ten and twelve you can see some of his profile that PPU have faxed over to me. His last conviction was over eight years ago and that's probably why he's not on the DNA database. He was done for gross indecency against two girls. One was fifteen and the other fourteen. What do you bet that G in Rebecca's journal is Geoffrey Collins?"

"My, my, we have been busy haven't we?" Looks like you've solved this all on your own. You'll be after promotion and a commendation next," Hunter replied.

"If the cap fits," she smiled back modestly.

"That is real good work Grace. Now you can help me get an operational plan drawn up with the SIO so that we can do an early morning knock on this Geoffrey Collins."

- ooOoo -

CHAPTER NINETEEN
DAY THIRTY: 5th August.

Geoffrey Collins lived in a one bedroom flat above one of the charity shops on Barnwell High Street. A decision had been made the night before not to contact his landlord for fear of word leaking out and Collins fleeing before the early morning raid. By 7am both marked and unmarked police cars lined the High Street. Overnight one of the evening shift detectives had secreted himself at the rear of the place to keep a check of Collins movements, ensuring he didn't leave before he could be arrested.

Hunter and his team were at the back of the queue of police vehicles, watching the Task Force don their protective gear and check their firearms. They were taking no chances. Ten minutes later the radios crackled into life, the Task Force Inspector had begun coordinating the operation. His instructions were short and precise and in a matter of minutes the immediate area around the flat had been cordoned off.

Hunter wound down the car window as the 'Strike...Strike...Strike." shout went out over the airwaves.

Two dull thuds pierced the stillness of the morning, followed by the shattering of glass and splintering of wood.

He knew at that moment that Collins door had succumbed to the Task Force battering ram. He listened intently to the radio chatter as the armed team swept the building 'clearing' each room, and in less than a minute his name was being called.

"DS Kerr?" The Task Force Officer requested.

Hunter responded.

"The flat is empty, Collins is not here."

Hunter cursed beneath his breath. Nevertheless he left the unmarked CID car, followed by Grace, Tony Bullars and Mike Sampson, already garbed in their forensic suits.

The detectives entered the flat via the ground floor door at the rear of the building. The firearms team were just 'racking' their weapons, clearing rounds from the chambers of their Heckler and Kock MP5s.

Hunter gave them a studious glance. He admired the elite team, always viewing them as a necessary evil in the fight against crime. It had always been his mind-set never to carry a gun. If truth be told he didn't trust himself with something which could take away someone's life from the slightest of touch. He had always been worried that with a gun in his hand he might get it so wrong – especially when the red mist came. No, he'd stick with his fists. He had more control over them and the damage he left behind was always repairable. He squeezed past them, over the bits and pieces of broken timber and glass, which had once been the back door. It had been well and truly knocked off its hinges.

Grace, Tony and Mike followed up behind.

They all cringed and screwed up their faces as a rancid smell reached their nostrils. Glancing around, the flat was a hovel, filthy and malodorous. A table in the centre of the room was covered in dirty crockery, a half eaten sandwich, and milk had curdled in its plastic container.

Hunter scrutinised the setting and wondered if it normally was left in such a state, or had Collins left in a hurry.

A bare electric bulb provided the only light, and wallpaper, the pattern of which must have come from the seventies, peeled in places from the damp walls.

In the bedroom a patch of light streamed through a gap in the curtains picking out objects within the sparsely furnished room. Against one wall was an old fashioned metal bed covered in an array of yellow stained sheets. The image reminded Hunter of Tracey Emin's Turner Prize submission to The Tate Gallery.

On a bed side unit laid a lap top computer. It was still switched on.

A bundle of newly printed photographs lay scattered over the floor. Grace picked one up, studied it, and turned it to Hunter's face. He instantly recognised the close-up shot of the pretty teenage girl - Kirsty Evans - who now lay critically injured in Barnwell General.

He shook his head disconsolately. "We need to nail this bastard, and quick before he attacks again."

Grace nodded in agreement, shook out one of the plastic exhibit bags she had been carrying in her jacket pocket and dropped in the photo. Pulling the top off her marker pen with her teeth she timed and dated the exhibit label and bent down to scoop up more of the pictures. They all appeared to be snaps of Kirsty, taken at regular intervals, and she instantly identified the background as the park where Kirsty had been attacked.

Hunter whipped out his police radio. It sparked into life as he pressed the open channel button "I want Scenes of Crime and the computer team up here immediately," he called in.

He knew they wouldn't be long. He had included them in his operational plan the previous evening, briefing the SOCO manager over the phone before leaving work, and ensuring that they were in their vans at the end of the street before the start of the morning's raid.

Though his team would be carrying out a thorough search to gather evidence he knew that he still required the full range of specialist skills to process the crime scene, and despite the fact that the firearms unit had trampled through most of the flat Hunter knew that there would still be some significant clues around.

Within minutes he heard the heavy footfalls of several individuals clomping hurriedly up the stairs.

Red-faced and breathing heavily, SOCO manager Duncan Wroe, whom he had known for many years, poked his head of straggling hair and unshaven face round the door. As usual the white forensic suit he wore hung limp on his rake-thin frame. He unfortunately always looked so dishevelled; yet despite that appearance Hunter knew that Duncan was one of the best SOCO officers around. So much so, that two years previously he had been selected by the Home Office as a member of a Forensic Science Team to travel to Afghanistan and train up newly appointed Afghan Scenes of Crime officers in modern forensic science methods.

Hunter knew he was going to get a thorough job done. He greeted him eagerly, snapping off one of his latex gloves to shake his hand. His part was over. It was time to update the SOCO manager and hand the crime scene over.

As Hunter briefed Duncan the computer technician slid past, making straight for the laptop. The pale-faced, spectacle wearing young man slotted a memory stick into one of the available ports and hit the 'enter' tab. The screen saver flashed on. The desktop image showed another picture of Kirsty Evans. It was a replicated shot from one of the photos Grace had already recovered as evidence.

The technician pushed his spectacles back over the bridge of his nose, entwined the fingers of both hands together and bent them back until they clicked. For a few seconds his elongated digits hovered above the laptop.

The image reminded Hunter of a pianist about to play a concerto.

As if reading his thoughts his fingers dropped onto the keyboard and began their dance upon the keys. After a few seconds he mumbled. It seemed more to himself than to anyone else in the room. "The guy's password protected his system. This will take me a little time." The techie began to work the keyboard again.

Around the room the Scenes of Crime officers' activity had also begun. They were setting up a camera to record the scene, and taping the unmade bed for fibre samples.

Hunter knew from experience that finding transferred fibres could link a victim to the scene. He tugged at Grace's elbow. "There's nothing we can do here for now. Bag up all the photos and we'll get back to the station. We need to get Collins circulated tonight."

She acknowledged with a nod of her head and finished sealing the exhibit bag.

* * * * *

Hunter entered the MIT office to find that Barry Newstead was its sole occupant. The big man was hunkered over a computer, laboriously plink-plonking the keyboard using only his index fingers. Hunter smiled to himself as he watched the seasoned ex-detective thump each key with his stubby fingers.

It was a complete contrast to the typing skills he had recently witnessed being performed by the young computer technician on Collins' laptop.

Hunter scraped back his seat with his leg, slipped of his jacket, dropped it over the chair back and flopped down. "Shall I get you a bucket of water Barry, that keyboard's going to be on fire soon," he said straight-faced.

"Piss off," Barry retorted, eyes still focussed downwards.

"Now, now Mr Newstead show some respect."

"Piss off Detective Sergeant." He glanced across at Hunter, pushing his spectacles up onto his head, catching his gaze.

They both cracked a grin.

"Bloody computers, they're more trouble than they're worth," Barry added, rolling his neck and knuckle-rubbing the tension from around his eyes. "Anyway Mr Sarcastic where's your side-kick?"

"Grace is booking in some evidence we got from Collins's place. We found a whole bunch of recent photos of Kirsty Evans. They look like they were taken in the park just before she was attacked. We've got him bang to rights when we catch him."

"Any stuff relating to the other girls?"

"When I left Scenes of Crime were just starting, and a computer whizz-kid was just going through Collins's laptop. Anyway I'm surprised to find you in. I thought you'd got a load of statements to get."

"I heard on the radio that you'd not got Collins and I guessed you'd want all his background stuff to track him down. That's what I was doing, or trying to do, when you came in."

"Okay what have you got for me then?"

Barry snatched up a bundle of papers and pointed them towards Hunter. "I got most of it from the Sex Offender Officer in the Public Protection Unit. He told me over the phone what they had got on the computer, which wasn't as much as what was held in a paper file they had, so he faxed me that. I've skip read it and it contains his entire prosecution file. I've also rung Probation and they've given me snippets from his prison intelligence record as well as info from all the meetings they've had with him. They've e-mailed me everything but I can't seem to pull the bloody stuff off."

Hunter couldn't help but grin again.

"It's alright for you. This technical crap is all new to me. Give me a phone and a pen any day."

"You've done a good job anyway Barry. It's saved us loads of time, but you didn't need to go to all this trouble."

"Oh I do, believe me I do. What I wouldn't give to be part of the team to track him down. Just a couple of minutes with him are all I would need."

During his detective constable days he had been with Barry on more than one occasion when he'd meted out his own form of justice on arrest, but it was the way in which he had almost spat out the first part of the sentence, which caused consternation in Hunter. "What do you mean?" he probed.

"Nothing Hunter. I just want to catch Geoffrey Collins like you do. The guy's got a lot to answer for, killing all those innocent girls."

Hunter thought that he faltered over his words and that wasn't like Barry. "There's more to this isn't there?"

"No, no. What makes you say that?"

Hunter saw that Barry was blushing.

"Come on spill the beans."

"Nothing to spill. You're reading too much into this."

It was the look on Barry's face, which caused the alarm bells to ring in Hunter's head. It was one of unquestionable guilt.

"Barry I'm not as green as I'm cabbage looking and you more than anyone should know that. We go back a long way." He stopped in mid-sentence. Things were clicking into place. "This is about Susan Siddons isn't it? All the work you did off your own bat when her daughter went missing. Susan was more than a snout wasn't she?"

Barry's face set grim. "Nail on the head Hunter. I wanted to tell you ages ago but I knew if I did, you wouldn't allow me onto the team."

"Damn right I wouldn't Barry." Hunter raised his voice. "Be straight with me now. How long were you and Susan carrying on?"

"On and off for years Hunter." He paused. "Carol Siddons was my daughter."

- ooOoo -

CHAPTER TWENTY
DAY THIRTY-ONE: 6th August.

Nursing a cup of strong coffee Hunter leaned back in his seat. He didn't normally touch coffee until mid-afternoon, but he needed the huge caffeine hit this morning. He felt so weary after another restless night. What with the images of his crazed father still replaying themselves in his sub-conscious, coupled with Barry's surprise revelation yesterday, he seemed to be spending more time worrying about people than this case.

Recounting Barry's confession he realised only too well the implication this could have on the investigation. True, Barry had shouldered this burden for too many years, but what a time to reveal it, thought Hunter. The ex-cop had fathered a child to an old informant. A child who featured centrally in a murder case. In fact one of the biggest murder cases Hunter had ever been involved in, and the ex-cop was part of the investigation. It could compromise the whole enquiry, Hunter said to himself. If defence council got a whiff of this the case might not even get to court. Hunter knew he had to keep this suppressed, and last night he had warned Barry not to reveal this to anyone else.

Hunter's head was beginning to thump. He reached into his top drawer, took out two paracetamol tablets, popped then into his mouth, and swilled them down with the remainder of the coffee.

Around him he noticed that the office was beginning to fill up ready for that morning's briefing.

Grace practically fell into the office, bouncing on the balls of her feet. She snatched the cup from Hunter's hands and made towards the kettle at the far end of the office. She sniffed at his cup before she set it down. "What's with you drinking coffee at this time of day?" She said, switching on the kettle and turning to face him. Catching sight of the dark rings circling his eyes, she quipped, "Jesus Hunter you look shit."

"Thank you Grace, for those words of comfort."

"No I'm being serious Hunter. Are you going down with something?"

"Could do with a good night's sleep that's all. This case is getting to me." He wasn't going to expand on his reply, not even to Grace.

She rinsed out his cup and dropped in a tea bag. "I'm making you tea, too much coffee's bad for you," she said turning back to her task.

"Thank you mother."

"You need mothering," she retorted, tapping one foot as she impatiently waited for the kettle to boil.

It raised a smile in him. She's like a breath of fresh air, he thought to himself, if he could only but tell her why he felt so low this morning.

She poured steaming water into two cups. "Anyway I've had a very interesting half hour with Duncan Wroe. I called in at the SOCO offices on my way to work, just to see if they had got anything." She stirred the cups, squeezed out the tea bags and then added milk.

"He's told me that despite the fact the place was such a shit-hole, most of the surfaces had been wiped clean – and get this - with concentrated bleach." She set down Hunter's cup in front of him and sunk into her chair opposite.

Hunter's face took on a puzzled look.

"That was my reaction," she added, pointing a finger at him. "Every flat surface; doors, and even the lap-top keyboard. The whole place is clean as a whistle of prints. They've found a couple of fresh blood spills in the bathroom; very minute, and they're fast-tracking those to forensics today."

"That's strange," Hunter responded. A frown creased his forehead.

"That's what I thought. And also get this - the computer techie says the images of Kirsty, together with its password protection code were only recently added to Collins's laptop. They think someone else must be involved with Collins, someone who wants to cover up every trace that they were ever there. That's the only explanation they can give to their findings."

Hunter pursed his lips, "Someone's testing us to our limits Grace, and the sooner we get hold of Collins the better."

A throaty 'gruumph' caught their attention and they turned their heads to the front of the room where Detective Superintendent Robshaw was standing in front of the incident boards. This morning another man was in tow, clutching a tumbler of water. Tall and slim in his late forties, stylishly cut gelled hair, tailored striped shirt and designer jeans.

Definitely not cop, thought Hunter.

"Dishy," whispered Grace in Hunter's ear.

"Gay," Hunter shot back.

She elbowed him. "Jealous."

"Morning Ladies and Gents" The SIO began his morning introduction to briefing. "Can I firstly introduce Dr Paul Stevens, who is a Home Office Criminologist from the Behavioral and Geographical Profiling Unit. Dr Stevens has been reviewing our cases, and visited some of the scenes and is here to give us an insight into the type of person we are looking for. It may help us especially now that we have a chief suspect."

The Criminologist stepped forward and took a swig of the water.

"Good morning guys," he began. "Why am I here? You may well ask. One thing I can assure you of is that I am not here to steal your thunder. Your force has asked me to look at all the stages of your investigation to see if I can give an insight into the profile of the person you will be looking for. I was told this morning that you now have a major suspect in the frame for this, so my arrival this morning might be too late. However my thoughts on this case may just assist your interview once you catch him." He stepped backwards and then began striding across the front of the four wipe boards, one for each of the girls attacked, tapping each one as he passed.

"Firstly let me say that although this may well be the first serial killer investigation you've been involved in, for many it may not be your last. At any one time it is statistically known that there are at least two serial killers operating across Britain. I have only to mention Hindley and Brady, Peter Sutcliffe the Yorkshire Ripper, Fred and Rose West and of course most recently, and the most infamous to date, Harold Shipman, to name but a few." His hands were becoming more and more animated as he got into his stride.

He had already captured Hunter.

"Serial killers fall into two categories, organised, and disorganised. I've visited each of the sites where the bodies have been found and also where his last victim was attacked. These are not easy to get to and in the case of the bodies, which have been hidden for a decade, the original tracks to those sites would have only have been known by someone who is local to this area. This is someone who feels confident that they can stop their car and have the time to dig and bury a body. In the most recent case, the attack on Kirsty Evans, that he can secrete himself until she arrives and then have enough time to carry out his attack. The jogger coming along was pure luck."

Dr Stevens moved across the wipe boards, snatching a quick look at the photographs now affixed to their surfaces. His eyes rested on the time lines of each of the murders.

"The intervals are getting shorter." He settled himself onto the corner of a desk, pushing back a thigh and dangling one leg for comfort. "He is killing to fulfil a need and the urge to kill is stronger. The nature of his attacks plays a big part in his psyche as well - the strangulation with the belt and then the viciousness of the stabbings. Its frenzy is almost revengeful, punishing."

"Do you think that's where the cutting of the word evil into the bodies comes in?" interrupted Hunter.

"Some of that yes. But my personal feeling is that the marking of the girls is about what he thinks of each of the victims. Looking into the background of all these girls, their rebellious social antics, and their activities have made them become his victims. Added to that their physical profiles are all similar, and I would think that somewhere in his past an abusive woman or girl has featured strongly in his life."

"We're looking at other girls who are currently outstanding as missing persons. Do you think there is the likelihood that he has killed them?" Grace asked.

"Without reading through their files that is difficult to answer. However, a serial killer does not just emerge by chance. He has grown in confidence and is prepared to let you know which are his victims, and as in the case of Claire Fisher, who he abducted and murdered. My guess is there are still victims out there waiting to be found."

"We know about his signature marks carved into the torsos of each of the girls, but what is the significance of the playing card?" interjected Hunter.

"I've given that some thought. In the Rebecca Morris murder he left the seven of hearts over a gaping wound just above her heart. In the case of the mummified remains of Carol Siddons, although you have not yet found a playing card, the post mortem revealed that her heart had been removed. Finally with Claire Fisher, she was a skeleton so we don't know if any organs were removed, but he left behind the three of hearts. I think what you have here is the part of the sequence of each of these killings. Claire being his third victim, and Rebecca his seventh. The card suit - the hearts, signifying he has taken their hearts literally and physically." Dr Stevens took another swig of water, clutched it in both hands and travelled his gaze around the room.

"You have a pattern here. I am pretty confident when I say this guy is local, and given his most recent attacks on Rebecca Morris and her best friend Kirsty Evans, still works or lives around here. He knows his victims, either from his past, or he selects them. He carefully finds a place where he can attack them and also has a safe place where he can dispose of them. This is someone who plans meticulously. It was purely by chance that he was disturbed after killing Rebecca and now this recent attack on Kirsty. It is imperative that you catch him soon because believe me he is not going to stop."

* * * * *

Katherine Winter loved walking her dog at this time of the morning; except for the wildlife she had the woods to herself. A fine summer's mist was beginning to drift up from the overnight damp floor, swirling around her legs as she broke into a jog. Whipping out the rubber ball from her fleece pocket she launched it towards a gap between the trees.

"Go get it Rusty." she shouted.

The Irish red setter spun its head in the direction of the flying ball and then shot after it at breakneck speed. Twenty yards ahead Rusty darted into the undergrowth out of Katherine's view and all she could hear for several seconds was the scratching of paws amongst the undergrowth. Her attention was distracted when above her she became aware of a cacophony of cawing, and looking up she saw a building of rooks, swirling and swooping, reminiscent of an army of apache helicopters, an image which she had seen so many times recently on the news broadcasts from Iraq. Within seconds Rusty's barking was adding to the discordant sound. She wondered what on earth was happening, and although she experienced slight trepidation she pushed past the bushes towards the direction of her barking dog.

She spotted her Irish red setter resting on its haunches, staring upwards, still barking wildly.

Her eyes followed the dog's line of sight. Nothing could have prepared Katherine for what she found herself looking at. Dangling from a rope, fastened to a large tree bough, was a man's body. The first thing she noticed was the colour of his head. It was purple, and hopping bluebottles covered its bloated flesh. Then the smell hit her. It was a creeping, cloying smell of tepid urine and faeces, and her stomach leapt to her throat. Gagging, she gripped her nose and reached for her mobile.

* * * * *

DC Mike Sampson shifted uncomfortably in his oversized forensic suit. Because of his body weight to height ratio he generally found that to find anything to fasten over his pudgy stomach the sleeves would always be too long. Tugging at his sleeves had become a habit, and this was what he was now doing in his blue plastic mortuary oversuit.

He dropped the exhibit bag he had been carrying onto one of the side tables in the sterile room. The clear plastic wrapper contained an A4 printed note SOCO had recovered from the pocket of the hanging Geoffrey Collins. In bold letters it simply stated 'I AM A MONSTER FORGIVE ME.'

Earlier that morning he had raced to Barnwell woods straight after briefing on the orders of SIO Detective Superintendent Robshaw, to take charge of a very active scene. Upon his arrival he saw that the uniform Sergeant and his shift had done a cracking job. The Police Medical examiner and Scenes of Crime had already been called out and were en-route, and a clear path had been roped off to the location where the lady walking her dog had discovered Collins's body

Because of the efficiency of the sergeant and his team he was merely there to check that everything which needed to be done, was being done. His role at the scene ended when they cut down Collins for removal to the mortuary, ensuring that the loop and knot of the rope remained in situ around his neck.

That had been two and half hours ago and Mike was at the mortuary to observe Collins's post mortem, confirm the suicide, and then they could wrap up this investigation and celebrate in the pub.

The post mortem was already underway by the time he had suited and entered the mortuary cutting room. Pathologist Lizzie McCormack together with a Scenes of Crime Officer were already moving business-like around Geoffrey Collins's naked corpse which lay on one of the stainless steel autopsy tables.

The Professor was going through the preliminaries for the purpose of the recording tape. Height; weight; state of the body. The soft Scottish twang reminded Mike of the Mrs Doubtfire character from the Robin Williams movie.

She hooked one hand behind Collins's head and raised it from the wooden resting block. Then carefully she began to slide the still knotted rope over the bloated, discoloured face. The SOCO officer clicked off several shots of the process with his Nikon camera.

Rolling the head from side to side she delicately stroked and touched several parts of Collins's neck.

"As a slip-noose was used, ligature was in contact with the skin right around the full circumference of the neck," she began. She moved the head again fixed a finger to an area of the neck and the SOCO officer racked off several more shots.

"Now this is interesting," she announced after pursing her lips for a moment, "although there is evidence of bruising on and around the carotid vessels on the right hand side of the neck, except for the uppermost part of that side the ligature marks are faint and deficient on the sides and back."

Mike took a step towards the body "What does that mean Professor?"

Lizzie held up a latex-gloved hand, a clear order that she wanted him to say nothing else. With her other hand she took up a scalpel from a tray next to her. Then pushing her spectacles up onto the bridge of her nose she began slicing into the soft tissue of the throat area of the cadaver. Diving her fingers into the incised front of neck, she began pulling and probing the larynx.

"There is bone injury in the air passage. There is a fracture of the hyoid." She gave off a long drawn out "Hmmm," before continuing with the remainder of the post mortem. Part way through she scraped under the finger nails, dropped some fibres into sample tubes and held the hands up for the Scenes of Crime Officer to photograph. Finally, after two hours she dropped the last of her instruments back onto a metal tray and snapped off her surgical gloves.

"Suicide by hanging?" Mike asked

"Oh indeed dear, this man's demise was caused by strangulation, but this was no suicide."

Lizzie McCormack's response took him aback. "Not suicide?"

"The evidence couldn't be much clearer. This man was murdered. See here." The Pathologist raised Collins's head from the support block and motioned a finger over the incised opening in the throat. "Contusions to the soft tissue and underlying muscle, and a fractured hyoid, all of which are indicative of manual strangulation. Coupled with the fact that the rope marks around the neck are merely superficial I conclude that he was already dead when he was strung up."

She took a long pause. "When it comes to murder they can't pull the wool over my eyes. I have a few more tests to carry out but I've also found trauma to the face which leaves me to believe he has suffered significant blows to the mouth and left cheek which could have rendered him either unconscious or semi- conscious. Finding those injuries caused me to carry out further examinations, particularly of the hands. I found that the majority of his fingernails are broken and there are fibres and possibly flesh beneath the remains of his nails. I bet if you go back to the tree where you found this man hanging you will find striation marks on the branch, which has been caused by the rope when his dead weight has been hauled up."

Mike gasped at the magnitude of these findings. His mind was racing. If it hadn't been for Professor McCormack's experience in dealing with murder victims this would never have been spotted. It could only mean one thing - Geoffrey Collins had been set up to make him look like the murderer. He pictured in his mind the recent bust at Collins' flat. The real serial killer must have somehow got into Collins's flat, assaulted and strangled him, used his computer knowing the police would trace it back to him, left the recently taken photographs of Kirsty and cleaned up any trace of himself before he'd left. And that's why SOCO found the surfaces wiped with concentrated bleach. In his head he tumbled around everything he had recently learned. There was only one conclusion. Kirsty Evans's attacker and the slayer of Carol Siddons, Claire Fisher and Rebecca Morris, had tried to throw them off his scent by killing Collins and making it look like suicide.

"The crafty bastard," Mike said aloud.

"Wash your mouth out with soap dear," Lizzie responded drily.

"Sorry Professor, I was just thinking aloud."

She smiled back. "I know, and you're right the person who did this is very crafty - and brutal, and if I wasn't so good, he'd have succeeded."

No pub tonight, Mike thought to himself. The hunt is back on.

* * * * *

I don't know why they call this a green room, Detective Superintendent Michael Robshaw thought to himself as he re-read his script, there's not a drop of alcohol in sight.

He shuffled uneasily in his seat as the male make-up artist flicked a blusher brush filled with foundation across his face.

"Do I have to wear that stuff?" he had barked earlier, grimacing at the thought of having to wear make-up for the first time in his life.

"Despite the fact that you look well for someone who is in their late forties we all need a little help in front of the cameras," the make-up artist said.

The SIO made final notes to the speech he was going to make. His second visit to the 'Crimewatch' studios was much sooner than he had anticipated, but he knew they had to 'up the ante' if they were to catch this killer. He had committed murder at least four times and would have added Kirsty Evans to his list had it not been for the quick reactions of a Paramedic out on his evening jog.

The numerous 'actions' were still being processed, and the new ones to find a link with Geoffrey Collins were being carried out at this moment as he prepared himself for the evening's live programme.

Detectives had already pulled Collins' prison and Probation files and were ploughing through them. They'd all come to the conclusion during the day's briefing that the killer must have known Collins was a convicted sex offender and that was why he had chosen him as the ideal candidate to throw them off his scent.

There had also been a very difficult debate during that meeting as to whether the use of the leather belt should be disclosed, especially as it was a significant piece of evidence. He had to argue strongly that they had very little choice. They had to act before someone else was murdered.

"And if showing that belt on TV will jog someone's memory and give us that golden nugget by which we can identify our killer, then it will be worth it," he had told his teams.

The buzzer above the door sounded and the 'three minutes' light flashed on.

The make-up artist pushed the handle of his brush underneath Michael Robshaw's jaw and manoeuvred the Superintendent's head from side to side.

"Pretty as a picture" he whispered. "Go break a leg."

* * * * *

She was following the light along the tunnel. Through the darkness she could see the trees and fields ahead and the summer breeze brushing her face brought with it the smell of freshly mown grass. But with every stride her experience was one of dragging feet through treacle and her pounding heart felt as if it was about to burst through her chest.

Though she couldn't see him she could sense he was getting closer, almost hear him breathing down her neck, and smell the foul stench of the halitosis from his mouth. Rebecca was shouting to her, waving her to safety. And then he was on her, grabbing at her hair and clawing at her skin. She was tugged forward so hard that her feet left the ground. Then something was tightening around her neck and the air left her lungs with a whoosh.

She tried to fight back, biting and scratching her attacker, but he was on top of her and she couldn't move. She was totally at his mercy.

He lowered his head and she caught the first glimpse of his face. It was a hazy image she saw but she thought she recognised him. Rebecca was trying to tell her who it was; she had been there when she had first seen him.

And the voice. It was growling at her, but she had heard it before, when it had been much softer and kinder.

The haziness started to clear. His face was suddenly unobstructed.

Kirsty Evans flicked open her eyes and gasped for breath "I know who it is." she screamed from her hospital bed.

- ooOoo –

CHAPTER TWENTY ONE
DAY THIRTY-TWO: 7th August.

The persistent ringing tone from Grace's desk phone was not going to go away. She mentally cursed herself for not putting it onto voicemail, especially as she had so much paperwork to go through.

She snapped it up and gave a curt "Grace Marshall MIT" and waited for the response.

There was a slight pause on the other end of the line, "Grace is that you?"

She immediately recognised the voice of the desk clerk from downstairs. "Sorry Cheryl," she responded pleasantly, "I've got so much work to do and so very little time to do it. I promised I'd take the girls to their netball training tonight. I'll really be in their bad books if I don't turn up."

"Tell me about it. What about that lump of a husband taking his turn? Or is he like mine, not much help?" returned Cheryl.

"Oh he tries his best, but it's the third time this week he's had to pick them up when I've promised. It's not been helped by him just getting a new job. I'll be getting the riot act read soon if I'm not careful."

"Well I might be adding to your burden Grace. There's a lady just turned up at the front desk. She wants to speak to a policewoman. She says she saw the Crimewatch programme last night and she's not exactly sure but she thinks the killer could be her ex-hubby."

The woman who Grace ushered into a side room within the foyer of the police station was nervous and twitchy and Grace being a non-smoker couldn't help but notice that she smelled strongly of cigarette smoke. She seated herself at one side of the fixed table in the room clasping her hands between her knees and introduced herself as Rachel Beddows, adding that she was twenty-five years old. With only a little eye liner on for make-up, Grace thought she looked a lot older.

"The desk clerk says that you believe the killer we're after could be your ex-husband," Grace opened, taking out her pen, scribbling onto a sheet of paper; testing it was working.

"I'm almost certain it's him," she replied. Her voice was raspy and gravelly.

"What makes you say that?"

"I've been following all the local news about the murders because a couple of weeks ago I did have a thought that it could be him and so when I heard it was going to be on Crimewatch I sat down to watch the programme. When I saw that detective – I think he was a Superintendent or something – show that belt I just froze. I heard him say it'd been recovered from the attack on the latest victim and they could link it to at least two of the murders. Was that the exact belt he showed?"

Grace nodded.

"Then I'm certain it was Gabe's. Well not exactly Gabe's as such, it belonged to his father and Gabe used to play around with it."

"What do you mean play around with it?"

"He used to twist it around in his hands whilst he was watching TV, as though he was getting it ready to throttle someone. It used to scare me."

"You call him Gabe?"

"Yes his full name is Gabriel Wild. The last I heard he was still living with his mum on the Tree estate."

"How long have you been divorced from him?"

"Oh I'm not divorced, but I've been separated from him nearly eight years now. I ran away and haven't seen him since. I've been too scared to go to a solicitors or anything. He always said if I left him he'd find me and kill me. I live in Sheffield now and I changed my name by deed poll."

"There's obviously some reason why you think it's him besides seeing that belt why don't you tell me a bit more?"

"I don't really want to get him into trouble if it isn't him," she retorted anxiously.

"Don't worry we have the attacker's DNA so if it isn't him a quick test will clear him."

Rachel unclasped her hands and set them on the table. She fiddled with several gold rings, which adorned a number of fingers on both hands. "I'll start from when we met, that'll give you a picture of what he's like." She licked her lips. "Gabe was into photography in a big way and was working as an apprentice at a big studio here in Barnwell. He used to come to our school to take all the form's photographs. He was twenty-one when we first met and I was almost sixteen, in my last year at school before college. He chatted up all the girls but I was the one who fell for him. He told me I could be a model with my looks and figure and asked if he could take some private photos for a portfolio for a model agency he freelanced for. Like a jerk I fell for it hook line and sinker. I posed for some innocent shots at first and then he persuaded me to have some more sexy ones done. His dad had made him a photo studio in the loft and he used to photograph me there when his mum went out. Then the inevitable happened and we started having sex. Within six months, just after my sixteenth birthday, I left home after a bust up with my mum and moved into his mother's house." She paused her blue-grey eyes focussed on Grace. It was a gaze filled with sadness and despair. "Am I going round the houses too much for you?"

"No you're absolutely fine. I've got bags of time," Grace lied. In the back of her mind she was thinking about her girls' netball practice, but at the same time she could see the tension etched on Rachel's face.

"He started to do 'kinky' things when we had sex. It scared me at first but I suppose I just got used to them."

"What do you mean kinky?"

"It's a bit embarrassing this." She wrung her hands. "Well he always wanted me to dress up in my schoolgirl stuff, which I could understand. But then he started asking me to resist so he could pretend he was raping me. Then one time he got his father's belt and put it round my neck and started squeezing it. That really freaked me out and we didn't have sex for a good few months after that. After he stopped sulking we talked about it and he said it was only a bit of fun, that he wouldn't hurt me and it was just bondage. Well after we had a good drink one night he did it again to me. This time he really hurt me. He squeezed the belt so tight that I went unconscious for a good few minutes. That's when I told him enough was enough. Things just soured after that. A couple of weeks after, he started to go out late at night and he would be gone for ages. On a couple of occasions he didn't get back until the early hours of the morning. One night he came in absolutely lathered in sweat and I asked him what he had been up to. He said he'd just been out for a jog. But I knew he was lying because he'd never jogged in his life; he hated sport. He'd sooner light up a fag than go for a run. Anyway the next morning I saw he'd put his clothing in the washing machine but when I went to hang them out I thought there were bloodstains on a T-shirt. I asked him about it but he just said it was some dye from his photography processing."

"When was this?" asked Grace, as she quickly started scribbling some notes.

"I'm sorry I can't remember the exact day or even month. It would have been about a year before I left him, so you're talking eight or nine years ago now. Why is that significant?"

"I'm not sure at this stage." Grace thought the timing could coincide with the disappearance of Claire Fisher but she also knew there were still a number of other girls outstanding in the missing from home files they had upstairs in the MIT Office.

"Anyway after the bust-up he asked me to marry him, to show that he still loved me. I said yes thinking everything would be okay but within weeks of the marriage he was wanting to use the belt on me again and we just had row after row. I told him he was perverted and I'd had enough and he told me that if I left him he'd kill me and bury me where no one would be able to find me. A couple of weeks after that I packed what I could, and when his mother was out shopping, and he was at work, I left. I never got in touch with him again. I went to a refuge at first and didn't even tell my parents where I was for fear he'd find me, and then they re-housed me to Sheffield and I've been there ever since."

"Besides the incidents you've told me about Rachel is there anything else about Gabriel's character which you found to be unusual or different?"

"Weird you mean?" She paused and ran a hand through her hair.

Grace couldn't help but notice its lack of style and the abundance of split-ends. She knew from her experience of dealing with domestic violence that this was a girl who had lost her self-esteem.

"Well there were the pictures he kept in the briefcase of some of the girls he had photographed at school. And he also kept some local newspaper cuttings about girls going missing. I never told him I'd found them. I was too scared. That's what's made me come to you."

Grace could feel the hairs prickle at the back of her neck. "Anything else about him?"

"He hates coppers – sorry police – he once told me he had been beaten up by a cop when he was a kid who had wanted him to confess to killing and cutting up a pet rabbit. He said the cop had been a close neighbour, a Mr Newstead."

That has to be Barry, Grace said to herself.

For another half hour Grace back-tracked on everything Rachel had said, testing to see if there was anything that had been missed. She had taken copious notes in preparation for a formal statement, and though she tried her best to stay focussed on the important task in hand, from time-to-time her thoughts had drifted. She couldn't help but bring to the front of her mind reflections of what might she might be facing within the next hour-or-so when she finally got home – late again.

- ooOoo -

CHAPTER TWENTY TWO
DAY THIRTY-THREE: 8th August.

"Does the name Gabriel Wild mean anything to you?" Grace grabbed Barry Newstead's attention the moment he had walked through the door. He was the first to enter the office, after her and she could hardly contain her excitement. She had to share with someone what she had learned late yesterday. Everyone had gone home by the time she had finished talking with Rachel Beddows and she had tried to get hold of Hunter before she left work but his mobile had been diverted to voicemail. It had been her intention to ring him later from her home but she thought better of it when she saw the faces of Robyn and Jade, who sent her on a guilt trip for missing their netball practice. She tried to remind herself that she had already put her career on hold on two occasions in order to bring up her daughters - that they were old enough to look after themselves and that this is what she needed to do for her own fulfilment. However, she still found herself apologising throughout the remainder of the evening, promising to do something or other with them at the weekend.

"Don't I get a good morning Barry how are you this fine day, instead of being quizzed about a little brat who once upon a time used to live near us?"

"Don't be such an old grouch. I got some information last night, which could end this enquiry. I hardly slept last night and look at me I'm as fresh as a daisy, not a miserable old sod like you."

"Less of the 'old' will you? Anyway what can't wait long enough for me to even have my morning caffeine infusion?"

"Gabriel Wild's ex-wife came in late last night telling me she thinks he's our killer. She gave me loads of examples and there's no doubt a lot of what she told me could fit the profile of our murderer, but I checked him out on the Intelligence system and he's got nothing at all recorded against him. She did mention however that he had had a bit of a run in with a Mr Newstead years ago when he was a teenager."

"A bit of a run in is an understatement," Barry snapped, setting his lunch container down on his desk and then removing his coat. "He was a right little bloody tearaway, and a pervert to boot. He became the bane of my life."

"Tell me about him and then I'll fill you in what his ex-wife told me."

"It really was a long time ago. I had just gone into CID when he turned up on my radar. He used to live a couple of doors down from us but I hardly noticed him as a youngster because whilst his dad was around he was a real polite kid. Then one day I remember his old man came home early from work and found his mother in bed with the guy from across the road. There was a hell of a bust up and he tried to throttle her. I was off duty doing the garden and could hear this commotion so I ran to their house and had to pull him off her. I managed to calm things down and I dealt with it there and then - like we used to in those days. I found out that a couple of days after the domestic he'd upped sticks and left. She was left to bring Gabriel up on her own." His eyes drifted up to the ceiling momentarily. Returning his gaze he continued, "Over the next few years I kept getting complaints about him following girls and playing with himself in front of them and I can remember one neighbour catching him peeping through her ground floor bathroom window. I had words with him in front of his mother and I know she gave him a real good hiding for that."

He paused a second and started stroking his bushy moustache.

"A few months after, I had to deal with him again. This time for giving a lad a right hammering. I think the lad had slagged off his mum. Well after that I used to see him hanging around the back of my house and when one day I told him to sling his hook he put two fingers up at me so I warmed his ear-hole for him."

She saw his expression harden.

"About a week later I heard Sarah screaming early one morning from the garden. I dashed out wondering what on earth was happening and found parts of her pet rabbit had been nailed up on the Wendy house. It had been cut to pieces with a knife or something similar. I just knew it was that little bastard Gabriel and so I went straight to his house. I tried to get him to cough that he'd done it but his mother just kept covering for him. Anyway shortly after that they moved. She sold the house and the next thing I discovered was they had gone to a council house on the Tree Estate. I kept a watch out for him but that was the last I saw of him. What does his ex say about him?"

Grace tried to contain her excitement as she re-iterated what Rachel Beddows had told her the previous evening. "I'm just waiting for Hunter to come in and then I'm going to feed it into morning briefing. Fancy a cuppa?" she finished.

"Bloody hell Grace, that's reminded me of something else involving him." He peeled off his jumper and chucked it over the piled-up paperwork on his desk. "It must have been about ten years ago now but I'm sure that he was interviewed over a girl's body that was discovered in some woods just over the border in West Yorkshire."

Grace studied the thoughtful look on Barry's face as he dropped silent. She could almost hear the cogs turning over inside his head. Then he raised a finger.

"I remember the gist of it now. A local peeping-tom out looking for couples having sex in a well known lovers' lane heard a girl screaming and from what I can recall he either shouted or dashed towards the sound. Anyway the next thing he saw was a young man with a small dog sprinting off along the lane. He guessed something had gone off and started looking around where he had heard the screaming coming from, and that's when he came across the body of a teenage girl who had been beaten and strangled."

Barry dropped his eyes down to his desk deep in thought. "I think it was South Kirby way, just outside our Force area," he continued, "I can remember seeing an e-fit of the suspect, but it wasn't a good one and I know that Gabriel Wild was interviewed as part of the enquiry, but I never got the end result. I'm not sure if it was ever detected or not because it was West Yorks' job, but I can make a quick phone call to one of my old buddies from there and get the heads up if you want?"

"Please if you wouldn't mind Barry and I'll make a brew."

Five minutes later, sipping at her freshly brewed coffee, Grace caught the sound of Hunter's voice outside in the corridor. As he entered the office she pushed herself up from her desk ready to greet him.

"Where were you last night when I needed you? I came back to the office from talking to a witness and it was like the Marie Celeste. I tried to ring you on your mobile but all I kept getting was your voicemail."

"That's because whilst you were downstairs in the interview room, me and Tony got called out to the hospital. Kirsty Evans came round yesterday afternoon. She knows who attacked her. It was a guy who took their school photographs. She knows him as Gabe."

"What a coincidence," Grace replied.

* * * * *

Avoiding the motorway Hunter took the A61, the less congested route into Wakefield. It was a good few years since he had travelled this road but as he passed certain landmarks the memories gave him a warm feeling. It seemed like yesterday, but he quickly recalled that it was in fact twelve years since he had made the regular twice weekly journey for a period of ten weeks to and from Detective Training School, which was situated in a side road on the edge of the city, and he just knew he would have to re-visit and view the centre before returning to Barnwell. He had had such a memorable experience learning there. He had returned to the district bursting with knowledge of the criminal law, and along the learning path had also made so many contacts with detectives from other forces, the length and breadth of England, which had proved extremely useful over the years.

As he slowed the car to join the crawling nose-to-tail traffic entering Wakefield he glanced across at Grace who he could see was still studying the notes she had made from her conversations with Gabriel Wild's ex-partner the previous night and also Barry Newstead earlier that morning.

Together with the revelation from Kirsty Evans, Hunter knew this was the breakthrough they had been waiting for.

After Barry's phone call to one of his old West Yorkshire colleagues Hunter had been given the telephone number of his counterpart in MIT in Wakefield. Immediately after morning briefing he had spoken with a Detective Sergeant Glen Deakins and arranged a meet at Wood Street police station situated in the centre of the city.

Following the Detective Sergeant's instructions Hunter parked the unmarked police car in a multi storey car park and he and Grace walked the few hundred yards to the old red-bricked police station opposite the Law Courts.

Despite an attempt to give its foyer a contemporary makeover the waiting area still had that dark and gloomy feel typical of the Victorian era. Showing their warrant badges to the front-of-entrance clerk, Hunter and Grace took up seats which had been arranged along the front wall below two large sash windows, the bottom section of which held toughened and frosted glass. A pale sunlight had managed to penetrate and was lighting the dimness around them.

Biding his time Hunter coolly eyed the numerous framed force publicity posters adorning the walls and couldn't help but smile, thinking cynically, as he read over the mission statements and modern day Whitehall spin which seemed to have even crept into the police service. 'All this bullshit', he said to himself, when what the public really wanted was cops on the streets.

Within a few minutes his attention was distracted by the sound of an electronic buzzer and a side door burst open. A tall, slim, steel-grey haired man appeared in the doorway. Wearing a two-piece pinstriped suit and sporting a good tanned complexion DS Glen Deakins looked more the typical business tycoon than an MIT detective. He greeted them and Hunter immediately recognised his strong Leeds dialect as he rolled his tongue around their names.

"Hi, I'm to give you the full works." He held out a hand to shake. "My DCI can't speak highly enough of Barry Newstead." He glanced behind them. "Barry not with you?"

Hunter shook his head.

"Pity. The DCI was hoping to catch up with him. It appears they worked together on some secretive joint force investigation into corruption in the Met during the early eighties."

He held open the door as Grace and Hunter joined him and then pointed an extended arm up the open staircase that connected all three floors of the building. "We're on the top floor. MIT has all one corridor. Too hot in summer and freezing cold in winter but whose complaining, still get the cheque in the post thirteen times a year, don't we?" The Sergeant grinned. His features were strong and his hazel eyes displayed genuineness about him.

The top of the stairway opened onto a bright and airy corridor that led to suite after suite of rooms and offices, each one seemed to be bustling with activity. Its airiness took Hunter by surprise.

As if reading his mind the DS offered, "This place was given a full refurb before we moved in eighteen months ago. Everything we need is here. You ought have seen the place before it got its make-over." He took them down the corridor. "I've got us a room at the far end where you can look at the files from the Kelly Johnson murder."

He stopped at a glass-panelled door and pushed it inwards. They entered an eight-foot-by-eight-foot carpeted room. It was lit by a pair of fluorescent lights set in a chrome frame for maximum brightness. Along one wall was a framework of metal shelves adorned floor to ceiling with boxed case files. Hunter guessed this was where they stored the cold case work; previously undetected serious crimes of rape and murder which required reviewing now that new scientific methods, such as DNA, had come into play. In the centre, two desks had been pushed together, the light oak surfaces almost covered by an array of paperwork, organised into piles.

"The Kelly Johnson case." DS Deakins pointed out with an open palm, almost as though he was introducing someone rather than something. "I know this job like the back of my hand. I worked on this as a young detective back in ninety-six. In fact it was my first ever murder case. I spent over six months on it before it was wound down to just a small team. It was filed as undetected after eighteen months and its one of our review cases now." He rested his hand on one of the piles. "Everything is here. The witness statements, door-to-door reports and suspect interviews in date and alphabetical order."

Hunter eyed the pile-upon-pile of paperwork. "You might be able to shortcut things for us without the need to plough through all this lot, especially as you worked on it for so long."

"Yeah, no problem. To be honest when the gaffer asked me to show you the case it gave me the opportunity to skip read back over some of the actions I did on the case. In fact now it seems only like last week when I was working on it." DS Deakins pointed out the chairs around the table to Grace and Hunter and lowered himself into one. Leaning forward, intertwining his fingers, he rested his chin, and flicked his gaze from one to the other of his guests. He paused for a few seconds as if gathering his thoughts.

In the background Hunter became suddenly conscious of the bustle of activity, which was coming from the rooms further along the corridor. He reckoned behind those doors would be similar scenes to those of his own murder team back at Barnwell. Officers busy on telephones or computers following up their leads to crack the case. Working practices the length and breadth of the country were distinctly similar despite each murder being different.

"Kelly Marie Johnson, thirteen years old," Glen unlocked his hands and spun an A5 size photograph of a smiling teenage girl towards them. The colours were still extremely sharp despite the photograph being twelve year old. A picture of a very pretty girl, and yet with many similarities to the other victims; dark collar length hair, glistening hazel eyes, and with an air of innocence about her.

Hunter noticed that the girl was wearing heavy make-up and the pose of Kelly appeared more confident than the photos they had of the other girls. This shot was more professional altogether.

Grace took the photograph from the DS's fingers, angling it slightly towards herself. "This is an unusual photo. Was it taken in a studio?"

"It was actually," Glen replied. "Kelly had just been taken on by a modelling company. She was doing shoots for catalogues. That photo came from her portfolio. As you can see Kelly was a very pretty girl, looked a lot older than her thirteen years, and because of that she attracted a lot older type of boy. It caused a bit of friction with her dad."

"What was she like as a person?" Grace continued.

"Well until she got the modelling contract just a normal teenage girl, but the six months leading up to her death her parents and her friends said her personality changed. She began to hang out with older teenagers. Putting jealousy to one side her closest friends painted a picture of a girl who suddenly got very cocky and arrogant and who began picking on girls who she considered less attractive than herself, humiliating them and even bullying a couple of them. She began wagging school and we found out she'd been meeting up with a couple of lads, sixteen and seventeen. We questioned them on several occasions and both eventually admitted they had had sex with her, but they insisted she had told them she was herself sixteen. What they did have however was unbreakable alibis on the day she was murdered. They were at work, witnessed by dozens of their co-workers."

He took back the picture and viewed it himself.

She'd begun drinking as well; cider; and heavily. She rolled in drunk on several occasions and had bust-ups with her parents. She'd also been warned by the modelling agency about her attitude."

"A girl with everything, pressing the self-destruction button," said Hunter. "How many times have we seen that?"

"These characteristics you are describing identically match our victims. All the girls seemed to have been going through a real chaotic phase in their lives leading up to their deaths," added Grace.

"In a short space of time Kelly changed from a naive young girl into a real wild child."

"What happened on the day she was murdered?" asked Grace

"She'd come home from school." Glen paused. "This was one of the rare occasions in recent times she had actually attended. She was on a final warning from the modelling agency. A clean up your act or your finished ultimatum," he continued. "Anyway she got changed and told her mother she was meeting a couple of friends and would be back for her tea."

He picked up some typewritten notes turned a couple of the pages over and then continued reading from one of the sheets.

"At four forty-five pm on the second of August nineteen ninety six Mr William Burridge was in woods at South Elmsall," he glanced up, "Billy was known as a bit of a peeping-tom in the village. He did admit under questioning that he used to visit the woods on a regular occasion because they were well known as a rendezvous point for courting couples." He returned his gaze back to the notes. "He heard a girl screaming. He could tell from its tone that it was someone in trouble and ran towards the sound and began shouting as he got closer. He described seeing a young man wearing a dark T-shirt and jeans running with a small wiry-haired dog before he disappeared amongst the trees." The DS looked up from his notes again. "He got a glimpse of his face, just for a split-second glance, but it was enough for him to do an e-fit picture for us."

He continued. "Then Billy found Kelly amongst some long grass. She had been strangled by a belt of some type and she had been stabbed. In fact when the post-mortem was done the pathologist stated that the killer had made some attempt to cut out her heart."

Hunter and Grace exchanged looks.

Glen Deakin ran his fingers down the typewritten script. "Uniform were first on scene. A dog man did a follow through the woods, and some farmer's fields, which led towards the village of Great Houghton, in your area. He lost the track there unfortunately." He set down the papers. "And that's where I came in. I was part of the team, which did enquiries in your area. We joined up with a few of your detectives and did house to house. We circulated the e-fit and got an anonymous tip-off, which pointed us in the direction of Gabriel Wild. I knew as soon as I started interviewing him that something was not right. He was so nervous and cagey. We found there had been a bonfire in the back garden, some clothing and what looked like a pair of trainers had been burned, but it was four days after the murder and everything was just ashes. His mother totally covered for him. Said he was with her in the house at the time of the murder. Gabriel hardly said anything in interview and we couldn't knock what his mother said. She stood firm even though we threatened her with perverting the course of justice."

The DS's mouth set tight. "Gabriel remained and still remains our strongest suspect for Kelly Johnson's murder."

"Just one question," said Hunter, "Did you find a playing card with Kelly's body?"

The enquiry caught Glen in his tracks.

"Do you know that rings a bell." He flicked through the mounds of paper and dragged out several stapled sheets. Sliding a finger slowly down the typeface he stopped halfway down the second sheet and averted his eyes to Hunter then Grace. "Yes, it's here, on the exhibits list from the scene, a playing card found in Kelly's left hand. It was photographed in situ; the Two of Hearts."

"Kelly Johnson was his second victim," rasped Hunter.

- ooOoo -

CHAPTER TWENTY THREE
DAY THIRTY-FOUR: 9th August.

The back door of the Wild's semi-detached, the original wood and glass one, from the early fifties when the house was built, lay in pieces. It had initially resisted the Task Force Firearms Team battering ram, but on the third 'run' the oak door had exploded from its frame in spectacular fashion. Splinters of wood and shards of glass had flown everywhere.

"Clear." one of the Kevlar-armoured firearms officers shouted as he swept the last remaining room on the ground floor and moved deftly on towards the stairwell.

Hunter and his team shared an air of nervous excitement as they stood outside, waiting and listening for their signal to enter. An earlier clear blue sky had given way to a slight drizzle and despite it still being the last dregs of summer the air seemed dense with cold moisture.

Set out in front of them was a meticulously tidy garden. Neatly trimmed hedges and tall bushes surrounded a newly mown lawn.

Hunter strained his ears following the sounds of the searching firearms team. They were currently moving rapidly through the upper rooms. Even though he was anticipating it, when the call for them to enter came it made him jump. Hunter went in first. He noticed that despite the daylight the lights were on in every downstairs room. A television was on somewhere in the lounge to his left; even though it was soundless he could see the flicker of blurred images against the dark patterned wallpaper. He bounded up the threadbare carpeted stairs quickly followed by Grace, Tony and Mike. On the landing he was surprised to be met by Paul Goodright, garbed head to toe in standard protective Task Force clothing with a Heckler and Kock rifle strapped across his chest. It had slipped his mind that Paul was part of the Firearms team. It was the first time he had seen him in uniform. He looked a quite a commanding presence.

"Fancy meeting you here," Hunter greeted him.

Paul's features were set grim. "The target's not here Hunter and you're not going to like what we've just found." He pointed towards the front of the house.

Hunter pushed the bedroom door fully open and the four MIT detectives trooped in. The room was gloomy. A single shaft of light pierced the dimness. One of the windows was open and the velvet curtains were lifting in the breeze. In the dullness he picked out the sheet-covered mound on the bed. Using thumb and index figure he carefully lifted the top edge of the white linen cover to reveal the figure of an ageing woman curled up in the foetal position. A gut-wrenching smell emanated from the body and he held his breath as he bent over the corpse. Lividity was rampant throughout her torso. A clear sign she had been dead for some days. Looking into her wide staring eyes he knew that the blood-shot effect meant that the blood vessels had blown, usually the result of strangulation. It was a feature in all the murders they had been investigating. A grotesquely swollen tongue had forced its way between her lips, filling the entranceway to her mouth.

"Looks like he's got to her as well. I wonder if she found out about him and was going to drop him?" Tony Bullars broke the silence.

"The bastard. His own bloody mother. The evil bastard." Grace seemed to stumble over her words. "I need some fresh air."

She trotted down the stairs and made her way to the back door, stepping out into the fine rain. She leaned her shoulders back against the house wall and took in deep gulps of air.

"How could he? I mean all those people and now his own Mother." she spat out.

Hunter joined her. "You okay Grace? This is not like you."

"Things have just caught up with me Hunter. It's been a long couple of months with very little break and now this." She pushed herself back off the wall. "I want to personally nick this twisted bastard Hunter," she announced quite loudly. "Want to look him in the eye, take a leaf out of Barry's book - hope he puts up a fight so I can give the bastard some of what he deserves." Her bottom lip quivered as she fought back the rage. She took a deep breath. "But we've dealt with his type all the time, haven't we Hunter. When they come up against someone who's a match they totally bottle it. They're wimps and cowards. And I bet this pervert's just the same."

"You finished venting your spleen now, because we've got work to do."

"Yeah, I feel better after that," Grace answered giving him a wan smile as she turned to go back into the house.

* * * * *

He wanted to ring that fucking woman detective's neck - just like his mother's. Saying things like that about him.

I'm not a wimp and a coward and I'm certainly not a pervert. I'll show her.

He slunk back into the bushes away from the officer's gaze.

He had only just managed to hide. The police's arrival had completely taken him by surprise. He had been in the shed looking for some sacking to take his mother's body away and bury, now that it was starting to smell, when he had heard the cars screeching up to the front of the house.

He knew that sound could only mean one thing. It confirmed in his mind that he had been right to do what he had done. Before he had ended his mother's miserable life she must have telephoned the police and tipped them off about him. What had she said to him?

"Enough is enough." Those were her words.

I knew she had, that's why she had to die.

By rights he knew he should have punished her a long time ago.

How could she betray me after all this time? I'd only let her live this long because she had helped me.

How many times had she washed his bloodstained clothing without question?

It wasn't just my secret. It was our little secret. It was the only thing we actually shared together since that day she caused my dad to leave.

When he had seen the armed police smash down the door and then watched them all scuttle inside to search he had decided it was time to make himself scarce. He was about to emerge from the bushes at the bottom of the garden when that black lady detective and her colleague had come out, and she had started to slag him off. She was just like all the others.

He had intended to call it a day and leave the area now that he had been found out but he knew he had one more job to do before he left.

She has to be taught a lesson. She can't say those things about me without being punished.

- ooOoo -

CHAPTER TWENTY FOUR
DAY THIRTY-SIX: 11th August.

Grace cupped her mug of hot coffee in both hands staring at the small TV screen in her kitchen. The sound was on low but she could still pick out the words of Detective Superintendent Michael Robshaw. The local news broadcast was replaying footage from last night's press conference held at the front of the Wild's home.

"There has been a significant development with the discovery of the body of an elderly woman, and a post mortem examination will be carried out to determine cause of death," he was announcing to the world's press in his best Police speak. "We urgently need to trace and speak with her son Gabriel in relation to this incident." His face was solemn on camera, though Grace knew that inside he was elated because they finally knew who the serial killer was. Gabriel Wild was on the run.

The next shot was from the air, of the Wild's rear garden, where a white forensic tent had been erected beside the wooden shed. She knew they had already dug up the remains of Gabriel's dog. More disturbingly however was the fact that the ground penetrating radar had indicated there was at least one more much larger form buried beneath the flowerbeds. They were expecting to find yet another teenage girl's body.

Grace flicked off the television set, trotted across the kitchen, snatched up the wall phone, scrolled down the contacts list and hit the speed dial button. She trapped it between her head and shoulder, listening to the ringing tone as she put the finishing touches to the polish on her nails.

"Come on, come on answer" she found herself muttering under her breath. She blew on her sticky nails. She had a lot to do after yesterday's discovery.

"Hello," the deep voice, at the other end of the phone, answered.

"Hi dad, it's me," she responded and removed the phone from between her head and shoulder, pressing it against her ear.

"Oh, hello Princess."

Grace found herself screwing up her eyes, again. For though she loved to hear the exaggerated notes in her father's Jamaican accent, and knew in her own heart that it was just his term of affection towards her, she still cringed when he used the Princess word.

"Dad I wish you wouldn't still call me Princess, I'm thirty seven years old."

"You will always be my princess, no matter how old you are."

Why on earth with the surname Kelly had her father and mother decided to call her Grace she would never know. Over and over she had bemoaned this to herself, from as far back as she could recall. As a young child she had not realised the significance of her name, but as she had got older, upon attending comprehensive school, she had found herself the brunt of so much taunting and mocking. It had been her first experience of prejudice because of her colour.

She shook herself away from her thoughts. "Dad I need a favour. I've got to work late again. Something really important has cropped up"

"I know it's been on this morning's news." he interjected.

"Can you pick up the girls from their school and give them their tea. I've got them booked into a holiday school sports scheme for this week. I wouldn't ask you under normal circumstances dad but David's still trying to sort out his new job so he's been working late as well."

"Anytime Princess. You know you don't need to ask. Me and your mother love having them."

"Thanks Dad you're a star." She didn't give him time to respond. She knew if she engaged him in any further conversation it would be lengthy. And she just didn't have time, especially as she had to drop the girls off before she drove in.

* * * * *

The Wild's home had become another murder crime scene. Mrs Wild's body had been removed on the instructions of the Coroner's Office and now lay with all the other bodies, in cold storage at the mortuary.

Hunter, Tony Bullars and Mike Sampson, together with forensics had been over every inch of the house, rifling through cupboards and drawers to search out evidence. On the second sweep of the loft area Hunter gave off a shout as he began prising a corner of what looked like a section of wall, but what was in fact painted plywood. He had discovered a false wall covering the chimney breast. He tugged it away from its frame.

"Bloody hell just look at this lot," he cried, reaching through and pulling out a glass storage jar. It had a label near its base and he turned it around and held it towards the single bulb, which lit up the loft space. The jar was filled with a discoloured liquid and something slopped around inside.

"Frigging hell," he exclaimed, recoiling, almost dropping the jar. He caught it with his other hand and brought it closer to his eyes. Turning the jar he held it up towards the low wattage bulb to get a better look. He read the label: Claire Fisher's name was emblazoned across it in bold black ink. Widening his eyes in the dim light he focussed on the contents.

Jerking his head back he thrust the jar towards Mike Sampson.

"Christ Mike is that what I think it is? The sick bastard. The press are going to have a field day when they get hold of this."

Mike scrutinised the contents and nodded. "It's a heart. The bastard cut out and stored her heart. And look there's a couple of more jars behind there as well."

Hunter handed the jar to Mike and leaned back into the space. He could make out three more lined up on a narrow shelf. Above, on another shelf, he spotted several box files and he took one down and flicked it open. It contained an array of newspaper's and photos, which he began to read. He recognised some of the faces in the photographs and yellowing newspaper cuttings. Claire Fisher, Rebecca Morris and Carol Siddons were amongst them. Sellotaped to Carol's photo was

The Ace of Hearts playing card: Foxed and discoloured, it showed clear signs of ageing.

She was his first victim, Hunter said to himself. He remembered hers had been the first body that they had found with its heart cut out. And he bet there would be a jar on the shelf with her name upon it.

There were other images of teenage girls that were familiar and he guessed that these would match some of those on the missing from home files back in the office. Filed in date order he speed-read the newspaper story lines of young girls who had disappeared over the last fifteen years. He instantly picked out the ones they had already found murdered. But amongst them were other girls' names whose bodies hadn't been found and Hunter knew in his heart that these were in gravesites not too far away waiting to be uncovered.

Inside clear plastic pockets he found photographs. Gabriel had taken shots of the girls after he had killed them. The images were graphic and gruesome. As he took out more files he found in the back of one of them a large scale local map of the Dearne Valley and its surrounding area. At the location of the old Manvers Colliery site were four ringed areas in red ink. As he scanned the map he spotted, circled, the old farm complex near to the village of Harlington, and at the top left hand section another drawn hoop covered a wooded area close to the village of South Elmsall.

Looking at the map Hunter knew that he was looking at the locations where Gabriel had buried his victims and realised that there was further digging to do, especially around the Manvers complex.

Outside Wild's home the media circus had gathered. The team could hear the Sky Newscopter hovering above. To feed their hunger a description and photograph of Gabriel Wild had already been circulated amongst them and that had been plastered across every news channel the evening before. Numerous sightings had been phoned in and these were currently being followed up.

They had also put out an 'All Ports Warning' to prevent Gabriel from leaving the Country.

The search to capture Barnwell's serial killer was in full flow.

* * * * *

It had been easier to get back to his car than he had anticipated. He slipped on his disguise, of the spectacles and his father's duffle jacket, which were still in the boot and then scooped out a handful of hair wax from its tin and rubbed it into his hair. He sat in the car for a good ten minutes cursing. Things had come to a head quicker than he had ever anticipated. He would be punished for sure. They'd found the body of his mother before he'd had time to bury her, and sooner or later he knew the detectives would tear apart the house and find all of his little secrets.

A tingling sensation coursed its way through his body as the images of all his victims washed around in his brain. He closed his eyes trying to hold the vision of each one as he recalled what he had done to them.

Their names slowly filtered through. Carol Siddons had been the first. A smile lit up his face. He could still see the surprise on her face as though it was only yesterday. Then there had been Kelly Johnson. She had been a right tart. He'd soon sorted her though. He would never forget the two girls from the children's home near Doncaster; Amy Clarke and her friend Katie Nichols. He'd met them on Nether Hall Road, a notorious place for prostitutes. He'd been cruising the area when he spotted them.

"Fifty quid for both of us" Amy had said "You're getting underage you know."

Those two bitches had chosen themselves.

Though, it had proved difficult killing them. The girls had been edgy the entire journey to the Manvers complex and when he had pulled onto the track behind the coking plant they had tried to escape. Thank god his car had only been two-door; they couldn't get out of the back.

They had put up a hell of a fight. He had scratches and bite marks everywhere and the car had been a real mess when he had finished. It had taken days of cleaning before he could use his car again. He'd buried those two together in the same grave. And then there was Claire Fisher – posh little rich kid. If only her parents had known what she was really like. He didn't need to rape her. She had given in to him so easy, but he'd still killed her anyway – gullible bitch. Three years ago there had been Zoe Green. She had been so pretty. He spotted her whilst he was mooching around Clifton Park, in Rotherham. She was walking her dog and had let it off its leash. Luring the dog to the bushes had been so easy and when she had come looking he had pounced. He could still see the shocked look on her face. She had just frozen and he had killed her in less than a minute. Smuggling her body into the boot of his car had been the hard part. He'd waited whilst dusk and then moved her before anyone had come searching. He'd driven home and secreted her behind his garden shed. He'd covered her with bin bags and garden rubbish, and the next day buried her between the hydrangea bushes and the back fence without his mother noticing.

Finally there had been Rebecca Morris. She had been his bad omen. Killing her had proved his downfall, but now wasn't the time for recriminations. He still had things to do.

Starting the engine he aimed a lengthy look up and down the street, and when he had satisfied himself that no police officers were in sight he set off in the direction of the quiet country lanes, which he knew so well.

Earlier that day it had not been too hard following Grace's people carrier.

She obviously has other things on her mind.

He smiled to himself as he wove in and out of the traffic, two, and no more than three cars behind. He had picked her up late into the evening leaving the police station and had followed her home. He had been elated that day when Grace had emerged at 8am with her two children. He hadn't thought about the detective having kids - and they were girls at that.

He liked the look of the eldest in her school uniform. He was surprised to see her dressed like that because he knew the kid's were on school holiday. Then he recognised which school she was at – private school. He guessed they must have different holiday's and he took a short cut, anticipating where Grace would be driving. He was right. He was comfortably parked, a good hundred yards from the entranceway to the private school when Grace arrived. He used the zoom lens on his camera to watch the girl's get out, and then snapped off a shot.

He was certain Grace would be working late again because of the ongoing hunt for him and he therefore guessed that her daughter's would be making their own way home.

The remainder of the day he put things in place and rehearsed his lines, and ten minutes before the school day was due to end he slipped his car into a marked parking bay opposite the school gates and sat back to wait.

It wasn't long before he spotted the eldest girl, coming towards him, chatting with a bunch of mates.

He slipped out of the driver's seat and strode purposely towards her.

"Miss Marshall?" he asked and he showed the fake warrant card he had made earlier on his laptop. He could see she was taken aback. "Miss Marshall I'm detective Wild. I work with your Mum. She's had an accident and I've been sent to take you to the hospital." He could see the girl visibly pale.

"I need to speak with someone." She reached for her mobile in her blazer pocket.

"We need to hurry Miss, your mum needs to go to theatre. You can phone who you need to tell on the way there."

She dropped it back into her pocket and followed him, picking up the pace to keep with him as he jogged to his car.

* * * * *

Back in the MIT office, Grace and Barry Newstead had been given the task of logging all the evidence, which had been gathered and brought from the house. They were in the process of separating the vast array of forensic bags when Grace's persistently ringing mobile phone disturbed them. The ring tone was a little baby continuously laughing. She loved the tone. It reminded her of her own two giggling girls when they had been babies, and how she had ended up in fits of laughter along with them. Every time she heard it, it had that same effect upon her. But this time she tried to ignore it. She had important work to do. It rang again and she snatched it out of her handbag and flicked up the screen. The screen told her it was Robyn. It had to be important; she knew not to ring her at work.

"Hello Robyn, mum's busy, tell me what you want quickly," she said disgruntled.

"I gather I am speaking with Detective Grace Marshall," said the man's voice.

She didn't recognise it.

"Who is this? Is that school? Is there something wrong with Robyn?" she asked anxiously.

"Not yet but there soon will be." The man's voice was cold and menacing.

Grace froze, her mind racing.

"You know who this is Grace, don't you?" He continued, "It's Gabriel Wild. You've been bad mouthing me Grace and you need to be punished."

"I haven't. Is Robyn there? I haven't been saying anything about you." she stammered.

"You're lying Grace. I heard you. I was hiding in the bushes. You said I was a coward and a wimp and a pervert. Those were your words Grace and for that I'm going to hurt you where it hurts the most."

There was a long pause on the other end. Grace's face turned ashen. In her line of vision she saw that Barry was trying to get her attention. She knew that he had spotted that something was wrong.

"Do want to speak to Robyn?" Grace could hear her daughter sobbing in the background. The sobbing got nearer.

"Robyn. Robyn." She virtually screamed down the phone.

The sobbing drifted away and Gabriel Wild was back on the line "Do you know what I did to all the other girls?"

"If you hurt her. If you harm one hair on her head I'll fucking kill you." She screamed back with an edge of hysteria in her voice. The tears of anger and desperation welled up in the corner of her eyes.

Without warning the line went dead.

- ooOoo -

CHAPTER TWENTY FIVE
DAY THIRTY-SEVEN: 12th August.

Detective Superintendent Robshaw was running the operation from the Command Suite at the police station. He had called in a Hostage Negotiator, had briefed Task Force Firearms Unit as to their duties and turned out as many police vehicles as he could muster and ordered them to park up at strategic points throughout the district. Finally, he had called in the phone technicians from headquarters to fix the tracking and recording equipment to Grace Marshall's phone. As soon as her mobile rung again they would be able to get a fix on the user.

In less than four hours he had managed to get everything into full swing, and he was praying that nothing had yet happened to Grace's daughter, and that Gabriel Wild had a big enough ego to make contact.

He didn't have to wait long. Grace's mobile started to ring.

Suddenly the ring tone was not so funny.

She watched the technicians operate their equipment and when they gave her the 'okay' signal she flipped up the screen.

It was Robyn's phone. "Hello Robyn?" she said nervously.

"Hello Grace it's me."

She recognised Gabriel's voice.

"Let me speak with Robyn," she replied.

"You're in no position to make demands Grace. And I'm guessing there's someone else listening to this so I'll be hanging up before you can get a trace. I just want you to say goodbye to your daughter."

Grace could hear Robyn's cries coming nearer to the receiver. Within seconds she was sobbing in her ear.

"Help me mum," she snivelled. Then her weeping drifted away.

"The next time you see your daughter, Grace, will be in the mortuary with all the other bitches," Gabriel hung up.

Grace dropped her mobile.

For several seconds there was complete silence in the room. It was broken by one of the technicians.

"Traced it." he shouted and stabbed an index finger on a blown up copy of a map of the District. "They're here, behind one of the units on the Manvers Industrial site."

* * * * *

The early evening sky was rapidly filling with grey clouds. With it came a fine rain. It sprayed across the windscreen of the parked MIT car, diminishing the view of the main Dearne parkway. Hunter and Tony Bullars were in the unmarked car. They had tucked the Vauxhall Astra into a lay-by and were monitoring the airwaves on their radio sets. Watching and waiting.

When the shout went up, indicating the location of Gabriel Wild, the two detectives bolted upright: Stirred into action.

Seconds after the radio broadcast Hunter locked onto a car that was screaming towards them.

Wild's Toyota rocked the MIT car as it shot past.

Hunter revved up the engine and slammed into first gear.

Tony Bullars snatched up the radio handset to call it in.

The wheels spun, churning up loose gravel, and Hunter pressed harder on the accelerator, spurring the car in the direction of Wild's speeding Toyota. Whipping through the gears Hunter soon had the unmarked police vehicle registering seventy mph and was making ground in their pursuit of the fleeing fugitive. He could hear from the radio chatter that other police cars were coming to their aid. The airwaves were awash with police officers' voices strategically aiming their vehicles to cut off every conceivable escape avenue to Wild. 'Whiskey nine-nine' - the police helicopter had lifted from its base at Sheffield to join in the hunt.

As an advanced driver, trained in the craft of pursuit from his drug squad days, Hunter handled the car faultlessly, jerking around the many roundabouts, before pointing the bonnet towards the middle of the road as he straightened out to continue the chase. He beeped wildly on the car horn then re-adjusted his fingers to flick on the beam of his headlights.

As Wild's car swerved up ahead and the brake lights illuminated Hunter knew his driving had had an effect.

Beyond the Toyota Hunter spotted whirling blue lights in the distance, heading towards them. The response on the radio told him that it was the marked firearms vehicle and he began to ease off. The Task Force vehicle had a far more powerful engine and was far better placed to take over the chase.

* * * * *

Gabriel Wild almost lost control when he spotted the CID cars flashing headlights in his rear view mirror. For a second his car snaked and he stamped on the brake and whipped down the gears. Hitting the accelerator he could hear the Toyota's engine scream as he began to widen the gap again. His concentration on the car behind made him completely miss seeing the oncoming marked police car until it was too late.

* * * * *

The police Volvo lined its bonnet up towards the Toyota and swung sideways across the road. The actions had the desired effect. The Toyota's tyres protested with a concerted squeal, jarring, as Gabriel braked harshly. He could do little to stop the car crabbing sideways as he began to lose control of the steering. In a fit of panic he hit the accelerator. The engine screamed, drowning out the bursting front tyre. It bounced up the kerb, onto the grass verge, smashed through wooden fencing, lining the side of the road, and picking up speed, on a muddy surface, it careered wildly down a small incline. The Toyota slid for ten yards before flipping over, rolling twice onto its roof, finally coming to a halt when it hit a metal gatepost.

* * * * *

Gabriel's head had taken out the windscreen and only the exploding airbag had saved him from being thrown through. As he kicked open the buckled drivers door he caught a glimpse of himself in the rear view mirror. His face was barely recognisable. His forehead had a wicked gash and blood poured from numerous cuts. His right cheek was already swollen causing his eye to close. He also saw that his lip had split in two. He reached up, fingers probing his blood-marked face.

"The bastards. The fucking bastards," he screamed.

Robyn was slumped forward in the passenger seat. He could see she was stunned but uninjured. He snapped off her seat belt and dragged her by her hair across the front seats, pulling her through the driver's door, snatching his Bowie knife from the door-well as he stumbled out onto the grass.

He saw that the CID Officers following behind had already alighted, as had the two uniformed officers who had cut off his path, and they were armed; their short rifles pointing in his direction.

Panic set in.

Gabriel pulled Robyn closer to him pressing his head tightly against hers. His focus was on the two armed officers. He could see their mouths moving but he couldn't hear what they were saying. The detonation of the airbag had temporarily deafened him.

He pushed the blade to her neck, digging the point into her soft flesh, drawing blood. "I'll fucking kill her." he screamed. "I'm telling you she's fucking dead."

* * * * *

If Gabriel Wild could have just looked in a mirror at that moment, he would have known how wrong he was.

But then he couldn't see the red laser dot from the tritium illuminated sight dancing on his forehead.

The 9mm lightweight round left the Heckler and Kock MP 5 muzzle at 400 metres per second. The illegal dum-dum bullet punched into Gabriel Wild's head just above the eyes, smashed through his skull and fragmented into the frontal lobe of his brain.

He had no time to realise why none of his limbs would move how he wanted them to. The force flung him backwards and before he hit the ground he was dead.

A little blood splattered Robyn Marshall's cheek and for a second she stood there frozen. Then she let out a shriek and the shriek became a scream.

The Officer secured the cocking handle of his gun, cleared the round in his chamber and then pulled away the fifteen round magazine holder. He turned and handed his weapon to his Supervisor.

"Sorry Sarge I felt I was left with no option. You heard me shout to him three times to drop the knife but he took no notice. I thought he was going to kill her," he said.

As he strolled back to the Armed Response Vehicle, Paul Goodright received a flashback of the night the CID car was stolen. Like the other times, he saw the image of his sister lying in Intensive Care, the doctors telling her that her boyfriend had been killed and that she would be crippled for life by the joyrider who had run them off the road.

He had sworn there and then to her that he would track him down, and after all these years of probing and searching his efforts had finally paid off.

Paul dropped his chin into his chest trying to suppress the smile, which was creeping across his mouth.

He had finally delivered Gabriel Wild's punishment for all the misery he had caused.

Now he could lay his own demons to rest.

* * * * *

"What were Gabriel Wild's last words to the firearms officer just before he shot him...?

In between drinks, sniggers and laughter erupted from the group of detectives at yet another one of Mike Sampson's serial killer jokes.

Hunter smiled and shook his head.

The MIT team had virtually taken over one half of the lounge. It was a good job the pub had only the handful of regulars that the team all knew. Anyone else other than the locals in the lounge and they might take offence.

An hour earlier he and others from the team had been so pleased to see Grace hugging her fourteen-year-old daughter so tightly in the back yard of the police station.

He'd tried to put a reassuring arm around his partner telling her it was all over but one look at her face told him her head was elsewhere. All she had kept repeating was that she needed to get Robyn home.

Grace had left with her daughter in the back of a traffic car, in a complete daze.

The Detective Superintendent had wrapped things up very quickly with one of the fastest de-briefs Hunter had ever known, ending the short conference with a promise of a more thorough scrum-down early the next morning and finishing the preamble by standing everyone a drink to celebrate the end of the investigation.

Hunter pushed his way to the bar half listening to the end of Mike's joke. He knew it was these moments that bonded a team.

On his way he spotted Paul Goodright tucked into a corner, hunched over a beer, rubbing a hand over his shaven head. He was alone.

He made a mental note to have some time with him once he had got himself a drink. He had not seen him since the shooting.

He ordered a pint and then sauntered across to his old colleague.

"How're we feeling?" Hunter asked, sliding onto a seat opposite. Paul's head shot up. He'd obviously been lost in his thoughts ruminated Hunter.

"Not too bad – had better days."

He made a brave attempt to crack a smile, but Hunter could see it was half-hearted.

"Glad it's over?"

"You bet." He pushed himself back against his seat. His squat muscular frame stretched his black T-shirt.

Hunter could remember when Paul had been a very slim twenty-something detective with a full head of hair. That's when the memories tumbled into his head. He would never have guessed that the decisions he and Paul had made that fateful night on the 12th October 1993 would have brought about such tragic chain of events involving so many people. As the episodes had unfolded during the last few weeks he had questioned himself so many times. Should he have done anything different? He had found himself unable to answer. No doubt that would be one of many things he would dwell on over the next few weeks.

"Thanks to you the result is good though eh?"

Paul tightened his mouth, rested his strong bare forearms across the table and gripped the bottom of his glass. His beer had lost its head.

Hunter wondered how long he had been nursing it.

"You say that but it doesn't really take away the feelings I have over what happened all those years ago. That psycho tore my life apart." He fixed Hunter with his hazel eyes. "I thought that when I shot him it would have made me feel better but its already short lived. I still feel so responsible for what happened. If I hadn't have gone off shagging that night this wouldn't have happened."

"Paul you've got to stop beating yourself up. You weren't to know what was going to happen that night. People happened to be in the wrong place at the wrong time. You have to put it down to sheer fate. The guy was a killer – born and bred – full stop. There was nothing – and I repeat nothing you could have done about it." Hunter pointed towards Paul's flat beer. "Let me get you a fresh one you've earned it believe me. There will be a lot of people out there grateful for what you have done. Just think about all those parents of the girl's he's murdered for one. Secondly we won't have the expense of a trial and the worry that some smart barrister will exploit a loophole or a jury will do an OJ Simpson and allow him to walk free." Hunter drained his own beer then wiped the edges of his mouth. "I'd be honoured if you'd allow me to buy you a drink."

Paul returned a weak smile. "Another beer would be great thanks."

Hunter pushed himself up from his seat and edged through the throng once more towards the bar. He ordered another two pints of Timothy Taylor and returned to his old colleague.

He placed the beer in front of Paul and then raised his glass. "Cheers."

Paul picked up the pint. "Cheers"

Hunter took a swig. "I'm gonna get some fresh air in the garden. You're more than welcome to join me but I'm going to have this and then disappear. I'm knackered. It's been a long day."

"No you get yourself off. I'm having this and then I'm going as well. Anyway I wouldn't make good company at the moment. We'll catch up some time eh?"

"You bet," Hunter acknowledged with a quick nod and then spun away.

Easing himself past a couple blocking his way Hunter pushed open the French doors that led out into the garden. The sunlight momentarily blinded him and made him close his eyes for a second. Blinking them open, he realised that the earlier evening drizzle had given way to the beginnings of a spectacular sunset. The temperature had risen, although the air was still fresh from the rain. He leant against one of the wooden benches and took in all the smells of the surroundings. That burst of rain had invigorated the dryness in the landscape. He took another swallow of his second pint, casting a glance over the hedgerow at the bottom of the beer garden, towards a view of the countryside beyond. For the first time he realised the pub's location gave him a clear view of the scene where this mayhem had first started five weeks ago. In the distance he could just make out the collection of old tumbledown farm buildings where Rebecca Morris's body had been discovered. That find had started this whole roller coaster of events, uncovering the actions of a demented killer who had devastated the lives of seven innocent teenage girls and their families, and culminating in the abduction of Grace's daughter – one of their own. It had made him realise just how vulnerable they could all be.

Yet somehow Hunter no longer had the appetite or indeed the energy to rejoice. It felt almost as if every last drop of adrenaline had been squeezed out of him. He was totally drained. The long days and sleepless nights had finally caught up with him. He'd only drunk one full pint, and a little of his second but he knew that had gone to his head.

He was so deep in thought that he jumped when the hand was placed on his shoulder. He jerked around quickly to be greeted by Barry Newstead's beaming face.

"Penny for them Hunter."

"Crikey Barry, you made me jump. I was somewhere else just then."

"Thinking about Grace and Robyn?"

"Yes, them and Paul Goodright, and the families of the other victims."

"Careful Hunter you'll have someone thinking you've gone soft."

They both cracked a grin.

"Anyway what are you doing out here?" enquired Hunter. "Why aren't you celebrating with the others? That's not like you? People will be talking that Barry Newstead is going on the wagon."

Barry dug Hunter in the ribs. "I'm on a promise."

Hunter widened his eyes. "My, my; we are a dark horse. Tell me more."

"Sue Siddons." Barry paused.

Hunter returned a pleased look.

He continued. "The enquiry got us back together, made us both realise what we had lost. Not just Carol, but years of friendship. She's going to straighten herself out now that she's got closure. She's started going to AA meetings."

Hunter patted Barry's upper arm, gave him a reassuring look. "Hope it all goes well for you Barry. I really do, you deserve it. You've been a good ally to me on this investigation..."

Barry pulled him up short. "Getting soft again Hunter." He winked and downed the remainder of his beer. Wiping the dregs from around his mouth with the back of one of his huge hands he said, "Fancy another?"

Hunter shook his head. He glanced at his watch. He knew at this time that Beth would be just getting the boy's supper ready before their bedtime. He emptied his glass and set it down onto one of the wooden benches.

"No thanks Barry, that's me done. I'm not even going to say goodbye to the team - I'm knackered. I just want to get home, put my feet up and watch the ten o'clock news for once."

As he made for the side gate he already knew what he was going to do. It seemed to have been an eternity since he'd last had some R & R, even though they'd done a family holiday at half term in Minorca. He was going to book a cottage on the North East coast for Beth and the boy's – at one of his favourite spots. He might even be able to smuggle along his paints.

- ooOoo –

Read the second book in the D.S. Hunter Kerr series

Cold Death

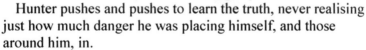

Taking a well-earned break from the 'Dearne Valley Demon' case, Detective Sergeant Hunter Kerr's rest is suddenly shattered when he witnesses a violent argument involving his father, shortly followed by a murderous road-rage attack upon his parents.

As he delves deeper, Hunter uncovers disturbing facts and suspects that his father is harbouring a sinister secret from his past; a secret, which he is desperate to keep buried.

In his father's native Scotland a sadistic and violent killer is on the rampage. Three retired detectives are found tortured and butchered. Is there a link? Or, is it someone who just likes killing cops?

Hunter pushes and pushes to learn the truth, never realising just how much danger he was placing himself, and those around him, in.

In Barnwell, Hunter's working partner, DC Grace Marshall, recovering from her own psychological problems arising out of the 'Demon' serial-killer investigation, is 'acting sergeant' in his absence and soon finds herself in charge of her first major incident; a young woman's battered body is dragged from the freezing waters of the local country park.

ISBN: 978-1-907565-28-1

Lightning Source UK Ltd.
Milton Keynes UK
UKOW05f1611310714

236117UK00002B/17/P